THE TRUTH HURTS

As she came to the end of her story, Eva's voice had slowed and become flat. She looked at Bowen over her knees, and he stared back dumbly.

"I see. I'm sorry, I had to know . . . I . . . I'll kill that bastard if I ever see him! I mean it, Eva. Anybody who follows us or bothers you—"

Eva came up on her knees. "No, David! No. I have talked with him. He will not follow us again. And even if someone does . . . You must not try . . . He, the men who work for him . . . they are very hard . . . They might . . . there could be violence."

Bowen stared at her for a moment, then smiled—but not with his eyes. "Really? Do you really think I could be so lucky?"

"Philip Ross does not cheat his audience as he peels away the layers."

—*New York Daily News*

TRUE LIES

PHILIP ROSS

TOR

A TOM DOHERTY ASSOCIATES BOOK
NEW YORK

TRUE LIES

A Tor Book
Published by Tom Doherty Associates, Inc.
175 Fifth Avenue
New York, N.Y. 10010

Tor® is a registered trademark of Tom Doherty Associates, Inc.

ISBN: 0-812-51376-2
Library of Congress Catalog Card Number: 87-50869

First edition: March 1988
First mass market edition: May 1994

Printed in the United States of America

0 9 8 7 6 5 4 3 2 1

CHAPTER

1

Standing together at the window wall that made a postcard picture of the palm trees, the long hillside and the green and blue ocean, they could see the car guarding the entrance to the drive up to their cottage. They could see the one man leaning with his elbows on the roof of the car, watching the cottage with binoculars, and the other lounging, waiting. They could see the second car coming along the main road, from the north.

"There he comes, Eva," Bowen said.

"Yes. This time we will not escape."

"I'm afraid you're right. But would you really want us to get away, Eva? Isn't this what the whole thing has been leading to?"

"I don't know."

"You don't?"

They stood at the window, not close together, not far apart. Her left arm lay across her body, her right fingers touched her cheek. He stood squarely, hands down in his trouser pockets. They watched the second car drawing closer.

"You were very amusing at the beginning, when we first met," she said. "We were, both of us, very amusing. Trying so hard not to show we were interested in one another."

"Yes," he said. "It was pretty funny."

He saw her first as she started along the row of seats. Her white-blond hair, her iridescent, magenta dress: She came toward him like a flame along a fuse. She was looking downward. He was able to watch her for several seconds before she caught him at it. He looked at his program. When she reached the empty seat next to him he glanced up at her and smiled politely. Her small smile and nod were equally vague and formal.

"How did you know I was interested in you?" she asked. "When did you know?"

"Right away. As soon as you looked at me."

"How did you know?"

"When we first looked at each other, before you sat down— Your eyes . . . they weren't opaque; you were looking at me—from someplace way back. And we held the look too long. Just a fraction of a second; but longer than we had to for the sake of being polite. Of course, I wanted to let you know I was interested. I had to make contact with you.

"When I first saw you I couldn't believe that you were so gorgeous: your hair and that dress . . . Your beautiful face. The glow of it. I almost felt like putting my arms

2

around you and saying, 'The hell with it all, the world's well lost for love.' That's the truth.

"I knew I'd have to be cool, not push you. But I knew I had a chance because you didn't break it—the look; not first, not turning me off. You were being cool, too; but I saw you were interested."

He returned to his program. He leaned to his left, deliberately: not as though any shyness had crowded him into a corner, but—a perfect gentleman—so that she might have all of her space, have uncompromised use of the seat arm between them.

"Yes," she said. "I couldn't believe my good luck. You were such a handsome man, David. Such a high, noble, intelligent forehead. Those deep lines on either side of your mouth—why, I could see at once you were a serious man, sometimes even stern, but a man who prefers to smile. So confident seeming, but you were being sensitive about showing your interest in me. I liked you, at once. But I didn't want you to know I wanted . . . to suspect . . . I didn't want you to think I was eager to know you."

She settled herself, crossing one slim leg over the other, and opened her own program.

He finished reading the concert notes, folded the booklet lengthwise down its middle, precisely, put it into the breast pocket of his jacket. He studied the musicians' platform, the wall behind it, the organization of the ceiling, undoubtedly preparing himself to reproduce them at a drafting table, later, from memory. With scrupulous care he did not look to his right.

She glanced up from her reading to watch a couple move across and take seats three rows ahead. She turned and stared at someone off to the right. She read again, briefly. She closed her program and looked forward.

"We sure were pretty funny," he said.

More people streamed into the hall; more and more. The ripple of voices gradually rose to a rush, then a rolling surf.

"Yes. I thought I would laugh aloud when you pretended to have an itch and scratched your forehead so that you could tip your head and look at my leg."

"You knew I was looking at your leg?"

"Of course."

"I thought I was very circumspect."

"You didn't just stare . . ."

Musicians began taking their places. The tympanist tuned, softly, quickly: boom, boom, boom. He tightened the tension. Bum, bum, bum, a quarter tone higher. He tapped the second drum, a tone higher yet. Then he compared the two: low-high, low-high, low-high.

One double bass player and then a second plucked strings, playing figures that tumbled over one another. People entering the hall now hurried to their seats. Program pages were quickly flipped, concert notes for the first piece skimmed. All the hall moiled with bobbing heads, twistings and turnings, flashing hands: No one could sit still.

She didn't look directly toward him again. In shifting position (only the better to stow her purse and program beside her, of course) she did catch sight of his broad hands—on which he wore no rings—and the peaty tweed of his jacket sleeve, and the honed crease of his twill trousers, and his burnished shoes. Then she leaned to her right. He leaned to the left. They looked at the platform. There might have been a wall between them.

He had seen, though, that her left hand lay composed within her right, that a clear polish coated her short fingernails. Except that she had crossed her legs, and the bottom of her skirt had wickedly fallen open to reveal her knee, she sat like a good little girl waiting for church to begin.

String players practiced swift finger runs. The piccolo raced up and down the scale. Then the concertmaster signaled, the oboe sounded, and chaos suddenly was concentrated and ordered into an A.

Momentarily hushed, the excitement of the audience rose again as the lights in the house dimmed and those on the platform brightened. Swelling applause greeted the conductor. He bowed, took his place, raised his arms. The absolute silence of anticipation was denser than the noise had been.

Bowen pushed himself upright in his seat, leaning a little forward.

"That's when I started to love you," she said. "When I saw how you loved music. I know you like it, in any case. But were you pretending—to impress me— There have been so many deceptions, so many lies, David . . . Were you only pretending to care so much?"

"No," he said. "I don't fake music."

It was an all-Prokofiev program. The first piece was the Classical Symphony, bubbling, frolicking, running, dancing, skipping, tumbling, turning cartwheels. Lightheartedness made even the stately pavane sprightly; and the final movement was a kindergarten let out for carnival. But the racing tempo, dynamic changes, tricks with tonal expectations kept a nervous tension under all the gaiety.

She didn't look directly at him, but he seemed to be responding with an intensity that suggested he had forgotten her—indeed, that nothing existed for him in the hall except the orchestra.

But at the end, as they began clapping, he turned and exclaimed, "Wasn't that delightful!" as though they had come to the concert together.

She nodded vigorously, and when the applause had ceased and the lights came up, she said something about the orchestra being in good form, and he agreed.

During the short pause while the piano was wheeled into place he said, "This is an exciting program, isn't it? Risky."

"Oh? Risky? Why? All three pieces are very popular."

"Yes. Because they're all so brilliant. Intense. Exciting. But with the three of them together, there's no letdown, no pastoral scene for relief, to set up the climax. Previn's risking burning us out before the intermission."

That they were strangers must have slipped their minds.

"Perhaps," she said. "We all must have come because we like excitement."

"Yes, that's my point. We came expecting it. We've had one dose, we're already high. The concerto's going to give us another big jolt. That means the *Alexander Nevsky* is going to have to be absolutely super or it'll seem like an anticlimax."

"What do you think the program should have been, instead?"

"Oh, I don't think it should be different. I like the risk."

"You like to live dangerously?"

They watched each other's eyes.

"I like calculated risks."

"You like the *illusion* of danger."

"I like to try risky things—when I have confidence I can succeed. Are you a lover of danger?"

"I would say no, except that I find myself talking about such a subject with a strange man."

"My name is David Bowen." He had rested his elbow on the seat arm between them. He turned up his palm as if presenting himself upon it. "Do I really seem strange to you?"

Laughing, she put her hand firmly into his for an instant. "Eva Kraus. No."

André Previn returned to the platform to conduct the Third Piano Concerto from the keyboard. He acknowledged the applause, sat, pausing for a moment like that between lightning and thunder, then signaled. The clarinets, and then the strings, high and breezelike, played the introduction: dawn, a broad landscape still dewy, tranquil, light filling a wide sky. Then all the rest of the orchestra entered: a galloping rhythm, softly at first as though behind a hill, sweeping up and over, the piano flashing, racing in the lead. And then image after image for the listener—sparkling streams, raging rivers, cataracts, winds sweeping across prairies of grain, lightning flashing, kaleidoscopes, bursting stars.

Whether Bowen had such visions, or felt the sound purely, he again sat upright staring at the orchestra. He looked galvanized, as though the music were dependent on him, arising from him as much as from the players, and would collapse if his attention failed for an instant.

Eva seemed to give herself to the music, her act of will to be without will, slack in her seat, most often looking at her hands lying one within the other in her lap. Sometimes her eyes were closed. Her shoulders swayed slightly, her fingers tightening, demonstrating the music's power to move her. Sometimes she gazed toward the upper corners of the hall, sometimes to the side, toward Bowen.

At the end of the first movement he turned and saw her looking at him. He grinned, nodding, sharing the experience. He did the same before the third movement. But each time when the music started again he was alone in the hall.

After the piano had pounded out the last chords of the racing finale, a hurricane of applause swept up from the audience.

"Wow!" he almost shouted when at last it began to diminish. "Wow!" throwing his arms wide apart.

"Oh, yes! Oh, yes, so exciting!" She shook her clasped hands before her like one in religious ecstasy. "Fantastic! Brilliant! *Wunderschön!* So . . . so . . ."

"Wow!"

She laughed, bowing in surrender. "So wow. You have said it the best."

They grinned at one another.

"You want to go out for the intermission?" he asked.

"If you like."

They moved to the doors into the lobby with the mass of people, but once through, Bowen—a polite halfback—forced his way across to a corner—"Excuse me, pardon me"—never shoving, really, but never allowing anyone to impede him. Eva slipped through close in his wake.

"Ah, this is better," she said. "I thought we would be trapped in the middle of everyone. You got us through very nicely."

"The trick is never to stop, or to let anybody think you're willing to. You're German?" he asked.

"Yes."

"I wasn't sure. Your English is excellent, but I knew you weren't British. I thought, maybe, Scandinavian —your hair is so light."

"My family is from the Baltic. So comes the hair. Also the cheekbones. You are American."

"How'd you guess?"

"Not only from your speech. You have the American face."

"There's an American face?"

"Yes: your own. Showing their own faces, not wearing a mask—that is the American face, open and honest. Not all Americans have it, of course."

"Thanks. I haven't met enough Germans to be able to say anything about the German face—if there is one. I think I could say a lot of nice things about yours, though."

"Since I have said you look honest, I would have to believe them. How nice." She smiled prettily in acceptance of his compliment, but changed the subject. "You are visiting London?"

"Yes, a kind of extended visit. I'm here for a month or two."

"How nice. You have business here?"

"Not exactly. I can handle my business from wherever I am, so I travel a lot. I like to travel. I was in Switzerland for a while this summer and now I'm getting my cultural batteries recharged. Are you visiting?"

"No. I am a resident. I came from Germany two years ago."

"Great—for a person who likes music as much as I see you do. Isn't it a great city? There must be half a dozen concerts almost every night of the year."

"Yes. Unfortunately, I cannot afford to attend more than one a week. And usually I sit higher. Someone where I work gave me the ticket for tonight."

"You work in London? I know it's hard for a

foreigner to get permission to live here unless you have a job before you come."

"Yes. I had such a position. I translate from German and English for a business concern."

"Ah. I see."

In their corner of the lobby, they stood apart from the press of people around the bar and the doors to the concert hall. They faced one another, but not squarely. He stood with his back close to a wall. She was half turned from him, her arms at her sides, or sometimes with the fingers of one hand against her cheek or the base of her throat, as she looked up at him. She might have looked at him almost levelly, but she kept one shoulder lower and her head tipped to the side. Although she glanced across the room sometimes, mostly she looked at his face and met his eyes.

"You listen to the music with great strength," she said. "Almost as if you think you are making it."

"I guess I do. Think I'm making it, I mean. At least, doing my part. Music is a communication—it takes both the people who are making the sounds and those who are hearing them to make it happen."

"Yes," she said. "Oh, yes. Music has meaning —deep spiritual meaning."

The warning chimes sounded. They returned to their seats. Now the chorus was massed behind the instrumentalists. Eva had to lean toward Bowen to make herself heard in the hive of noise from the audience.

"No one seems to feel 'burned out.'"

"I'm certainly not," he said. "This is the most exciting time I've ever had at a concert."

They continued looking at one another. When he looked *at*, he tightened his eyes, as if narrowed sight were sharper. Her eyes were as blue and open as the sky, but she tilted her head, looking at him from her own angle, and so seemed both innocent and knowing.

André Previn returned to the podium.

He lifted his baton, and Russia groaned under grinding chords of oppression. The chorus offered hope as they sang of the hero, Alexander Nevsky. But, chanting beneath iron crosses, the horned-helmeted Teutonic Knights burned forward over the Motherland. "Arise to arms, ye Russian folk," the chorus called. So stirring was their song that their hundred voices seemed thousands as the common people rose in wrath against their foe.

In the eerie stillness of morning mist, unable to see but knowing one another's presence, the two armies poised on the frozen lake. Softly at first, the strings sounded the rhythm of running. It grew louder, the Russian army running, sweeping, smashing like a hammer onto the Teuton's steel. The battle raged. The Teutons drew together—a solid block of armor, a wall of spears. Then, under their weight, the ice broke!

The voice of one woman, full of sorrow and yet proud, mourned those Russian warriors who had fallen. And, finally, the entire host, every singer, every instrument, lifted in a song of triumph and glory.

Exaltation brought the concert audience to its feet, filling the hall with a roar greater than that of the battle.

When the house lights came up at last, Bowen and Eva turned toward one another, faces flushed, eyes shining, as though their spirits still soared over the field of glory. Then they were back in the concert hall realizing they would have to leave it. Bowen hesitated, holding her eye. "Would you . . . There's a nice pub over by Waterloo. Would you like to go for a drink?"

She took a moment. "If you like," she said then. That was how they met and began together: as though by accident, as though the meeting hadn't been carefully arranged and the traps set.

They walked quickly; the pub would close in thirty minutes. Their footsteps clicked in an intricately interweaving rhythm. Suddenly Bowen halted them. "Listen."

"What?"

"Hear the city." No cars passed along the streets behind the Festival Hall, the traffic on Waterloo Road was light; yet the warm night hummed. "It's like we can hear the sound of its bloodstream."

A high haze held the city's glow. He gestured upward. "Look: It's like we can see it—the energy, the excitement that it gives off."

She looked up, then at him. He smiled, shrugged dismissively. "We'd better keep moving."

They crossed a street. Eva said, "You love music very much, I think."

"Yes. It's about the best thing there is—even ahead of sex and serious intellectual discussion, the two next best."

She laughed. "A very interesting trio of preferences. And laughter? I think laughter should be there also."

"Absolutely."

When they had gone a little farther, she said, "And among the things that are most important—love? Should not love be there?"

"Love's more problematic."

After a moment still as a pool she said, "Yes." After another, she said—brightly again—"All of these things have in common: They are sharing."

"I guess you're right. I'll have to think about that."

They continued a little way in silence.

"You have begun to think at once?" she said.

"Sorry. I didn't mean to go away."

"It is all right. I like it that something I have said, you should wish to think about. Please, though, to tell me—after you have thought—what you think."

He halted, stopped perhaps by the deeper, quieter tone more than the words. He looked at her levelly. Sudden seriousness, more than shadow and the slant of streetlamp light, made her delicate face seem more defined.

"I will. I certainly will."

They reached the pub. Surely all of the regular patrons and half of the concert audience had sardined themselves into it. Bowen pried his way to the bar and then back with her lager and his half of bitter. All the talk, the laughter, thick and turbulent, pressed on them. They had to shout into one another's ear even though they had space enough only to stand toe between toe.

Leaning toward him, she asked, "Do you visit London often?"

He could smell her scent. "I've been here once before. I only started traveling about a year ago."

They had to hold their glasses up and to the side, turning their heads to sip. A rose-colored light in the ceiling played down on them, making his face all the more craggy. Hers, lifted just a little, glowed.

She began, "Perhaps you won't think that I am rude to ask—"

Someone bumped her. She jerked her head enough to avoid hitting Bowen's chin, but for an instant was thrown fully against him. He had set his own back against a pillar; he couldn't move. She recovered, saying, "Sorry."

Looking embarrassed yet pleased, he said, "Not at all."

She was turning, but a split-second pause and pursed-lip smile showed she had caught both meanings. Then she went on to glare over her shoulder at the red-sweatered bear who had backed into her. He said, "Beg pardon," but didn't seem to have any way to move farther from her, nor regret enough to keep him from rocking for emphasis when he returned to roaring at his companions.

Bowen looked from side to side, and tried to shift to give her room; but there wasn't any. He twisted so she might move closer to the pillar. She smiled and shrugged, turning and putting her shoulder into his. Perhaps she thought oblique contact less suggestive than facing him at a minuscule, merely provocative distance. She didn't hold herself stiffly, but neither did the movement have any snuggle to it. It appeared to be simply an accommodation to circumstance she didn't mind making.

She finished her question. "What is your business —that you can travel wherever, as much as you wish?"

"Well . . . I manage money. I used to work for a brokerage house—investment counselors—in New York: Merrill Lynch—you may have heard of them."

She nodded. Her thigh just touched his. They could feel one another's warmth.

"I was an analyst, an advisor. I analyzed the economy, and the market . . . prospects for investment . . . advised clients where to put their money. I got good enough at it that I built up some capital of my own . . . I'm not really rich, but I am able to get along by managing my own money, along with commissions for advising a few private clients I kept."

"I see," she said, "how very nice for you," her voice full of pleasure at his good fortune.

"I'm not really rich," he said again. "People usually think I must be."

"I think you are," she said seriously, guilelessly. "You have enough—it seems—to satisfy you; so you can live as you wish. That is to be rich."

"You're right. But I think probably, maybe in another year, I'll get tired of it and want to do something serious. For now for several reasons, I decided to just take some time—a kind of sabbatical."

"I see."

He was holding his glass in his left hand, curled up by his shoulder. His right hung by his side. It brushed her bottom. He pulled it away. "Have you left Germany permanently?" he asked.

"I think so," she said. "I do not know."

"I wondered if you were working over here just for the experience," he said, "for the language." Holding his arm down but away from her was awkward, and he touched the leg of a man leaning against the side of his pillar. He started to slip his hand into his trouser pocket, but his knuckles touched her thigh. He pulled them out again.

"Yes," she said. "The experience is very valuable."

Tentatively, as properly as a cadet leading a dowager duchess out to waltz, he put his arm across her back, his hand on her waist.

"But I left to end an unhappy love affair."

He lifted his hand away.

She glanced over her shoulder, then up at him. "It is all right."

He put his hand on her waist again. "You're a very straightforward person."

"Sometimes. I tell you—straightforwardly—not always."

"Oh?"

"No. You are straightforward, I think; but you like sometimes to say one thing and mean another."

"Ah. But that's just a kind of a game."

"And you never do something indirectly?"

"Sometimes."

"And you never say something that is not true?"

"If I told you 'no,' I guess I'd be proving I did."

"So. But I think, David, yes, you are straightforward and serious most of the time. I am also," she said, and smiled again. "But"—she tipped her head to one side—"I think we should not be too serious all at once."

"Okay. All right, to change the subject, what do you like to do besides go to concerts?"

She liked to walk in the country. Why, that was one of the things he liked best, too! He'd just been in the Alps, was thinking soon of going up to the Lake District. How wonderful! She wished so much to walk there, herself. And she liked to go to dinner at little Greek restaurants and talk about books until late in the evening. Oh, yes, she read a very great deal. Oh, yes, he did too. Everything that one of them liked so much to do was also a favorite of the other. Oh, yes!

"I just can't get over it, Eva—the luck, that we met. I mean, it was only luck that I was at the concert at all. I went to the box office two days ago to get some tickets for things that are coming up—I knew the concert tonight was sold out. And when I was leaving a guy stopped me and asked if I wanted to buy a ticket he couldn't use. The official price—he wasn't scalping.

"Just think: If I hadn't been there at exactly that

moment, you might be having a drink now with . . . I
don't know . . . a billionaire oil sheik."

"If the woman at my office had not had unexpected-
ly to visit her mother, you might be here with a"—she
said trippingly—"very pretty lady from Scotland."

Their smiles seemed equal. It was impossible to
detect who was lying.

"Time," one of the bartenders shouted. As though
his was the voice of Doom, the din in the room
rose—final words, everyone rushing to tell it all, at
last. "Drink up, please, it's time."

Bowen and Eva continued looking at one another. It
was too late to begin a new topic.

"I'd like to see you again, Eva."

"I would like to see you again, David."

"Soon."

"If you like."

"Tomorrow?"

"If you like."

Her outward hip pressed against his thigh. He took
the next to last sip of his beer. "I wouldn't want to spoil
this, Eva . . . I do want to see you again, tomorrow, so
I don't want to offend you . . . But you are very
beautiful, and I feel close to you. Would you think very
badly of me if I said I'd like to spend the night with
you?" For an instant he almost hid behind his glass,
but stopped himself and waited.

"No, David," she said after a moment. "I would not
think badly of you. If you did not have such a wish I
would be disappointed. But I think you would think
badly of me—if not now, perhaps later—if I agreed."

"Why?"

"You would think . . . not that I also felt such closeness; not that we already saw one another and knew

one another well enough, so that more time was not needed. You will think those things did not matter; that I am an easy woman."

He laughed. "No, no. But I won't argue. I don't want you to think that's the most important thing to me." He drained his glass, said, "Well, how about tomorrow —for dinner or a movie, I mean?"

Eva laughed and leaned her head to touch his shoulder. "Yes, I would like that very much."

When they came out of the pub she put her arm through his, pressed her shoulder to it for an instant.

"I'll get you a cab," he said.

"No. The Underground is just there, at the station. I am on the Northern Line—I do not have to change. It takes only twenty minutes. And it is much cheaper."

"Can I ride with you? I mean, just to see you home."

"If you like."

"I'd like."

"I would like it, also."

Arm in arm, holding tightly, smiling at each other, they floated across and into Waterloo. If either noticed in the darkness the two men who had followed them into the station from the Festival Hall, neither he nor she made mention.

The men did not get onto the train with them.

At that hour, the car was only half full, and people left it at each stop as they traveled out from the center of the city. Bowen had guided them to a seat in a corner of the car. With no one sitting next to them, with all the noise of the train like cotton wool insulating them, they were able to talk freely. At first they shared again their excitement of the concert, and talked of what they might do the next evening.

Then, after a moment of silence, Bowen—his eyes assuming that assaying squint—said, "I guess I really should ask . . . I've taken for granted . . . You said you'd ended a love affair. I take it you're not . . . seriously involved . . . with anyone right now."

"No. And I take it that you are not?"

"Right. I was married for eleven years, but that ended three years ago."

"Ah."

They had hurtled along through that tube of solid noise, talking intimately. But when they came up out of the Underground, Eva and Bowen walked through the soft-aired side streets without speaking. That blood-rush and tone of the city—never still—was distant. Off the amber-lit avenue, away from traffic, for the first time all evening they were alone in silence, and could have talked together quietly, and they said nothing.

Finally, stopping them, Eva said, "Here. My flat is in this house."

He pivoted to put himself at an angle to her. They had been side by side; now, though still linked arm in arm, they were a figure of distinct—and separable —elements.

"Did you think," she asked, "that if you saw me home, I would change my mind and invite you to stay?"

"No, I didn't think you would." Lightly, with a smile, he said, "To be honest, I wanted you to."

She didn't smile. "Do you always get what you want?"

He was serious again. "No. Not at all. But sometimes I do. When I want something, I do try to get it. I don't think you get anything unless you keep trying."

"A man of persistence."

"Yes. Look, I'm not pushing you, Eva. I think that if

we do make love—whenever—it'll be good. But I'm not pushing you."

The stiffness went from her neck, and she nodded. "I understand." Once more she laid her head against his shoulder; and they stood in silence.

"The quiet," she said.

"Yes." He was looking at the house. Of the last century, it had a sense of scale and elegance. A sundial had been built into the frieze above the portico. He gestured to it, and recited.

"'The curve of time is lost to sight. Care halts its march from mark to mark. We lie at that still point of night from which is swung the arc of darkness.'"

"What is that from?"

"It's not from anything. That's all of it."

"Who is it by?"

"Nobody. A very minor poet. An amateur."

For a moment she looked at him. Then she raised herself and kissed his cheek. "I hope you will not think badly of me, later," she said. "But I don't care."

CHAPTER

2

At a few minutes after five P.M. the next day he knocked at her door.

"Who is it?" she called from the other side.

"It's me."

"Oh! One moment." The chain rattled. She swept the door open. Huge magenta flowers splotched the white dressing gown wrapped and sashed tightly yet sloppily around her like a counterpane pulled hastily over an unmade bed. A towel turban hid her hair, narrowing her brow, broadening her cheekbones. She wore no makeup. Her face looked flat.

"I am not ready," she said unnecessarily. "Is it already time?"

"I'm early, I guess." He glanced beyond her as if

checking whether someone else were there. "I'm sorry. I hope it's all right." He stood stiffly; not shrugging or swinging his hands in embarrassment at coming too early; not smiling and reaching for her because it didn't matter. He simply stood and looked at her—like a totem pole.

"Come in. It is not all right, David. It is never all right that a man should see a woman when she is not expecting that he should see her. Your punishment is that you must see me looking so. Worse, that you must kiss me."

She closed the door and came to him. He put his arms around her, and met her lips. The thin fabric of the dressing gown scarcely veiled her to the touch; but she might have been embracing a tree.

She drew away. The flush drained from her face. "Good. I do not look like myself, and so you have no desire; you are faithful. Sit down, please, and wait a little moment, and your Eva will come back again."

She crossed the living room toward the hall and the bathroom, asking, "Did you have a pleasant day?"

"Yes," he said, rooted where she had left him, looking after her.

"Did you think of me?" she called from the bathroom.

"Yes. I thought about you a lot."

"Good. You must tell me everything you thought."

"Yes. Well . . . I do want to—"

"In a moment. I can't hear you now," she called, and turned on a hair drier.

For a few more seconds he stood like a person let down from a bus in a strange and possibly hostile neighborhood.

Apartments had been crowded into the house by ramming walls through once spacious rooms. The partitions that now cramped length and breadth rose to the original ceiling, though, twelve feet high. The disproportion, the volume of space unusable by people in the room, could easily give them the sense of a presence peering down on them. Perhaps that sense made Bowen scan back and forth and up all around before he moved. Then he began a careful circuit of the living room.

He stopped first at the bookshelf. There were several dictionaries in English; beside them what looked to be others in German. A two-volume encyclopedia, in English. A thick, old, leatherbound Göthe. Several thin books. He pulled out one of them. It was in German, but by the irregularity of the lines he could tell it was poetry. Paperback editions of novels—modern English writers: Virginia Woolf, Iris Murdoch, Doris Lessing, Evelyn Waugh; Thomas Mann and other German names he didn't recognize.

On a cabinet stood a portable radio, the BBC guide open beside it, programs of classical music underlined. He looked at several. He ran his finger across the cabinet top, examined it and then the line he'd drawn. Only a little dust: at most, two or three days' accumulation. When he looked at an angle, he could see no more than that behind the radio. She was not only neat, but fastidious.

In a corner by the window was a small desk. Letters in envelopes lay on it, stacks of papers, all in little square-cornered piles. He stood, staring down at them, reading the return address on the top envelope. He poked at it so as to reveal the next.

The hair drier stopped.

Quickly, he went on around and sat at one end of the big couch that faced the chimneypiece. The couch was upholstered in a blue fabric not as dark as the color of

policemen's uniforms but as cheerless. Pillows covered
in pink, lime green, red—geometrics, floral patterns
—made the drab shade a foil for gaiety. Eva had told
him she'd taken the flat furnished. Most of the pieces
were old and had never been of good quality. She must,
though, have put the pillows and the draperies and all
the other splashes of color in the room, herself.

Not with the care of a man really searching, but not
quite absentmindedly either, he ran his fingers under
the pillows and then along the crack between the
cushion and back.

"So," she called from the bathroom doorway. "Tell
me about your day." She laughed, "No, tell me first
what you thought about me," brushing her hair as she
spoke, standing one hip out, her head tipped, bare-
footed, in that splotchy, blotchy, flimsy, rumpled wrapper: a picture of domestic intimacy.

"Well . . . I guess I'll have to do both," he said. He
had craned his head to look at her over the couch back,
over his arm stretched like a bar along it. "I mean,
what I thought about you varied during the day. At
different times I thought different things."

His head was twisted to look at her. He let it swivel
to an angle away from her.

"This morning—when I went back to my hotel—I
guess I was in a daze. It was like waking up from a
dream—you know, a really vivid dream: the kind you
have in the morning just before you wake up, sometimes. Maybe an erotic dream. You can still feel her,
feel her body against yours. You close your eyes
again—you're awake, now, you know it—but you're
still in the dream. Seeing her, feeling her, is almost
more real than the daylight you can see through your
eyelids, than the bed you can feel. You think—you let
yourself think—that if you just keep your eyes closed,

you can stay in the dream." He turned his head toward her abruptly. "You know what I mean, Eva?"

"Yes." She had looked at him steadily while he spoke, while she brushed her hair. After another moment she turned and went back into the bathroom.

"Well, that was the way I felt," he said, speaking more loudly. "At first." He put both hands into his trouser pockets, pressing his elbows against his ribs.

"I had a shower, went down and ate breakfast. I went out and got tickets for that concert Saturday. Then I started walking. I vaguely had the idea of going to the National Gallery. I started walking in that direction. I must have known I wasn't really interested in looking at paintings, because I didn't take the Underground, I just started walking. I mean, my mind was elsewhere. I was thinking about you."

"That's nice, David," she called. "If you were thinking nice things. Were you thinking nice things?"

"Yes. At that point I was thinking about how wonderful last night was. About the concert—how we really shared it, shared the music. How we both let ourselves go when we were hearing it—you know? Nothing held back? Nothing hidden?"

He paused for a moment, like someone who has shouted into a cave and is waiting for the echo.

"Wasn't that wonderful, Eva? That sense of nothing hidden?"

"Yes, David."

"Yes, I thought that really was wonderful. That openness. But we both like sometimes to come at things indirectly. To say one thing, but let there be another meaning. You know what I mean?"

"Yes, David."

Bowen got up, went into the hall opposite the bathroom door, where he could watch her. Slouched, leaning against the wall, hands in his pockets, one leg crossing the other and resting on toe point, he looked as relaxed as a men's store mannequin tipped against a shop window wall.

Her back was to him. She faced the mirror. She was lining an eyebrow. The color of the pencil she used was very light.

"I didn't realize you used eyebrow pencil," he said.

"Good," she said. "But my hair is so light, I must. If not, I have no eyebrows at all. I look like I am always astounded by everything I see."

"Yes," he said. "I see. But it's not like you're faking anything, is it. You're just . . . giving more definition to what's there, aren't you."

"Yes. I am pleased that you should think of it that way, David." She began on the other brow, looking at it in the mirror. She didn't look at his reflection. "And then what did you do, David? What did you think?"

"Well, as I say, I had in my mind that I was going to go to the National Gallery—if I really had in my mind to go anyplace. Actually, I was just wandering. Just walking along, thinking about you—the things I said. And more. I was remembering us making love—I had never imagined that even just having a shoe taken off could be that wildly erotic. God, it's a wonder I didn't let myself walk in front of a bus or something, letting myself think about that. Probably—if a cop had seen my face—I'd have been arrested for indecent exposure."

She had lined her left eyelid. She looked at him in the mirror. It was as though he were being regarded from around the edge of a veil.

"I shall never be able to touch the buttons of that dress again without thinking," she said. She lined the other eyelid. Then she put down the eyeliner, took up a small jar and began brushing color onto her cheeks.

Crossing his arms, Bowen leaned back against the wall. "So, I was wandering along, thinking, keeping myself in a dream, as it were; and then—this is what I wanted to tell you about: my confrontation today between dream and reality. Lo and behold! There I was—nowhere near the National Gallery: I must have turned the wrong way on Charing Cross—I was up just across Oxford Street from the beginning of Tottenham Court Road.

"Well, now, I can't tell you whether that was pure coincidence, or whether—since you had been talking about your work just before I left you this morning—I had headed unconsciously straight to you—which, of course, is where I wanted to be. Still in a dream, as I say. I really didn't know you used so much makeup."

"It is not very much. Only a little color. When I have brushed it properly it will not look like makeup at all."

"I guess not, if that's what you had on last night.

"Well, so, when I realized where I was, I said, 'You can't see her, she's working.' But I looked at my watch, and it was eleven-thirty, and I thought, 'Maybe we can have lunch together.' But then I thought that maybe you didn't go out for lunch; or you might go out with people from your office; and in either case, I shouldn't bother you.

"I almost turned right around and went back. I really almost did. But then I thought of a great idea: I would go up and find your office and wait outside—across the street someplace. That way, if you didn't come out, or if you did and you were with other people, I'd just go away and see you tonight. But if you came out alone . . . So I found a place up the street in a doorway, and I watched for you.

"It was just like I was a kid. I used to do things like that when I was a kid—you know, if I had a crush on a girl I'd ride my bicycle around her block, pretend I had excuses for hanging around, in case she came out. That's what I was doing today, acting like a kid, feeling like a kid with a crush. I had a balloon in my chest, and it was being pumped up bigger and bigger every minute.

"Well, in about ten minutes you did come out, and you were alone. And I started out of the doorway and to hurry across to stop you, but—much to my surprise —this other guy—who had been standing outside your doorway, I realized—I hadn't really even noticed him— Well, he steps up, and you go right to him— obviously you knew he was going to be there, waiting for you. And he put his arm through yours—clearly he was somebody who knows you pretty well—and the two of you walked together down toward the corner. Him leaning down and talking close into your ear.

"Well, I have to tell you, Eva, I was pretty shocked. That balloon inside me: It didn't deflate, it just—the air inside it suddenly chilled down to absolute zero, and it froze solid. I was jealous and I did a terrible thing: I followed you. I followed you while you walked the couple of blocks, and saw when you went into that little restaurant. I could see through the window that the restaurant was full—it was just after noon then —but you and the guy were shown to a table. Obviously, he had reserved it."

Holding her head back, Eva put color onto her lips. She concentrated on them, not looking at him.

"Now, I thought to myself, 'Dave, this is a terrible thing you're doing—getting suspicious, and jealous. Following her. The guy is just some business associate.'

Except that the way he took your arm wasn't like he was a business associate. 'Well,' I said, 'he's an old friend of the family.' But he wasn't old. He must have been about my age. Really good-looking guy, too. So I said, 'Stop this, Dave; it's her brother.' Was it your brother, Eva?"

She put her lips together, looked at them. She blotted them with a tissue, studied them for another instant. "No."

Not looking at him, she reached for a bottle, unstoppered it. "The man's name is Gert Nagler. He is an acquaintance from Germany." She tipped the bottle against a finger, put scent behind one ear. "He is a man I do not like very much because he is arrogant. He believes he is so good-looking, so charming, that no woman can resist sleeping with him. He does not fear to offend by suggesting it." She tipped the bottle, touched behind the other ear. "He believes he can touch a woman, he can put his arm through the arm of any woman when they walk on the street, without hesitation." She tipped the bottle, brushed the base of her throat. "He does not really believe me when I refuse to go to bed with him. He believes I am merely playing hard-to-get."

She looked at Bowen's reflection. "As you know, David, I am not hard to get when I wish to be gotten."

Her eyes left his. She put the stopper back into the bottle, and replaced it. "He is certain that, eventually, I will give in: He expects always to get what he wants. But he is too vain to press me too hard, to suggest my refusal really troubles him. So, beyond taking my arm, his attentions are not a problem.

"I see him, sometimes—even though I do not like him—because we have mutual friends in Germany.

Friends who are quite dear to me, whom I will see seldom—if ever again. He goes back and forth often, so he brings me news of them."

She stood looking at Bowen in the mirror again, not turning to him; her hands down, fingers on the edge of the vanity.

"So," she said, "that is the story behind my luncheon hour 'assignation.'"

"I see," he said. "Well, if it's true, then I've made a damn fool of myself, haven't I?"

"Yes."

"I guess there are worse things than being a fool. That's why I'd like to believe your story."

"Then believe it," she said. She turned to face him, leaning against the vanity and crossing her arms. "Or do not."

They looked at one another. Her expression was one he'd never seen before, but her face now was.

"I'm sorry," he said. "I guess you're angry with me."

For a moment she seemed to consider reply unnecessary. "Yes," she said.

"Very angry?"

This time she did keep silent. He raised his eyes and nodded once, agreeing about the stupidity of the question.

"I'm sorry. It's because I do love you."

Her face—so beautifully composed—didn't react. She looked at him without seeming ever to need to blink. "That is not a kind of love I want. That is not love at all. Love trusts."

"Yes," he said. "I know. That's why it hurts so much when you're betrayed." He paused, perhaps waiting for a response, a further reassurance; but she offered none. Finally, he seemed to accept having to decide without any.

"I'm sorry." He swung his arms forward, but she would not unfold hers to take whatever he was offering in his upturned hands. After a moment he put his hands into his pockets, and slumped backward against the hall wall. They stared at one another. She didn't say anything.

"So, I guess either you forgive me, or you don't and I go away. Please forgive me."

After one more moment she uncrossed her arms and pushed herself away from the vanity. "I will forgive you."

She came out of the bathroom and across the hall to him. She put her fingertips on his shoulders and stretched up and kissed him lightly. He put his arms around her and started to pull her close. She leaned back and said, "But I was very angry with you. I am still very angry."

Clasping her tightly he kissed her mouth and then her neck. "I'll have to try to mollify you," he said.

Tipping her head so he could kiss her throat she said, "Oh, yes. Please try. But I am *very* angry."

He pulled at her dressing gown so that he could kiss above her collarbone. He put the tip of his tongue to the hollow there, and then touched it up her throat, and kissed her under her jaw. "How's that?"

"Oh, that is nice. That is very mollifying. I think I am completely mollified there." She giggled. "But I must tell you, I am angry with you *all over.*"

"I think we'd rather sit back there," Bowen said, indicating a table at the rear. The restaurant was nearly empty at that hour, and the waiter had gestured toward one close to the front window.

"This one is very nice," the waiter said, the gracious smile with which he had greeted Bowen and Eva comfortably fixed in place. He was handsome, dark-haired and mustached. Clear in his bearing was a sense of himself as a paragon of masculinity.

Bowen didn't draw himself up in confrontation. He simply stood as he was, staring into the man's eyes.

After an instant the waiter inclined his head and said, "But, of course, as you prefer."

So they dined near the rear of the narrow room, by the light of a candle burning and dripping picturesquely in the neck of a bottle, its glow reflecting up at them from the red tablecloth. Its flickering animated their faces. Each of them, but perhaps Eva in particular, had that kind of face that shows emotion almost like a Japanese mask: With tight skin over high bones, there is little actual change in the features; a wonderful variety of expressions can be seen on it, but they are made by slight changes in eyes and mouth, the way the head is held, the way light then plays on the features. Seen up close by candlelight, Eva's face seemed wonderfully alive—and even Bowen's showed a range of feelings. Neither seemed to be guarding thoughts and emotions, even concealing them.

They ate *taramasalata* and talked about Thomas Mann.

"I'm glad we were too late for the film," Bowen said later, after the *stifado,* the *baklava,* when they were lingering over the tiny cups of dark, sweet coffee. "We've had more time just to talk."

"Yes," Eva squeezed his fingers interlocked with hers on the table. "Better to talk. To know one another better, David. But you know, we do not talk about the things people talk about when they want to become acquainted: 'Where is your home? Do you have brothers and sisters?' We talk about books, and music, and what we think, and how we feel."

"Which is probably why we are really getting to know each other. Do you have brothers and sisters?"

"Two sisters."

"I have a younger brother." He shrugged. "So what do we know?"

She shrugged also, but apparently decided to play out the line. "And did you live in the city or the country? Did you have a happy childhood? Do you get on well with your younger brother?"

"The suburbs. No worse than anybody else, probably. Not particularly. He's six years younger, and . . . It's classic sibling rivalry, I guess: I was the center of the universe, and then he came in, and my mother and father . . . He was the cute baby, and got away with things I couldn't get away with, and got all the attention." He had turned and told the last of his story to the candle. He swung back abruptly. "How about you?"

"We lived in a town. I remember my childhood as happy, for the most part. Sometimes not, of course. My sisters and I . . . we were rivals, sometimes, I think. But also were we very close. My father was the old German type of papa. When we pleased him, he was very jolly with us; but when we did not . . . He could be very severe."

Bowen nodded, shrugged. "So. Well. I think knowing how you feel about Schubert and Thomas Mann tells me a lot more."

"Yes."

"I really like what I know about you, Eva."

"Thank you. I like you, David."

Their hands tightened on one another.

After a moment he asked, "You ready to go?"

"If you like."

* * *

They paused outside the restaurant, to take the air.

"Nice," he said.

"Yes. So pure, clear. Like . . . what? The sound of a flute?"

"Yes! Exactly! The sound of a single flute after an hour of listening to Mahler or Bruckner."

She laughed. "You do not like our post-Wagnerians?"

"Well, they have some nice stuff, and some good tunes; but they never know when to quit."

"Was the restaurant too thick for you? Should we have gone to a Norwegian one with white walls and eaten cold fish?"

"No. I love Greek food; this was great. I didn't even realize until we stepped out that it was a little . . .." Turning his head in the coolness he hesitated for an instant. Down the block and across the street, a man stood back in the shadow of a doorway. ". . . Stuffy in there," Bowen finished. "Let's walk this way."

"My flat is—"

"Yes, I know. But let's just go around the block for some more air, and work off some of that dinner."

She took his arm, and they walked along the street busy with traffic even at that late hour. Several times he slowed them briefly to look into the windows of darkened shops. At the end of the block they turned left, then left at the next corner, and made their way directly to her flat from there.

"May I come in?"

"Of course."

When they went into her bedroom, he started to take her in his arms; but she said, "No. You were very nice to me, before, when you were 'mollifying' me. You worked very hard at it, and it was *very* nice. Now it is my turn to be nice to you."

"You don't have to—"

"I know I don't have to. That is why I want to. Now lie down and be still."

"Was that nice? Did you like that?"

"Do you have to ask? My God, I don't think I've ever . . . You? Did you . . . ?"

"Oh, yes. Oh, very much yes."

"Then I guess a good time was had by all."

She giggled against his shoulder.

"Are you ready to go to sleep now?" he asked.

"Yes. I will turn out the light."

"I'll get it. You've done enough; and I want to see if I've still got legs. I'm still numb all over."

He got out of bed and turned off the lamp on the dresser. "I'll open the window blind, so the light'll wake us in the morning." He adjusted the cord. He paused there, looking down at the street.

"What is the matter?"

"Nothing. I just . . ." He started to turn away, but appeared unable to.

Eva came to the window. "What do you see?"

"Nothing."

"What?"

"It's probably nothing. Just a car. There's somebody sitting in it. You can see. He's smoking a cigarette. It's probably just somebody bringing his date home."

Eva looked. "David, when we came out of the restaurant, and you wanted to walk around the square, did you think someone was following us?"

"Why should anybody follow us?"

"Did you think there was someone?"

"Well, I did see a guy down the block I thought I'd seen before. But he didn't follow us—and there's no reason why he should—so I don't know why I was worried. Too much time in New York, I guess. You always have to be on guard in New York. That's all it was."

"I'm sure," she said. "We must go to sleep."

"Yes."

They got back into bed, and kissed and held each other, and then turned back-to-back to sleep. But although they were still, and breathed regularly, neither did fall asleep for some time, one wondering why the watcher was there, one knowing.

CHAPTER

3

"Oh, David, how nice! Thank you!" She sat down at her place in the kitchen. He had put yellow placemats on the white plastic table, and orange napkins, and had brought a small vase of golden and amber strawflowers from the living room.

"You have brought sunshine inside!" Her eyes filled, which must have embarrassed her. She kept looking down and then up at him again, so they really did seem to flash.

He was standing, on the other side of the table. "Well, with that little window facing a brick wall . . ." He gestured toward the window over the sink. "I thought it would be nice . . ."

"It is, David. It's lovely."

He poured coffee for her.

"Oh, such service. I must see that you get a nice tip."

"Ummmm, well!" Clicking his heels, he bowed. "Would you like me to shine your shoes, ma'am? Walk your dog?"

"Just give me a kiss."

"Yes, ma'am! Any particular place, ma'am?" wiggling his eyebrows.

Laughing, she said, "On the cheek will do for now."

His voice went very low. "Whatever you like, ma'am."

He kissed her cheek, and poured coffee for himself, and sat opposite her.

"This is very thoughtful of you, David. I don't think any of the men I have known . . . I mean, my father, my friends' fathers . . . Men in Germany do not make breakfast for their wives—their women."

"Well"—he shrugged—"I have my problems, but making breakfast isn't one of them."

"No," she said. "I see that. I think it is very nice."

"Is that toast going to be enough?" he asked. "If you'd like an egg . . . I saw you have eggs in the frig . . ."

"This is fine, thank you. Please have an egg, yourself, if you would like."

"No. I'll get my breakfast when I get back to my hotel. I might as well get some use out of the place."

She spread marmalade on her toast, thinly. Working it out toward the edges even more carefully, and without looking at him, she said, "Is your room very expensive? It must be, all hotels in London are."

"Well, it's not too bad. It's one of the cheaper ones—twenty pounds a night. Most of them are fifty or sixty and up."

"I know. But still it is much money. Especially since you are not really using it."

She took a neat bite of her toast. He stirred his coffee, and sipped.

"David . . . would you, perhaps, wish to stay here —during your visit in London?" She looked quickly at him, then down at her toast again.

"Yes!" he said.

She laughed. "A man who makes decisions quickly."

"There wasn't any deciding to do. Thank you."

They gazed into one another's eyes.

"Now you really will learn all my bad habits," she said.

"Yes. And you, mine. I guess that's the next thing for us to do."

"Yes." She drank some of her coffee. "Do you think this is happening too quickly, David?"

"No. I mean, it sure is happening quickly; but I don't think it's too . . . Look at Romeo and Juliet—he just saw her across that crowded room. Didn't Shakespeare say something about nobody ever loving who didn't love at first sight?"

"How do we know it truly is love, that it will last?"

"We don't. How can anybody ever know that? You think it will. You stand up there in front of God and everybody and vow 'till death shall part us.' You go along for ten years, still believing . . . And then, one day, pow! You can never be sure, Eva. You can hope; but all you can ever trust is *right now*. Right now . . . I like the way you butter your toast. You know"—he sang—"Da dum, the way you hold your knife . . . I like the way you sit and tip your head when you're thinking. It feels right to me."

Bowen came down the four-stepped stoop, pocketing the keys Eva had given him, and paused. Pale-yellow sunlight, warming the morning, brightened clumps of chrysanthemums planted along the base of the house front. He took a deep breath of the freshness, newness. He looked at the flowers, at the street left and right. He might merely have been enjoying the nascent glory of the day; but his survey also allowed him to be sure that the car he had seen the night before wasn't there; nor was there any other sign of a watcher. He turned to his right, started briskly to walk, then hesitated, apparently remembering something. He spun around, strode back to the house, went in again.

Coming up to Eva's flat, he bent close to the door, bringing the key up to the lock. He paused, listening. Eva was speaking on the telephone, rapidly, in German. There was a slight pause. Then, "Gert?" she said; "Eva."

Bowen stood listening, bent forward, head turned, his ear an inch from the door.

That door, a blue rectangle in a white wall, the similar door of the other flat, hallway walls, ceiling, floor, carpet runner: all straight lines, rectangles, planes, plain surfaces; Bowen held himself as rigid. Sunlight slanted through the half-circle window over the stairs, softened by a screen of grime but bright enough to reveal the faintest swirl of dust motes raised from the old, thick carpet. The rush of a bus blocks away was a whisper. Tinkles minute as the dust motes shimmered down from a radio in a flat on the floor above. But no such sounds had strength enough to suppress even one of Eva's words before it reached him.

When he heard her finish, he backed away and left the house quietly.

The quick-twist click of her key in the lock. She flung the door open, "Oh, you're here!" She shoved it closed behind her, spinning, her blue plaid skirt flaring, her face flushed, eyes wide and shining, stopping abruptly, almost teetering. "Oh, I hoped you would be; but I thought perhaps . . ."

"Hi," he said. He had been sitting in one corner of the couch, his jacket on. A book of poetry lay facedown beside him. Somber light from the early evening sky lit the room coolly, but he had turned on the lamp beyond the end of the couch. He got up, went to her, put his arms around her, kissed her gently.

"Oh, wait one moment," she said. "I must go to the W.C. I come back directly."

When she returned, he was sitting again like three sticks hinged together, both feet on the floor, looking toward the chimneypiece, the book replaced on its shelf.

"When did you get here?" she asked, grinning.

"I brought my bags just before lunch." He nodded toward the large and small suitcases he'd left at the side of the room. "I went out and ate, and sat in Hyde Park for a while. Eva, come sit down."

"You did not unpack your things? I showed you where . . ."

"Yes. I know. Come sit down."

She did, guardedly, at the other end of the sofa, looking at him just a little sideways. "What is wrong, David?"

"I want to trust you, Eva," he began, leaning a little toward her, his hands open to prove they held no weapons. "But I have to know . . . about this Gert person."

"I have told you," a furrow came between her eyes—concerned, still questioning, she seemed not yet angry but about to be.

"Yes. You said you didn't like him; that you only see

him occasionally. Well, I'm not going to be cute and play games with you. I know you've been in touch with him today."

"I have not seen Gert. You have no reason—"

"I didn't say you'd seen him. Listen, this morning, after I left . . . I was just starting down the street, and I thought—why not meet for lunch, just like I wanted to do yesterday. So I came back up. And just as I was about to put the key in the lock, I heard you talking. On the phone. I heard you say, 'Gert?' and 'Eva.' I don't speak German, so I don't know what you said, but I got that much: You were calling him. And you talked for a while, and for a minute you sounded angry. I heard a lot of *'Nein,* Gert, *nein.'* *Nein* is one of the few German words I know. But then you calmed down again, and it sounded like everything was all right; everything was very sweet, and *'Ja, ja, ja.'* And then you said, *'Auf weidersehn.'* That's another one I know: 'See you again.'"

She was a spike of anger. "You were spying on me!"

"No, I just happened . . ."

"You were spying on me! I don't believe you— It doesn't matter! You listened!"

"I couldn't help— Yeah, I listened! After yesterday . . . you call this guy . . . Damn right, I listened!"

"I will not be spied on!" she shouted.

"I wasn't spying— Don't avoid the question! Why did you call him?"

"You are spying! I hate it!" She yelled, both fists thrown up and then pounding on her thighs, "I hate it! I hate it! You are jealous maniac!" Wheeling on him, pounding the sofa cushion between them, she screamed, "Crazy! Bastard! You bastard! Son of a bitch bastard!" Throwing herself toward him, swinging her fists, trying to reach him, "I hate you! I hate you!"

He caught her wrists, she struggled, he flung her away, sprang up and around the end of the couch. "Crazy? *You're* crazy! What's the matter with you? I only asked— I've got a right—"

"Frigging, bloody, bloody bastard!"

"Goddammit, Eva, I'm only asking—"

She shrieked—a terrible, cornered animal scream without words.

"I'm only—"

She thrust herself upward, onto her knees on the couch, arms raised and shaking, eyes to incinerate him, a scream to shard him.

"All right, goddammit! Goddammit, I'm leaving!" he bellowed back at her.

She lunged at him as he passed, then fell facedown on the couch, sobbing, her face twisting against the cushion, against one fist, the other pounding beyond her head.

"I couldn't do it," he said. He stood in the hallway with his bags, the big one in his left hand, the smaller under his arm, just the way he'd carried them out. He'd stood there, holding them that way, for the whole minute and a half after he'd pushed the chime button, until she came to the door. He continued to stand there, holding them, while she looked at him.

In the ten minutes since he'd slammed and banged down the stairs like a loose piano, she must have stopped crying and washed her face in cold water. The flesh around her eyes was swollen, her face puffy, but her cheeks were dry, the terrible glitter of tears gone. She looked at him as though through frosted glass, as though through a dirt-filmed window at a distant figure: a little curious, not very.

"I couldn't break up, go away, mad, like that. We've

got to at least talk, Eva, even if all we say is . . ." He shifted his shoulders against the weight of his load. "Could I come in?"

Her hesitation might have been more a time for comprehending than deciding. Then she stepped back.

He came in, put down his bags. He opened his arms, and she drifted a step to stand within them, let him enclose her. They stood so, for some time, his hand on her head, holding it against his shoulder. After a while, she pulled her head away, and touched his cheek with her fingertips, and wiped away a new tear with the back of her hand.

"Could we sit down?" he asked. "Could we talk?"

She nodded, and—arms around each other—they walked to the couch and sat together.

She took a deep breath, drawing herself upright. "Yes, we must talk." She pulled away from him. "I must. There are things I must tell you." Looking away from him, brushing her hair back from her face, she slid to the end of the couch, turned to put her back against the arm, her feet on the seat, her knees up. She covered her legs with the full skirt. The lamplight, shining from behind him, fell on her softly. It flattered her, making her look almost young and beautiful although her eyes seemed very, very old.

"There are things I hoped I would not have to tell you, David. That was foolish of me.

"About Gert; what I told you is true. But it is not all of the truth."

Bowen nodded. He slid down to the opposite end, sat against that arm, his palms pressed together and shoved between his thighs.

"I told you," she began, "that I left Germany to end an unhappy love affair. That is true. Now I tell you about it.

44

"In Germany, I worked for a large business. Translating—translating from English into German: technical studies, articles from technical and scientific journals, that sort of thing. I worked in a little cubicle in a large room with many other translators. Our section was part of a department that was part of a unit that was part of a division of the company. At the head of the division was a man—you might call him a vice-president.

"His first name is Heinz. I would prefer not to tell you his last name. I would prefer that you should not perhaps read his name in a newspaper, or see his photograph, and know who he is.

"Heinz knows everyone who works under him: everyone in every section of every department of every unit. Heinz knows everything about everything. He is called 'Heinz of thousand eyes.'

"Among the things he always knows is when a new girl comes to work in his division. You know what I mean? Especially if she is a pretty girl.

"Everyone in the company knows this about Heinz. Perhaps you would think the . . . president of the company, the . . . board of directors would disapprove. Perhaps they did. But Heinz is very, very good at his work. The . . . productivity . . . of his division is outstanding. He is a brilliant, brilliant man. And he is clever enough to have put people who are intensely loyal to him in positions of authority within his division. If he was removed, it might be difficult for a new chief to . . . get so much productivity. And he has friends in other divisions, and among the directors, as well. He is a very strong and powerful man.

"The other girls told me about him on my first day. I was not surprised when he called me to his office soon after.

"I was frightened. But I must tell you, David, that I was not unpleased. Heinz is the head of a division, and he does not . . . interview . . . *every* girl who comes to work. For him to take an interest, it is flattering. Also, he is a very exciting, strong, handsome, interesting man. He is . . . I think, now . . . fifty-eight. His hair is color of steel. His face is—not handsome, like you—but . . . Yes, perhaps like you, but more. Even more the strong bones, deeper the lines. Almost too much. Almost, perhaps, ugly—but only just not.

"When he calls a girl to his office . . . 'so that he can meet the new colleague,' he says . . . he does not chase her around the room. He says nothing suggestive, does nothing to embarrass her. He knows, he *knows,* that when he wants her in his bed, she will be there. So he is charming, and gracious, and discreetly flattering. He flatters her by showing he has inquired about her and knows much about her. And he flatters her by asking questions to show he does not know all, and wishes to know more. And he speaks with knowledge, and intelligence, and sensitivity about whatever she says she is interested in. And he lets her know that he is pleased and surprised that she is so intelligent and sensitive about whatever it is—not that he thought she would be stupid; but that he is always surprised to find anyone as perceptive as she.

"And he looks at her with total concentration—the way you do, David, as if he were seeing her, aware of her and nothing else—perhaps only for that moment, because he is, of course, an important man of great affairs—but, for that moment, caring for nothing else in the world but her."

Eva was sitting with her arms around her knees. For a moment she rested her chin on one knee, and gazed off toward a dark corner. As dusk had thickened in the room, the lamplight showed stronger upon her.

Then she turned her head farther, her jaw against her shoulder, and half her face went into shadow. "Oh, yes, he knows. He knows that when he wants her, she will be in his bed, her clothes thrown off, her legs spread, gasping for him, before he even takes off his necktie." Biting her lower lip, she stared away over the back of the couch.

Bowen brought his hands up, his fingers curled but not tightened. After a moment she looked at his eyes again and said, "Of course, I fell in love with him instantly," and his fists clenched.

"The first time we made love, I pleased him. Because I am, of course, attractive; and because I so much wanted to please him. Not because I had skill in making love. I had no skill. I did, some few times, sleep with a boy at the university; I was not a blushing *Mädchen* with no idea of what she was supposed to do. But I knew only a little to do.

"So, I knew that when the excitement of my being new to him was over, he would not call me—except," she spoke with the lightness and precision of a torturer making very careful cuts with a razor, "perhaps, when he had had several dark-haired women, and wanted a blond again."

Although Bowen had become granite, his eyes seemed to show he felt the blade.

"So, I told him how much pleasure he gave me, and how I wanted to please him, only I had no skill, I was so innocent. I asked him to teach me. I asked him to get me books.

"That amused him. It kept his interest—just the idea, at first. He got me books.

"I studied them. I am a very good student, a very serious student. That is how I got high marks in the *Gymnasium* and received scholarship to the university; and then got high marks there, and was selected for the position at the . . . with the company that hired me. Always, from a little girl, I studied hard. My father —we were only the three girls, no boys—my father said therefore we could not be only *Hausfrauen,* making *Pfannen* and babies.

"So I studied the books Heinz brought me. What does one learn from such books? The serious ones, they tell you only things you do not want to know about . . . about . . . the machinery; and then they tell you —either that this experience they do not describe is full of spiritual beauty, or that certain gears may be engaged to good effect. The fiction is better. It tells you what might be done and how to do it in wonderful detail; but much of it is preposterous when you try it, and doesn't feel the way they say it feels."

She paused. "Do you know about this?" She spoke matter-of-factly, now; as if her pain had subsided to a tolerable ache.

"Not really." He looked down at his hands, then at her again as though he didn't want her to think he didn't want to. "I haven't read much of that kind of stuff."

"Well, I know about it. I am an expert."

"Yes, I know."

"And now you know how I know. And does it . . . disappoint you? Does it offend you?"

"I'll have to think about it."

"Yes. It is all supposed to be spontaneous, unlearned, I know. At least for a woman. When you think about it, David, think, perhaps, that having studied a skill does not make using it have no feeling."

She stared at him levelly for a moment, then looked up toward the high cornice. "Heinz was not offended. He was pleased. He was amused, as I have said. He would laugh aloud when I would show him something in a book and then we would attempt it.

"But with practice, skill was acquired. Even Heinz learned things to do, better, although he would never have admitted it. We became quite good at it.

"So, at first he had stayed with me because of the amusement, the novelty. Then, as we practiced, because it became more exciting; more exciting than what he got with any of his other women. And then he began to be in love with me."

She had sat back against the end of the couch. After a moment, leaning forward abruptly she said, "You must not think—I must not make you think—that making love was all we did. Even from the beginning: Heinz considered it unsophisticated to go to bed without first a dinner, a concert, something."

She relaxed again, folding her arms, looking away, this time toward the chimneypiece. Now she appeared as soft and warm as the light through the rose-tinted lampshade.

"We went to concerts, to the theater. We went, sometimes, to dinner parties: Heinz began to take me, socially, to the houses of his colleagues. I am attractive. I am intelligent. I had some culture, already. Heinz introduced me to more—there are so many things he knows about.

"I was—for that time, at that time—so happy. I loved him. Oh, I did so love him." She turned to Bowen again, and the lamplight glinted from her tears. "Do you understand?"

Still stonelike, he nodded. "Yes. I think so. He sounds like what every guy wants to be when he gets older. What you'd imagine every woman would admire. If you're asking me, 'Do I blame you for loving him?' no, how could I?"

"Good," she said. She sat up straighter. "No, David, I was not asking if you 'blame' me. I do not blame myself. But I am glad that you understand.

"I loved him, and then he began to love me. The making love—that is, the time with the books, the learning—that was like the *Thousand and One Nights*. Not so many, actually. I was Scheherazade. I kept him interested for long enough until he fell in love with me. That was when catastrophe began."

For a moment her eyes went past Bowen and seemed to look over a November landscape. She nodded slightly. "He loved me. What Heinz loves, he must have. He must own it. It must be his, totally, absolutely, in all its soul and being.

"I will not tell you everything—every step, every day by day, every bar by bar, how he built the cage around me. The man who worked in the cubicle next to mine was moved. All the cubicles were reassigned, all the men put at the other side of the room from me.

"I should have said that, of course, I continued working at my job. Although I was the mistress of the head of the division, that did not change my work. Heinz is too good at his job ever to show favoritism to one of his lovers. That would affect the morale of other workers. It might harm productivity.

"If you know that about him, then when I tell you, later, what happened—the things he did—you will understand that he is mad.

"So, first the men were given new places. Then they would not speak with me: only *'Guten Morgen, Fraulein Kraus'; 'Auf wiedersehn, Fraulein Kraus.'* With their eyes down. Then, when Heinz was busy—we were not together every night—if I went to a film, or to visit a woman friend—someone would follow me. Then Heinz arranged to have me taken from my flat to the office by auto, so that I would not have to ride the tram.

"I did not want this. I told him. We quarreled. He said he wanted only to protect me, because he loved me. He said he loved me to distraction. He asked if I still loved him. I still did. He was contrite. He promised to undo what he had done. What he had done only because he so loved me. I was forgiving. He wanted to make love. It was not satisfactory, because he did not wait for me. But I thought only that he was too eager to show how he loved me.

"The next morning, the car was there to pick me up. Nothing was changed.

"And at the office, now the other women would not speak to me. Those who had been my friends, who talked with me, were called in and asked what we talked about, what I said.

"But then I did hear—someone I knew, who knew someone who knew someone, whispered to me that Heinz's superiors knew about what he was doing. That it was hurting morale in my section. They knew about his using . . . company men to take me to work and watch me. They told him he must stop. He said he would.

"But he did not. There was no change at all.

"After a little while longer, I couldn't stand it. I asked for sick leave and went home—to my mother, my father is since nine years dead.

"The next day, men came from Heinz, and began watching my home. I went back. We quarreled. I was very angry. He begged me to forgive him. He said he loved me so much that he was in agony when he didn't know what I was doing. I was sorry for him, but I was still angry. He asked me to understand, to help him, to assure him of my love so that he wouldn't have to do such crazy things. He asked me to make love with him, right then. I didn't want to, but I agreed because I still cared for him, and I wanted to end the quarrel and have us be the way we were before.

"But he didn't really want to make love with me. He wanted me to make love to him. To do things only to give him pleasure, while he did nothing. When I said now he should do something for me, he said no, I should go on. When I said no, he . . . he was bad and cruel with me.

"Then I stopped loving him. I told him to go away. I didn't want to see him again.

"He went away. And the next morning the men took me to work, and they brought me home again and told me I was not allowed to go out until the next morning."

"How could they stop you?" Bowen asked.

"They . . . they said if I went out, they would go to the police and say I was a prostitute; that I had tried to pick them up. They told me Heinz told them he would go to the police and say I had stolen from him. I would lose my work . . . I wouldn't be able to get another job . . . he has so much influence he could keep anyone from hiring me. I believed it.

"So I went back to my flat each evening, and stayed there, and I began to hate him.

"I heard again that the president of the company had told Heinz he must stop. That he was misusing the . . . resources of the company, and that he was making himself ridiculous, and that his own work was suffering. I thought it would be over.

"But nothing changed. I knew Heinz must be absolutely mad to defy his superiors. But then I thought, perhaps he could. As I have told you, he is so important to them . . . he has such power. Nothing changed.

"After a week, Heinz again came to my flat. I must tell you, it was a special flat. I could never have gotten . . . I could never have afforded such a flat, myself. And—from the books—we had made it . . . In the bedroom, mirrors. The ceiling, the doors of the closets . . .

"Heinz came, late at night. I was in bed. I did not think he would come there, that way; and—there he was, in the doorway.

"He said, 'Was I sorry I had hurt him?' His voice is very deep, and strong, but he speaks quietly. He asked me, so quietly, was I sorry I had hurt him? If I was sorry, he said, he would forgive me. He did not want to treat me harshly, he did so only because he loved me so much. He could not bear to be apart from me, to think of me with anyone else.

"He came into the bedroom. He was wearing his black raincoat. He came into the bedroom, he was everywhere. Standing behind himself beyond the foot of the bed, four of him in the closet doors on the side of the room, walking upside down on the ceiling. I knew that if I turned I would see him behind me, coming toward me from above the head of the bed, too.

"I told him to go away. I told him I hated him.

"He began shouting. He is not so tall as you, David, but broader across the shoulders—an older man, heavy in the chest.

"He came toward me, shouting, shouting, 'You are mine! You belong to me! I love you, you are mine!'

"I screamed back at him. I lost my head, as I did today. I screamed—I don't know what, like today, filthy words, every filthy word I knew; and that I hated him! I hated him!

"And then . . . I will not talk about that. For the first year—more than a year—I had the dreams . . . the nightmares. And if I saw . . . I will not speak of this."

Bowen's hands were fisted tightly, now, and pressed against his legs, as if only that could keep them still.

Eva went on, her voice low. "After perhaps a year and a half I thought, 'Must I never love a man again? May I never let a man love me? *Does* Heinz own me?'

"I met, at my work—I was here, in London, then—a very young man: a sweet and gentle young man. I talked with him each day when we had our lunch. After a time we went to the cinema. And after we knew each other, I brought him here, and we made love. It was not good, but he was kind and gentle with me, and I knew I could love a man again.

"But that is not the part I must tell you about.

"The next morning, after the night that Heinz . . . I was in bed. I did not think, I could not think, of going to work. I was trying to think of nothing.

"His men came in, and told me I must go to work. I can only think, now, that Heinz imagined that I could, that I would, that if I went to work as if nothing had happened, then no notice would be taken. He could go on, disobeying the orders of his superiors.

"They made me dress, they drove me to the office, they walked me to my section. I didn't know. I went into my cubicle. I sat down. I started to work. Yes! I actually started to work.

"Then—I cannot tell you exactly. Screaming, I knew somehow I was screaming. Throwing books and papers up over my head, over the walls of the cubicle. I must have run out of my cubicle and begun tearing at things on other people's desks. I must have fainted.

"When I woke, I was on the bed—the daybed, in the first-aid room for our building, on the first floor. A man was there, sitting beside me. It was the . . . the president of the company! I knew him. Only from Heinz. I had been, twice, in his house. He is a . . . he can be a kindly man.

"When he saw I was awake, he took my hand, and asked if I was all right. And then he told me everything would be all right. He would take care of everything. And then someone gave me something to drink, and I fell asleep again.

"To make this story short, now, the president arranged that I should leave Germany. He arranged that I should come here and have work here. He knew Heinz would never leave me alone if I stayed in Germany—"

"Why wouldn't he come after you here?" Bowen's voice was very tight.

"Because . . ." Eva paused but continued looking at him steadily, ". . . because he does not like—he is afraid to travel. Yes! He needs always so much to have power that he does not want to go to a foreign country—where he does not have the language; where he is not in control. Perhaps he might . . . but no, it is like a fear. It is a fear. Two years, now, I have been in England. He will not come here.

"So, the president and the directors, they did not want to lose the work of Heinz; he is too valuable to them, too important. So, they do this for me, to end the situation.

"But . . . now . . . Now I tell you about Gert Nagler. What I have told you is true. All but one thing: Gert does not ask me to sleep with him. Gert works for Heinz. When he touches me, it is for Heinz, not for himself. If he touched me for himself, if he wanted me for himself, Heinz would kill— I don't know what Heinz might do to him.

"Gert gives me news of people I know. That is true, that is why I see him. He sees me in order to check on me for Heinz. And to remind me—only by touching on the arm, only by taking me to lunch—that I still belong to Heinz.

"He—men who work for him—have been watching us. I did not know, but . . . when you saw . . . last night . . .

"I called Gert this morning to say that this must stop. It is too much. I said I would not tolerate it, not even for the sake of . . . for the news of my friends. I told him it must stop or I would go to the police. He finally agreed. This is the story of my phone call."

As she came to the end of her story, Eva's voice had slowed and become flat. She looked at Bowen over her knees, and he stared back numbly.

"I see," he said dully. "I'm sorry, I had to know . . . I . . . I'll kill that bastard if I ever see him! I mean it, Eva. And I'll kill that shit Gert, too. Anybody who follows us or bothers you—"

Eva came up on her knees. "No, David! No. I have talked with Gert. He will not follow us again. And even if someone does . . . You must not try . . . Gert, the men who work for him . . . they are very hard . . . They might . . . there could be violence."

Bowen stared at her for a moment, then smiled —but not with his eyes. "Really? Do you really think I could be so lucky?"

CHAPTER

4

"You would *like* to fight them?" Eva asked.

"Yeah," Bowen answered, looking like an ax. Then he glanced down, perhaps into himself to check who was there. "If they'll give me the chance. I don't hope they'll bother you just so that I can get them. And I'm not hoping I can pick a fight on the street with this Gert or somebody. I'm hoping they pick a fight with me."

"These men can be dangerous, David."

"Well, so can I." With a tight smile Bowen held out his hands toward her, palms down. "Eighteen years of karate ought to be good for something. I've been a black belt for twelve years. Only for sport—never even fought off a mugger. But I've made life hell for several punching bags."

"You are not afraid, then?" It sounded less like a question than hope.

"No. I'm not going to let these creeps hassle us. I love you, Eva. I'm going to take care of you."

". . . Two tails, six feet, and three trunks?" she repeated, still giggling from the previous one.

"That's right," he said.

"What?"

"An elephant with spare parts."

"Oh, David!" She swung across the table as though to slap him, and then fell back laughing.

"What has big ears, weighs two thousand pounds, and has *two* trunks?"

"I don't know."

"An elephant going on vacation."

She exploded again. "That is terrible. These are all terrible! Terrible! Terrible!"

"How can you tell if there are elephants under your bed?"

She was laughing so hard she couldn't ask.

"Because you can touch the bedroom ceiling with your nose!"

Squealing, she flung herself back, and then forward again, wiping the tears from her eyes, brushing at the strand of hair that kept falling over them. Bowen grabbed her plate away just before she would have flailed one arm down on it. He had cooked an omelet for them, she had made a salad, and they had almost finished a two-liter jug of Rhine wine.

"What did the banana say to the elephant?"

Still gasping, she flung her arms out, shrugging.

"Nothing! Don't you know bananas can't talk?"

Twisting, she turned and half knelt, half fell out of her chair. "Oh! oh! oh!" She sat on the floor beating her fists against her chest.

She was already in bed, the covers up to her chin, when Bowen came in from the bathroom. Her face still was puffy and flushed from the crying, the laughing, the wine, but now it showed no emotion: a face after a desperate fever has finally broken.

"You look exhausted," he said.

"I am. It feels good. It is all right. I am all right."

"Good."

He undressed, hanging up his trousers and shirt carefully, setting his shoes side by side under the bed. He put out the lamp. He opened the window shade and looked down at the street. A light rain fell. He checked thoroughly, one way and then the other, looking as best he could through the windows of parked cars. "Nobody there," he said. "Not that I can see."

"There will be no one. I'm sure."

"Never hurts to check. But I hope you're right."

"I'm sure." Her voice was soft, without inflection. She lay on her back. He could see the shape of her hands clasped on her chest. Her eyes were closed.

He got into the bed carefully, trying not to disturb her, reached over only to touch her shoulder. "Hey! What's this?"

"My nightdress."

"I didn't think it was your jogging suit! What is this?" Propped up on one elbow, he stared at her.

She glanced at him, then away. "I felt . . . shy. I thought perhaps you would not want to . . ."

"What? Why?"

"Because . . ."

"Because of you and Heinz? Because you had a lover? Because you practiced from dirty books?"

"Yes."

Bowen sat up. "Eva . . . You said you were in love with him. You were in love with him?"

"Yes. For a while."

"Well, I was in love with Ellen. And we . . . we may not have taken quite the scholarly approach that you did; but we thought about what we were doing, and we sure tried a lot of different things."

"When I told you . . ."

"Yeah. I guess I was . . . shocked . . . for a minute there. But it doesn't matter. The minute we met, that was time zero in the year one. After then is all I care about. I love you. You love music. You're beautiful. And you know you're beautiful, but you don't keep looking in mirrors, you don't look at me like I'm a mirror—just to see me admiring you.

"I love you because . . . you like poetry. Because you like me for writing some—*that* was what made you decide to sleep with me. And I even love you—this is harder—but I even love you for putting on that goddamned nightgown so you could get me to say all this without your asking me, 'Do you love me?' " He shook her. "Now take the goddamn thing off!"

"The word 'antiques' seems to be applied pretty loosely," Bowen said as he and Eva paused by one of the tables that lined the curb, looking at a Toby mug with the face of Ringo Starr.

When they had arrived at the weekly antique fair on Portobello Road, the street already seethed with people moving like multicolored grains of sand in a slurry

—thickly, yet swirling past one another into and out of the shops, around the tables and booths at either side.

"'Old things' might not attract so many people," Eva said.

"And 'junk' probably fewer, although it seems to me that would be more accurate. Hey, look at that little box on the next table; the blue enamel one. That's not bad."

"Where?"

"This end, near the back corner."

"Oh, yes. How do you do that, David? Out of all these things, you see one thing."

"It just caught my eye."

"No. You do that. Things you see . . . From many noises you pick one sound. How do you do it?"

"It's a trick, I guess. A kind of concentration; except instead of concentrating on a particular thing, you concentrate on emptying yourself and being ready. And then when the particular thing does come to your attention, you're prepared to see it or hear it."

"How do you know which is the particular thing?"

"You just know."

They walked on.

Sunlight glinted on chrome, on stainless steel, and here and there on a piece of real silver. It gleamed in bits of brass, even gave a glow to the old gilt of ornate but tarnished picture frames. All up and down the street—in the windows of the antique shops, on the tables set up for the Saturday market—treasures lay heaped: objects old and new, from near and far, of every style, for every taste.

"There are some nice things," Eva said encouragingly. "I think more inside the shops than here on the street. And, of course, so much depends on what one likes; what one person thinks—"

"Yes, I know: One person's junk is another's treasure. When I was a kid, we used to have yard sales and exchange things from each other's attics. Let's go into that one. It looks like they have smaller things. Maybe we'll see something you like."

"David, we said we were not going to buy anything."

"Well . . . If we see something . . . I'd like to get something for you. To commemorate our meeting."

"David . . ."

"Maybe a pin or something. I mean, maybe an antique hat pin you could jab me with if ever I get jealous again."

"Ah. Sentiment and practicality combined."

"That's me."

Collectors, traders, tourists, gawkers: They streamed and eddied along the narrow street. Serious shoppers looking for bargains, impulse buyers ready to splurge, pickpockets, confidence men spotting prospects, people with no interest at all in the goods displayed, who'd come to be with other people, people watchers.

The two men watching Bowen and Eva enter the shop had no difficulty doing so despite the crowd. Eva's hair—platinum and spun gold in the sunshine —was a beacon even though her pink sweater didn't set it off like the deeper colors she usually wore. And some contrast was provided by Bowen's dark-blue shirt.

"Seventy-five pounds," Bowen said, indicating a bulbous vase glazed with swirls of bilious green and purple that stood in a case at the back of the shop they'd entered.

"Too much," Eva shook her head. "I don't think we'll take it."

"Not enough. If they want me to take that, they'll have to give me at least a hundred fifty."

One of the men had gotten ahead of them, sixty feet

farther north along the street. He stood at a booth there, apparently considering whether to buy from a collection of belt buckles. The other man, the one wearing a gray plaid sport jacket and wine-colored shirt, was nearly a block south of the store. He stood beside a window, waiting for Bowen and Eva to emerge.

Although the sunlight sparkled on all the metal and glass, brightening every scatter and splash of color, occasional shadows of scudding clouds swept along the road. The sky had that intensity of blueness that follows one shower and forecasts another. The breeze was cool.

The shop Bowen and Eva had entered sprawled through what from the outside appeared to be two separate stores. The second, on a corner, had a door on the side street.

"Now here's something," Bowen said, stopping near that door at a case displaying antique jewelry. "Look at those earrings. They look like amethyst. I think they're nice."

Eva bent to look. Small, faceted purple stones were centered in tiny, ribbed silver petals. "Yes. They are very lovely."

"Would you like them? I'll get them for you."

Eva looked up at him like a child at Santa Claus, "Oh, thank you, David!" then back at the earrings again. "How much do they cost?"

"Don't look at the price."

"Of course I will look at the price."

"*I* looked at the price. You just look at the earrings."

"No. They cost too much."

"They do not. I can afford it."

"Good. I am glad. I am glad I am attached to a man with so much money." She linked her arm through his.

"I am sure we can do many things with it better than to hang it on my ears." She was smiling, but Bowen wasn't. "Have I offended you, David?"

His arm, stiff, gave no responding pressure to hers. "Yes, I guess a little. I'd like to give you something. I think you should take them."

"You have given me something—everything I want —only by wanting to. Did I offend you to say I am attached to you?"

"No!" He did press her arm with his. "God no! That's the most wonderful thing . . ."

"And for me. That is what you have given me: That I have the right to say to you, 'Thank you, but it costs too much.' Do you understand what I mean?"

"Yes. I understand." He put his hand over hers in the crook of his arm.

"I would like—if you wish—you *should* give me something. When we go back, next to the Underground, there is a flower-seller. I would like—if you wish—that you might buy me some flowers. They do not cost too much, and for you to give me them would make me very happy."

For an instant Bowen looked like his face would crack. "That would make me very happy."

A woman coming into the shop brushed by him.

"You want to go on?" he asked.

"Yes. One moment, though. The wind is a little cold." Eva slipped into her dark-blue jacket, pulled a blue scarf from the pocket and tied it over her head.

"Yes. I think I'll put mine on too." Bowen put on his tan raincoat, turned the collar up. "Okay?" They went out onto the side street, crossed, and came back to Portobello Road. Eva had taken his arm again, and he lowered his head to speak to her.

Neither of the watchers recognized them. The one to

the north didn't move to keep his distance. The one behind, to the south, didn't follow; but after another three minutes he began to go along the shops toward the one he'd seen Bowen and Eva enter.

"Now that is nice—that chair." Eva stopped them at a window. "Don't you think?"

"I think it's very pretty. It's graceful, and the carving is excellent. But I wouldn't want to sit on it for more than five minutes."

"You are not supposed to sit on it. You are supposed to put it against a wall, next to a little table, and look at it."

"Right. Of course. I guess I'm just too practical." With Eva's arm still linked through his own, they drifted along.

The plaid-jacketed man reached the shop. He glanced in once, then looked more carefully. He went farther along and looked in through the adjoining front, then walked quickly to the corner and stared down the side street. He scanned down Portobello, didn't see the couple he sought. He did pick out his partner. He began moving toward him, walking quickly, but not rushing, looking over the crowd and into the shops he passed.

"Do you like winkles?" Eva asked, indicating a booth. Her English was excellent, but the word still came out halfway to "vinkles."

"What are winkles?"

"A kind of shellfish."

"What do they taste like?"

"I think like a piece of rubber that has been soaking in a bucket of low-tide sea water for six months."

"No, thank you. I think I'll pass this time."

"Some people like them."

They ambled farther.

"Why are you smiling that way?" she asked.

"Because everybody turns to look at you."

"Oh, David."

"It's true. And I'm sure you know it."

"The women are looking at *you*. And I'm sure you know *that*."

"The men look at you, the women look at both of us."

They stopped at a table on which stood boxes of old photographs. Releasing Bowen's arm, Eva began looking through them. He glanced at one or two, then idly examined passersby. He saw a man who looked like a rat: narrow-faced, sharp-nosed, furtive-eyed, hunched. Trying not to be obvious about it, Bowen checked that his billfold was in place. A young woman stalked up the middle of the street. She had a burr haircut and no eyebrows, and her lips were painted the color of over-ripe plum. An elderly gentleman with a white mustache, wearing a Norfolk jacket and a stick, never looked at her as he bore what was left of the Empire past her. Over by a table diagonally across and back up the street a tallish man in a trendy leather jacket—an Italian designer neo-Nazi style—was talking with a short, blue-chinned Mafia type in a plaid jacket and dark shirt. They spoke to each other sideways while casing the crowd; obviously they were either crooks or policemen. The tall man caught Bowen's eye for an instant, but his gaze swept on down the street.

"I think you are getting bored," Eva said.

"Oh no. Not if you're enjoying yourself."

"I am surprised, David, that you do not take more of a professional interest in things here."

"Professional interest?"

"Possible items for investment."

"Oh. No. I deal more in corporations and bonds and that kind of thing. Not artifacts."

"Isn't it the same idea? Seeing what you can buy cheaply and sell at a profit? I would think it would intrigue you."

"Well, I guess it just doesn't seem the same to me. Don't you want to look around some more?"

"I have been enjoying myself, but it is enough. We can go."

"Okay." They linked arms again and began strolling back up the street. "What do you want to do?"

"We are going to have supper after the concert tonight?" she asked.

"If you still want to. I like that better myself."

"Yes. We will not be sleepy during the concert. So, we should have a hearty lunch, don't you think?"

"Sure. Where do you want to go?"

"There is a Pakistani restaurant on the high street near my flat. They do carry-out. We could buy something and eat at home. I think it will rain again this afternoon. We could stay inside, and have lunch, and a nice nap before going out this evening."

"No."

"You don't like that?"

"We could have lunch, and then make love, and *then* have a nap."

"Why, what a lovely idea, David!"

"I know you wouldn't have thought of it if I hadn't."

"Perhaps it would have come to me."

The concert was one of a series presented in a church at the edge of Belgravia. The Harmonia string quartet played. Neither Eva nor Bowen had heard of the group but the program concluded with the Schubert quartet in A minor, and that was reason enough for them to want to hear it.

When they came out onto the street, a warm mist —golden from the sodium-vapor streetlamps— glowed in the air.

"Oh, David! Look: the color! It is what they say is around angels: a glory! Let's walk to the restaurant! It's not far, is it? I think it will take us less than half an hour."

"Sure. It's just on the other side of Belgravia. Just south of Brompton Road. Let's do it."

They started along the north side of Eaton Square.

"Look at the light on these houses," he said. "In daylight, they're white. Austere. They were built— Did you see any of *Upstairs, Downstairs?* They were built for the upper crust. All those porticoes, columns, all the same down the whole row: all formal, dignified, elegant. This neighborhood is strictly for the patricians: no plebeian passion around here. But look at them now: That light is like apricot jam; and it's turned them all into marzipan! And look at the shadows: Your eye makes them purple. All the houses—they've been turned into palaces out of the Arabian Nights. Pleasure domes. Not to suggest houses of pleasure, although . . ."

"Yes, David! Or, perhaps, palaces of *enchanters* who lure unwary people inside and turn them into toads!"

They walked hand in hand, smiling, only beginning to descend from the realm to which the music had transported them. Although the color of the streetlamp light dulled and darkened the greenery in the park along the other side of the street, the mist softened even the deepest black.

Nothing in the night seemed sinister until Bowen

—aware by some instinct that they were walking off course—stopped, took out his map, and, looking around, realized that a person who had been walking on the other side of the narrow park had stopped too.

Bowen couldn't see him. He had noted the presence of the man across the park, and now the man—instead of appearing in the next break between bushes—had stopped where he couldn't be seen.

"Eva, keep looking at me," Bowen said tensely, quietly.

Eva stiffened as he had done.

He in his tan raincoat, she in her dark blue, both with their collars turned up, standing at a quiet corner under the streetlamp, holding open his pocket map of central London—they could have been posing for a Burberry's ad.

"Don't turn right away. I think we're being followed," he said. "He's across the park, behind the bushes. You can't see him. Maybe he can look through and see us, so don't look at him."

"How do you know he's following us?"

"Because he's stopped."

"Perhaps . . ."

"Well, we'll see. Look," Bowen pointed to the map again. "I had it in my mind that these streets run east and west, but they don't. They go northeast-southwest. We're heading south of where we want to be. We have to turn right and go up this way. But we're going to make a couple extra turns, and see. We're just going to act like we're sightseeing—looking at the buildings, okay?"

"We should take a taxi. We shouldn't do anything—"

"There aren't any taxis. We'd have to get to a busier

street, anyway. And I am not running away, Eva. I'm going to check this out, and if this guy *is* following us I'm going to deal with him."

"David . . ."

"Come on." Bowen took Eva's arm, and turned her, and started up Lyall Street. Halfway up the block he turned them right again into an alley.

Small square stones paved the way, which led between two rows of low buildings that had been the stables at the rear of the townhouses facing the gracious streets. Although now they were, themselves, posh places to live, the alley was still a back-behind, not municipally lighted. Here and there an electrified lantern over a red- or black-enameled door splashed skim-milk light that soaked into old bricks and trickled away into the black crevices of the paving stones. At farther distances down the alley the lamps grew fuzzier; Belgrave Place crossing at the end was a bright smudge; and overhead the fog held that golden glow. But close by, the mist was too thin, the lanterns too pale to fill it. Bowen and Eva might have hidden themselves in the dense blackness of a shadowed doorway. Or they might have hurried down the long lane, veiling themselves in those layers of mist and disappearing in who-could-say-which-direction at the end.

When the man who was following them came up Lyall Street, on the side opposite the mouth of the alley, he paused and looked in. He couldn't see Bowen's and Eva's silhouettes, nor could he tell what they might have done. He spoke into the tiny microphone pinned behind his lapel, and continued up to the next corner, at Eaton Place. He went on around to his left on Eaton Place, giving himself as much distance and cover as he could while still being able to see where

Bowen and Eva had gone into the alley. In a moment, his partner drove past him on Eaton to check Belgrave Street at the far end of the block.

The driver was just reporting to the first that the alley had an exit out to Eaton Place halfway down the block, when Bowen and Eva came out of it. He continued to Belgrave, turned left and out of sight, and halted.

Bowen and Eva came out onto Eaton Place, and turned left—back toward Lyall Street, toward the man standing just beyond the corner. The man instantly pivoted and began walking away on Eaton, as though he'd been going that way all along.

"I was right," Bowen said.

"How do you know? He is not following, he's ahead. He's going away from us."

"He must have come up along the street behind us, and he was waiting there to see which way we went."

"How can you know that? How do you know it was the same person who was across the park?"

"I don't. I didn't see that guy clearly at all. But the guy who's ahead of us now was on Portobello Road this morning." Bowen's jaw was set, his eyes sharp. He looked grim, yet pleased.

They turned and went north on Lyall, passing between the masses of the buildings that walled each side of the street like mausoleums. The orange light lay slathered on them, makeup on the face of a corpse.

Bowen strode along with his hands fisted in his raincoat pockets, determinedly not looking over his shoulder. "Don't look back, Eva. He won't be behind us now. If he picks us up again, we'll spot him later; but don't show we're looking for him."

Eva's hand was linked through his arm. She squeezed it for emphasis as she spoke. "Gert promised me, David. I was very firm, and he promised, and I don't believe he would have us followed. Perhaps you were mistaken."

"You were lied to before about this kind of thing, weren't you? Why should you believe anything he said? I wasn't mistaken. I recognized that guy. I recognized his sport jacket. I recognized him. He was on Portobello Road this morning, and I don't believe it's a coincidence."

"But he went away from us."

"What else could he do? Maybe now he'll drop it, for tonight. Maybe he'll come around the block and try to pick us up again. Maybe he's got partners. We'll just keep going the way we were going, and watch."

"And what will we do if we are being followed?"

"I don't know—exactly. Find some way to confront them. I mean, catch them out, show them we know —and that we're not just going to complain about it over the telephone."

"David, no! You must not begin a fight with them. They are—if it is them—they are truly dangerous."

"I'm not going to pick a fight. But if I can get one of them off alone, and he wants to start something . . . I think I can handle this, Eva. I really can."

At Pont Street Bowen and Eva turned left. As they approached the district south of Knightsbridge more people were about. They had to wait for the crossing signal at Sloan Street because of the traffic. Other colors of light cut the lurid yellow from the sodium lamps. But whatever their hue, they gleamed from puddles on the sidewalk, from the roads, as though from pits filled with black oil. Cars swished past on the street, flecks of light glinting and streaking along their sides, like sleek predatory fish.

After Bowen and Eva had crossed Sloan Street, the

men following them took advantage of the traffic to let the one who'd been on foot out of the car again. He was wearing a hat now, and he pulled on a dark raincoat before starting to trail them.

At the fork at the end of Pont Street, Bowen led Eva left a few paces and stopped opposite the church there.

"Now we look at the church as if I were telling you something about it." He gestured. Then he led her back to the junction and across Pont Street.

The follower was on that side, sixty yards back. Not stopping, he took shorter steps and slowed his pace, and let a couple pass him.

Bowen had halted again, and once more pointed across the street toward the church. "Okay," he said. "I've got an idea who's behind us now. We'll go on and see if any of them keep with us."

They crossed Walton Street and entered Beauchamp Place. The restaurant where they'd planned to eat was near the other end, but Bowen stopped them at the first one they came to. "Now we look at the menu on the post here," he said.

Many people were entering and leaving the restaurants and coffee houses, strolling, stopping to read the menus and notices posted outside, just as Bowen and Eva were doing. Back on the far side of Walton Street, the follower shielded himself behind a post-box pillar. He had contacted his partner. As soon as that man had gotten around through traffic and found a place where he could watch the other end of Beauchamp, keeping the quarry in sight wouldn't matter. Eva and Bowen could dine wherever they wanted; they'd be picked up again afterward. But to make sure they didn't wander right out of Beauchamp and go into some place on Brompton Road unseen, he had to stay close until his partner was set.

"Yes!" Bowen exclaimed. "I see him!"

"Where?"

"Don't look!"

"How can you be sure? How could you see him —there are so many people?"

"I saw him because I was ready to see him. Now come on."

"Where are we going?"

"Just around the block. I think I know how to catch him. When I was here before, when I found the restaurant . . . Come on. I'll show you."

"David, no!"

"Yes."

She had turned at an angle to him, pulling on his arm. He put his hand over hers and pressed hard.

"I'm going to take care of this. If you want, we'll slip you into a café or something and I'll go on. But I am going to deal with this." He spoke softly, his voice pitched low. "But, on second thought . . ." he said after the pause in which she didn't retort, ". . . while I really don't think there is much danger—right here, in the middle of the city—if *you* do, then we *had* better get you out of it."

"No! If you do this, I come with you!" Her head was set squarely, her chin thrust toward him in a way he hadn't seen before.

For another moment they stared at one another, two boulders of determination.

"Okay," he said. "There isn't going to be any problem, anyway. Come on."

As though having decided on a destination, they walked directly to the end of the street and turned onto Brompton. The man following used other pedestrians for cover as best he could, closing the distance, keeping Bowen and Eva in sight along Brompton, and saw when they turned right again. His partner still wasn't in place.

"Have you seen this street before?" Bowen asked.

"No."

"I'd have wanted to show it to you, anyway. Look! Right here in the middle of all this commercial stuff —it's like it doesn't know: It doesn't know it isn't still in the eighteenth century."

Small, red-brick Georgian houses lined the narrow sidewalks. Warm light shone on frilly curtains in the many-paned windows. The mist that haloed the lanterns on posts seemed thicker, more dreamlike, than it had on the busy thoroughfare.

"But how . . . ?" Eva started to ask.

"I'll show you. Come on. Hurry."

The man following must not have known Beaufort Gardens was a dead end or he might simply have decided to hold back and wait for Bowen and Eva to emerge again. He came up to its corner, stood out at the Brompton Road curb, waited until a group of people were passing so he would have cover, then quickly moved to peer down Beaufort and get back out of sight again. In that one glance he'd taken in that the street had been empty. He spoke with his partner, who even then was pulling into the clear space of a bus stop two blocks away, and started down the way Bowen and Eva had gone. The street was short. Despite the fog, he didn't have to go far to see the curb at the end joining the ones at the sides of the street without a break.

The man halted, listening. From all around, constant as the sea, the city roared. But the little mist-muffled street was a cave holding its own silence to itself. There were no voices. No footsteps. His own barely sounded as he continued toward the dead end. He was a short man, stocky—even heavy—but he wore crepe-soled shoes, and put his feet down carefully. He could see that the street had no outlet for cars, but perhaps he knew that such cul-de-sacs often have passages at their ends for pedestrians.

This one did: a narrow alley between the last house on his right and the buildings blocking the end. As soon as he saw it, the man stepped from the sidewalk out into the middle of the street so that he could look through the gate at a better angle. The passage seemed narrow. Short sections of wall ending at brick pillars flanked the wrought-iron gate. The gate was not quite closed.

The man stood still for a moment. Then carefully, but not furtively, he came toward the gate. He halted three feet away. The passage was unlit, although he could see light at the end of it. He could see no one within it. He stepped forward again, and listened. He put his hands up, and began to push the gate inward. Its hinges ground and squeaked.

"Looking for somebody?" Bowen asked sharply, stepping from behind the pillar and yanking on the gate.

The man had been pushing with his palms, but he wasn't jerked inward, off balance. He gasped and jumped back with an alacrity surprising for his build.

Bowen swung the gate in, looming forward into the opening, his own hands up, keeping the man within range of a kick. Eva came into sight behind him.

"Okay, buddy. Now I'm telling you: You leave this woman alone!"

The man stared back at him for an instant, then raised and showed his palms. "Hey, fella," he said, "I don't know what your problem is, but leave me outta it. I'm just a tourist here myself."

CHAPTER

5

Without saying another word to the man, Bowen backed into the passageway, taking Eva's hand and pushing her before him toward the brightness at the other end. The man continued to stand framed by the gateway, looking after them—his figure growing smaller with distance, losing definition in the mist, but always there until they came out at the other end.

"Who *was* that?" Eva asked.

Bowen said, "We've got to get out of here." Stepping to the curb, he flagged one of the cruising taxis.

"David . . ." she started to question again when they were inside and the cab had pulled away to carry them back to her apartment.

"Later," he said firmly. "I'll explain when we get

there." His voice, his grip on her hand, had the grim, high-tensile calm of a man steering a runaway truck down a mountainside. Several times he turned to peer through the cab's rear window, evidently assuring himself they weren't being followed. Then he stared straight ahead as though that runaway truck had crashed and he was just beginning to know he'd been injured, and was trying to feel whether he could move.

When they reached her house he looked up and down the street from inside the taxi before getting out. He led them up the stairs to her flat quickly but on guard; went inside ahead of her the same way —reaching and turning on lights before entering. While Eva stood in the living room staring after him, he looked into each of the other rooms and out through the windows at the street, then pulled the blinds.

"Okay," he said, "I don't think they're out there yet."

"David, what is happening? Who was that man? He wasn't from Gert, he wasn't German. He looked Italian, but he spoke like an American."

For a moment Bowen stared back at her from the window. "Italian . . . yes, he did," he said as though that aspect of the man's appearance hadn't registered before. "You're right." He hesitated. "Eva . . . First, thanks for riding with me, not pressing me till we got here. I'll tell you, now. But come into the bedroom. I've got to pack."

"David . . . ! Why?"

"Come on. I've got to hurry."

In the bedroom he gestured for her to sit on the chair while he grabbed his smaller suitcase from the closet, threw it on the bed. Then he paused, looking at her. The furrow had formed between her eyebrows, but she had clasped her hands to confine the worry or anger that caused it.

"I have to tell you something," he began. "I guess we both have things in our pasts we didn't want to talk about. We wanted it to be 'time zero, year one,' like I said: forget the bad things, start our whole lives new. And also . . . You were afraid of how I might feel about you if I knew about your past?"

She nodded. Now she looked like someone who knows a story will be tragic even before all the characters have been introduced.

"Well, the same with me," he said. He opened the suitcase, and laid back with careful precision the internal straps meant to hold clothes in place, and then stared at the empty bag. As always, he stood solidly, but now he spoke without looking at her. "The way I got the money I'm living on now, that I invest . . . just what I told you: I was a financial analyst. But my clients . . ."

"Yes," she said. It wasn't a question, but he must have taken it as a prompt.

"You were right about that guy tonight looking Italian. I worked for the Mafia. You know what that is?"

She hesitated, then said, "Yes, of course."

He wheeled abruptly, and from the chest of drawers took underwear and socks, placed them beside the suitcase. "There was a guy I knew in college—when I was an undergraduate. From New York. I guess you could call him an Italian-American Prince. There were rumors about what his father did, but . . . I didn't know him well. Anyway, after I went through graduate school and started working for Merrill Lynch, he looked me up. And—to make the story short—I worked for him, for his family."

He took a shirt from the closet, laid it on the bed, began folding it. "I didn't do anything that was actually illegal. I mean, they had money, they wanted to invest it—just like anybody else. I didn't have to know where the money came from. I did assume they wouldn't want anybody else to know either; so I advised them about how they could move their assets around, make them difficult to trace. Actually, that's something that a lot of financial counselors do for a lot of clients."

He began folding another shirt. "So, I told myself I wasn't doing anything wrong. Not really wrong. That's what I told myself: I was only a professional person providing a service to people who were entitled to buy it, like any other members of the public. Just practicing an honest profession. And I sure was doing myself a lot of good by it. They paid me very well—I guess a lot of people won't work for them, and they wanted to make sure I'd keep doing it. And—as I told you—I really am good at what I do, so I made more for myself out of what they gave me."

He took trousers from the closet, folded them, put them into the bag, talking as though practicing a speech in an empty room. He avoided looking at Eva. All that time she watched him with a serious but distant amazement, like one atheist hearing another tell about seeing an angel.

"I worked for them for almost five years—not just a little while. I did them a lot of good. We did each other a lot of good."

He put in a sweater, then began placing the shirts and underclothes, making the most efficient use of the space. "After a while, I finally decided I wanted out. I decided I really didn't like what they did—when I finally let myself think about it."

He put the last of the clothes into the suitcase, and

then stood looking down at it. "I'll have to get my things from the bathroom," he said, but didn't move.

"So, you see, Eva," he said after a moment, his eyes still away from her, "I'm not quite the sensitive, honest, principled, high-minded guy you thought I was." His voice was low and soft, like a man with a chest wound. "I had hoped you wouldn't have to know that."

Eva's expression had been one of astonished disbelief. But then she responded to his pain. "You left them," she said quietly.

"Yes. Eventually."

"So, it would seem, David, that you became high-minded and principled."

"Yeah," he said. He put his hands into his pockets, turned his head toward her. "Maybe I did. I'd like to think so. However, my conscience didn't really start bothering me till I'd made a pile and didn't need to work for them anymore. And until I began realizing that the kind of people I was coming to like to be with wouldn't approve of what I did. I mean, would you approve? If—when we met—I'd introduced myself saying, 'Hey, guess who I work for?' would you have been interested in me?"

"I am 'interested' in you now, David. I approve of you now."

After a moment, he said, "Thank you." But he didn't turn to her until she rose and came to him and touched his shoulder. Then they held one another tightly.

"I've got to get going," he said, pushing her away and striding into the bathroom.

"Why?" She came as far as the bedroom door.

He swept his things together and into a plastic-lined pouch. "You don't just walk away from those guys,

Eva. If you've got something they want, they keep on wanting it—and they get it. They don't mind paying for it, but they won't let you not give it to them."

Grabbing up the pouch, he brushed past her to the bed again. "And, I'm a danger to them. The things I know . . . there are a lot of people who would like to know what I know about them."

"So they are following you? Here? They are a danger to you?"

"Yes. I knew they'd come after me if I tried to leave them. When I decided to go, I planned . . . I was able—people I met—I was able to get myself a false passport." He had tossed the pouch into the suitcase. From a compartment in its lid he took a folder, waved it toward her, and shoved it into his jacket pocket. "When I travel—cross a border—I use a different name. I never thought they'd trace me once I started moving around in Europe.

"When I saw somebody watching us the other night, I was worried. But when you said it was Gert . . ."

"It was: his men."

"Then these guys have picked me up since then. I don't know how they did it. Anyway, I've got to shake them, Eva."

"Where will you go?"

"I don't know. Out of London. You don't have to show any papers anywhere when you travel in England. Later I can get out of the country."

"David . . ."

"I've got to, Eva. Later—as soon as I can—I'll get in touch with you."

"No! Let me go with you!"

"No. You can't."

"Are you afraid for me? Is there so much danger —right now? Then we must call the police!"

"No! That's just what I can't do. I call the police, tell them why— They'll contact the States, and I'll be held, maybe . . . subpoenaed, forced to go back, testify. Then I'd really be in danger. No, the best thing is to get away. There won't be any danger if I move fast enough."

"Then I go with you!" She seized his arm.

"No!"

"Yes, David. I can help you. Two are better for watching, and— I must go with you, David. If you go alone, I think I will never see you again!"

"Of course you will. I'll get in touch as soon—"

"I'm afraid you won't."

"I will! Eva, I love you. I don't want to leave you; I don't want ever to be away from you. Believe me. Believe me!"

For a moment he stared at her with all that concentration he could bring to bear. Finally, she released her grip and said, "All right, David, I will believe you. But what am I . . . ? To sit here, not knowing? Sick from not knowing, worrying, terrified for you—" He didn't look persuaded. Another idea seemed to strike her. "And what will they do to me? Perhaps they will watch me, follow me, waiting for you to call . . . Perhaps they might try to make me tell them where you have gone!"

"They wouldn't hurt you. Maybe they'd watch . . ." But he faltered. "I don't know. I don't think they'd . . . But they're capable of anything if they believe . . . Oh, God, Eva, if I've put you in danger . . . !"

Down on the street a car passed slowly. Even the spinning of the shaft inside the electric clock on the bedside table was audible.

"Okay," he said, suddenly solid again. "You come with me for a couple days—call in sick for work, whatever you have to do. By then I'll be able to get out of the country without them being able . . . Then I'll send a cable to them telling them you don't know where I am; that if they bother you, I'll go straight to the police and tell everything I know. That'll keep them away—even if they watch you, which they won't do for very long, anyway. We'll have a way to be in contact. When it seems safe again, we'll find a way to meet."

"David . . ." Then Eva flipped her hand dismissively. "Now is not the time for arguing. Yes." She gestured to his suitcase, "Are you finished?"

"Yes."

"Please move your bag. I pack now, too."

As Bowen closed his bag and lifted it from the bed, Eva pulled one of her own from underneath it. "It is a good plan, David: to go away together for a little time. Then . . . we must see." She began gathering clothes and putting them into the bag. "What else can we do? I can tell you that there is nothing here—in London, in my life—that I could not leave tonight and never think about again."

She paused, holding a folded sweater, and looked at him where he stood in the doorway. "And there is nothing I would not leave, I think, to be with you." She placed the sweater into a corner of the bag, went on swiftly poking other things around it. "I think that is true," she said. "I think it is possible for a person to come into one's life—for Life to come—and take one's hand, and one goes and never hears the door closing behind, and never regrets. I think that if one will not take that hand when it is offered, *that* is what one will regret—sitting alone behind that closed door —forever.

"But I do not know . . . I know we have only four days together." She looked at him quickly, shook her head. "No. Four nights. Only one full day. So we cannot speak of such things, perhaps, with good sense. So, we go away together now, and we do not say what we do after that."

She looked at him steadily for a moment, then down at her bag again, and gestured toward it. "So, where do we go?"

"I don't . . . The Lake District. I was going to go hiking there anyway; I've read up about it."

"Good. I wear my walking shoes." She got them from the closet. "I put on trousers." She stepped to him, turned her back. "Do my zip." He unzipped her dress, and she stepped away, slipping it down. "And you should take your heavier sweater. Have you warm stockings?"

"I'll wear it," he said. "I'll wear my hiking shoes, too. Anything else we need, we'll just buy. I've got plenty of traveler's checks, and three credit cards."

"Good. How do we go away? Do you think they will be outside?"

"They could be, by now. I'll check through the window, but . . . I think we'd better just assume they are."

"Five minutes, I will be ready; but do you think there will be a train? So late, on Saturday night?"

"I don't know. I . . . I feel like we've got to get out of here as fast as we can. But . . ."

"If there is no train until morning, where do we go?"

"I don't know." Bowen stared back at her, then rapidly from side to side as if uncertain whether the closeness of the walls protected or confined them. "I don't know . . . I . . ."

Suddenly he straightened, his fists against his hips. "I'm running scared. That is a bad thing to do. Let's just take a little minute and breathe deeply." He took that breath. "Okay. The first thing is, we find out about trains. Then—if you're right—if there isn't going to be one before sometime tomorrow morning—we settle down and try to get some rest. Whatever those guys might do . . . I don't see them trying to blast in here in the middle of the night, waking up all the neighbors, to get me. We're probably much safer in here than wandering around London between now and dawn, with no place to go. And then—when we've got our brains in gear again—we figure how we're going to get to the train without being followed."

"How can you get into this building other than through the front door downstairs?"

"That is the only way."

"There's no back entrance?"

"The flat on the ground floor has a door to the garden behind the house, but there is no stairway up from there—it must have been taken out when the house was made into flats."

"There's no fire escape?"

"No."

"How could they rent apartments without . . . ? In the States . . . Okay, it doesn't matter."

"You said you didn't think they would try to get in."

"I don't. I think they'll wait and try to get to me when I'm off alone someplace. The only reason they might move sooner is that they know I know they're watching me. So I don't think . . . I just want to be sure that when we open the front door to your apartment here, somebody can't be waiting in the hall. The only way they could get in is through the street door?"

"Yes."

"Okay. Then we can watch from the window here."

Bowen was on guard at the side of the bedroom

window, looking down through the slanted slats. He could see the sidewalk in front of the entrance, and up and down the street. He and Eva had turned out all the lights in the flat. Their suitcases stood ready at the door.

"Are you going to stand there all night?" she asked.

He turned to her for a moment. "No," he said. "I'm going to sit." He pulled the small armchair over beside the window. "Why don't you lie down? Try to get some rest. Sleep, if you can."

"And you?"

"I'll be all right."

"We can take turns."

"I'll be all right," he said again.

"We can take turns," she repeated, lightly but firmly.

He turned and stared at her. She stood at one side of the bed, so thin, so delicate, so pale in the streetlamp light, so slight and fragile-looking; yet there was the sense she was so weighted, centered, that no matter how one pushed or tugged her she could not be swayed. "Okay," he said after a moment.

Eva sat on the edge of the bed, removed her shoes, swung her feet up.

"Thank you," Bowen said. "For wanting to help me. For sharing this."

"I love you, David," she said as though he had asked a question and that was the answer.

"I believe you do, Eva. I . . . I'm sorry. I should have told you about me—all of it—when we first met."

"No. How could you? Why would you? I did not tell you about Heinz. Surely everyone who meets someone has something to hide: has a past, has a secret, something of which to be ashamed. I think two people must begin with what is lovable. If that is enough, if they fall in love, then the strength of the love can be tested by what is brought up from hiding. No one would ever fall in love, David, if they began by saying, 'How do you do? Let me tell you about the horrible person I have been.'"

"You think people can love when they've deceived each other?"

"Yes." She made that affirmation in the same soft but certain tone as before.

"But love is trust," he said. "That's what you said. You're right—you have to be able to trust. And if there's a deception, sooner or later—"

"Sooner or later it will be known. No, the deception cannot go on forever. The truth will be known. And then the love—which also is a truth—will be put beside it. I do love you, David."

"I do love you, Eva." He looked away to check through the window. Without looking back at her he said, "I'm sorry I've gotten you involved in this. Whatever happens, I want you to know I mean that."

"Yes. I am sorry there is something to be involved in. I am sorry I have involved you with Gert Nagler, with Heinz."

"Well, they don't seem to be our immediate problem."

"No."

They were silent for a time, Bowen watching the street, Eva looking at the pattern of shadows on the ceiling. She stifled a yawn.

"Are you sleepy?" he asked. "Do you think you can sleep for a while?"

"I think perhaps."

Dashing down the front steps and across the sidewalk, Eva and Bowen reached the curb as the taxi halted. They had been standing just inside the entrance, watching through the glass panels beside the door.

Eva grabbed open the taxi door, ducked in and slid to the far side of the backseat, swinging her bag ahead of her. Bowen came immediately behind, slamming the door and saying, "Victoria Station, and hurry, please, we're late for our train!"

As the cab sped off, Bowen stayed hunching forward, watching for any movement ahead or to the sides. Eva kept herself strained around looking out the back. "Yes," she said as they reached the first cross street and turned.

Bowen glanced back. Another car had pulled out from the curb at the far end of the block. His and Eva's eyes met for a moment, but they said nothing.

Early on an overcast Sunday morning: All of London seemed to be sleeping-in behind a drawn window shade—a translucent mother-of-pearl fog just above the chimney-pots. Its brightness showed the sun was up and about and would soon raise the curtain and rouse the slug-a-beds.

All the shops on the main road were shuttered. Ahead, a bus heaved itself away from the curb and lumbered along with a kind of somnolent momentum. A few other taxis cruised drowsily, two men were delivering newspapers from a van, here and there sleepy-looking people drove private cars. Traffic increased as they neared the center of the city, but the car behind had no difficulty following. It caught up with them to a distance of one block, then maintained that interval.

Bowen and Eva didn't watch it all the time. Looking ahead as well, they were aware that after they had

turned onto the Great Albert Road another car
—perhaps only by coincidence—moved along exactly
at their speed a block and a half in front of them.

They passed a woman wearing a trenchcoat over her
pajamas, walking a poodle. At another place a young
man stood on a corner staring across the street, looking
as though he'd stuck his finger into an electric socket
and the current had made his hair stand on end and
burned out his eyes. Along the edges of the parks,
where in the filtered light and unmoving air great trees
stood as still and flat as those in a watercolor landscape, joggers ran, and what traffic there was swept
around, avoiding the maze of inner streets.

Despite that traffic, the two cars stayed with them all
the way. The leading car had already halted, double
parked, when the cab drew up at Victoria Station. The
second car stopped a little way behind. Bowen couldn't
see whether anyone had gotten out of the first one. He
shoved bills over the seat, saying, "Keep it," and was
out of the door helping Eva and glancing toward the
other car all in a moment. Its door was opening. But
then Eva was on the sidewalk and Bowen slammed the
cab door and they turned and darted into the station.
They didn't look behind. They assumed men would be
following.

Bowen grabbed Eva's hand, and—as always—she
matched his pressure. They started toward the ticket
windows, then suddenly swerved and headed away,
making for the Underground. They dropped hands as
they approached the ticket machines, each reaching
into a pocket for the exact change they had counted out
and put there. Side by side they went through adjacent
gates, the way they'd planned it. They walked together
quickly to the escalator, then Bowen stepped ahead

and led the way, walking down the moving steps. He didn't look back, but he could hear Eva in step right behind him.

They went down, down, deep under the ground where the light never changed direction, brightness, color.

At the bottom of the escalator Bowen took Eva's hand again, and they walked rapidly along the platform, stopping halfway toward the other end. A few people already stood there, waiting; but not enough to form a crowd within which Eva and Bowen could hide. They hadn't expected to do that. They had hoped to find a train when they reached the platform; one just about to leave, that they could board before anyone else could follow. They weren't that lucky.

Other people came from the escalator: the three that Bowen and Eva had walked down past, then a haughty, heavyset woman in a Queen Mother hat, twenty seconds later two men in dark overcoats, in another ten seconds a single man wearing a tan raincoat. A few more people reached the platform by the stairway at the other end: two heavily made-up young women who revealed—whenever their shiny plastic raincoats opened—legs uncovered to their upper thighs, then a man wearing a black anorak, then a dark-skinned man in a bus conductor's uniform and a turban.

Bowen and Eva didn't put their suitcases down.

The people who came onto the platform—and others continued to arrive—spread themselves along it. None came as far as the middle. Travelers on a sleepy Sunday morning: going visiting, going home, going about their innocent businesses. None of them looked sinister. "What do you think, David?" Eva asked quietly.

"I don't know. None of them is anyone I've seen before. I don't think it would be the duchess or the tarts."

"No. Perhaps the family there—the little boy could be a dwarf," she said with speculative seriousness.

"My guess would be the Sikh; he's got a transmitter in his turban."

Eva looked at the man, nodded slightly, appraisingly. "Perhaps." No strain showed on her face, but she was clutching his hand, and he squeezed back as hard.

The little boy piped questions continually at one end of the platform; the two young women crooned fluently to one another in vowels alone.

The place had a sense of cold on the heart rather than on the face. Not a chill to make the body shiver to warm itself, but a lack of living warmth that made the soul shudder. Eva must have felt that: There wasn't any other danger closing on them, but she pressed her shoulder to Bowen's. He felt the tremor in her, and held her arm tightly under his.

Then—before any sound—there came a sense of distant motion: a quivering in the concrete underfoot, a tension in the rails. The tan-raincoated man drifted a few steps toward Eva and Bowen, halted again. But the woman in the hat, and two later arrivals, also moved to find less congested places from which to board when the train arrived. None of them looked at Eva and Bowen, but Bowen looked at them all suspiciously, including the woman in the hat.

Far off in the tube there was a low rumble and a soft rush. The air began to move—not yet a wind, merely a sense of stirring.

The man in the anorak sauntered nearer.

The rumble became a thunder, then a regularly pulsing, rocking roar.

More people were coming to the center of the platform. Both the man in the raincoat and the one in the anorak did that. Neither came as close to Bowen and Eva as did some others.

The roar became almost deafening. Light glowed on the curved wall in the tunnel beyond the platform. It flared. And then suddenly the train hurled itself out of its lair.

Bowen and Eva stood still, hand in hand, holding their suitcases while exiting passengers came through the doors and strode away. They stood while the people on either side of them went onto the train. The matron went on, the family went on, the two men in dark coats went on, the one in the tan coat went on—he had shifted his place enough so that he boarded one end of the car Eva and Bowen stood before. On the other side of them, the Sikh boarded, and the girls, and all but one of the other people. The man in the anorak waited. Evidently, this wasn't his train. Evidently it wasn't Bowen's and Eva's. They stood, waiting, just two steps away from an open doorway.

Waiting was a strange thing for any of them to do: There were no branches on that line; all trains followed the same route to the same destination.

"Mind the doors!" a disembodied voice called.

Moving as one, Eva and Bowen leaped forward, and the paired doors slammed closed behind them. Through the glass panel in one of them, Bowen caught the eye of the man in the anorak. He didn't look dismayed, nor any more surprised than anyone might have been to see them jump at the last moment like that.

The car was only a quarter full. There were seats for everyone, and all of the passengers sat—except Bowen and Eva. Perhaps because they continued to stand, perhaps because they were such a handsome couple, many of the riders glanced at them. Some stared. The tan-raincoated man merely glanced, then seemed to withdraw into his own meditations, his eyes fixed straight ahead. That meant, of course, that he could have been watching Bowen's and Eva's reflections in the window opposite him. He had taken a seat next to one of the doors.

The train stopped at Green Park. Eva and Bowen picked up their suitcases. Two people left the car, three got on. None used the door the luggage might have obstructed. When the doors closed Bowen and Eva put the bags down again. As the train began moving, they could see that one of the pair of dark overcoated men who'd boarded the car beyond them at Victoria had gotten off. He didn't look at them as the train carried them past him.

As the train slowed coming into the Oxford Circus Station, where three Underground lines come together, Eva and Bowen once again lifted their suitcases. Again they stood as though ready to step aside should anyone use their door. And again, as the motorman's voice came over the loudspeaker, they stepped through the doors just before they closed.

Bowen didn't notice whether the man in the raincoat was looking through the window at them as the train began to move away. He was too busy checking the platform.

Just ahead, the other one of the pair of overcoated men stood apparently reading the exit signs to see which way to go. He didn't decide until after Eva and Bowen had passed him.

They let the escalator carry them up the long, steeply inclined shaft past the posters advertising chocolates and cigarettes and women's underwear.

Because they had so far to rise, and the stairway glided so smoothly, it soon seemed that they stood still while the posters floated by them; the handrails' black ribbons were stationary bars between which the jointed shining sheet-metal flowed. Eva stood a step up from Bowen, gripping his hand tightly against her back. The other people who had gotten off the train seemed fixed at nearly equal distances ahead and after them. No one climbed. The man in the overcoat kept his place two dozen steps behind.

And then—perhaps because the sense of motionlessness had been so strong—the rise ended almost like a flash. The last posters swept by them, and Eva and Bowen suddenly were forced to leap or be thrown from the escalator. That impetus sent them nearly running across the concourse and onto the next, shorter, escalator that would take them to street level. They climbed quickly up those steps, and so reached the top just as the man hurried onto the stairway below them.

He also started to climb, then halted as Bowen and Eva wheeled on around and came clipping down the other run, descending to the concourse again.

The man might have turned and tried to run down the rising escalator; or he might have dashed up and then back down the other side. In neither case could he have reached the bottom in time to see which way Eva and Bowen ran. Perhaps he accepted being outmaneuvered philosophically. Perhaps he wasn't really following them at all. In any case, the man let the escalator carry him up, and went out of the Underground.

"We did it! We did it! Faked them out!" Gasping from excitement and exhilaration, laughing, Bowen hugged Eva and swung her from side to side. She giggled and squeezed him back.

"But do you think they might—"

"No way! There's nothing they can do. I know he didn't see us come all the way back down here. You were right. We could have gone any way to any station in London: back to Victoria, or on to Euston or King's Cross; taken the Bakerloo line to Paddington . . . They'll never know. We did it!"

CHAPTER

6

"How could you just . . . leave?"

"I close the door."

Bowen and Eva seemed to have the train to themselves. Four other people had entered the car with them at Euston Station, but all left by the time they passed Manchester. Only the conductor, passing through, had come in since then. The train's regular clickety-clickety, the world rushing past, gave them a sense of being cocooned.

"Just walk away from everything?" he asked.

"The furnishings in my flat are not mine. The few things—the radio, the clothes . . . they can be replaced. I would be sorry to leave belongings, food in

the frig, that someone else must dispose of, but . . .
The circumstances are extreme."

"Don't you have friends?"

"No. I have been only two years in England. It is
difficult to make friends with the English. Or, perhaps,
it is difficult for me to make friends. I have only
acquaintances."

"Your job?"

"I would be sorry to cause difficulty for my employ-
er. He has been kind to me. But he can—no doubt
—within two days find a replacement for me. And I
am sure I could find work again."

"I suppose so. I don't know that you'd have to: I can
bring in enough . . . but I'd think you'd want to do
something that you enjoy—that you're good at and
you can't walk away from without caring."

"Of course I like to have interesting work. But it does
not matter so much to me; or where, or exactly what."

"What is important to you, Eva?"

"To live—to read, to think, to listen to music, to see
beauty. To love. I think 'to love,' although I have little
experience. Perhaps that is only a dream. But it is my
dream—all I want from life: to love, and be loved, and
live. What more would you want?"

"To do something. I want all of those things that you
want. But beyond that, I like to feel there's something I
can do pretty well, and do it. I like to solve problems;
face challenges. If possible, do something that's of
benefit to other people."

"Yes, I see that in you, David: overcoming challenges. I am surprised—forgive me if I offend you
—that you chose for a career economics, managing
money. I would expect you to have chosen something
with more excitement."

"Investing is pretty exciting. It's a form of gambling,

after all. It is challenging to make the right choices with a lot riding on them. And to be successful you have to know what you're doing."

"Of course. I should have understood that. Still, I would have thought something more active."

"Well, that's probably why I've kept up my karate as a sport."

"And benefiting other people?"

"I thought when I go back I might work for some good cause—a foundation, a charity, something like that."

"Yes. That is admirable. I suppose it has never seemed to me that anything I do could make much difference to the world."

Bowen nodded, looking past Eva through the window, but not seeming to see the green and tan fields blurring by. "You seem sure of yourself. You go at things in a determined way."

"Oh, yes. But they are the small things, David. The specifics. I did not, for example, *decide* to go to university and to become a translator. When I was a child I worked hard because it was expected of me, and, I suppose, because I enjoyed it. And so I was *sent* to the university. And I worked hard there, because that is what I do. And because I was good in English, it was decided that I should be a translator.

"I have always had direction, David—whatever direction is given to me."

"I see." Again, Bowen was silent for a time. "And so when Heinz decided he wanted you for a lover, you fell in love with him and worked hard at being a good one."

Eva returned his steady stare. "Perhaps that is so," she said at last. "And that troubles you."

"Yes."

"Because you think I love you only because you wanted me—because you decided."

"I guess so."

"I understand. It is not so. But, David, if I do love you, why would that matter?"

"I don't know. Maybe it shouldn't. There's just something about the passivity . . ."

Now Eva seemed to be looking ahead at a distant village, but her eyes didn't move. "I do become dependent. I allow others—" She turned to him. "I think I do not know *how* to decide, to determine some things: the big things . . . so I allow others . . . But you cannot say that—after that—I am passive."

"No," he said. He smiled, and touched her hand. "No, I certainly can't say that."

"Good," she said, and squeezed his hand, and pressed harder against his shoulder. "So, I think it is better we do not both have great determination about the big things, David. If we should make life together, you decide where we have our house, and I make sure the pantry is full and all the linens and towels are clean."

"What a team," he said. "What a team."

So they rolled along, hand in hand, seeming to be happy, seeming to be escaping, letting the train carry them, carrying the lies with them all the way.

Before they had boarded the train at Euston Station, Bowen had arranged with the Godfrey Davis Agency office for a car to be waiting at Lancaster. They ate a quick tasteless lunch in the station café when they arrived there. No one seemed to be watching them. Then they headed north, Bowen driving, and the soft, old hills began rising ahead of them. After they went off the motorway at Kendal, he turned quickly several times, pausing on lanes leading off to the side, to make sure no one was following. No one was.

"What a beautiful day!" he exclaimed, framing it between his palms, the heels of his hands at the top of the steering wheel.

"Yes. So clear! The hills, they are so . . . *full.*"

"I guess it's the angle of the light: throws shadows, brings out the contours; makes them that vivid. And the afternoon light has more color in it."

She chuckled. "You have analyzed the cause and effect."

"I guess." He laughed.

She sighed. "Yes, so beautiful! I am so happy to be seeing this with you."

"I wish we were coming here under different circumstances, but I'm glad we're doing it."

"Yes. I am sure, David, all will be well. We will think, and make a plan, together, for the future. Now that we are together, I am sure that everything —always—will be well."

Bowen kept his eyes on the road and nodded.

At Borrowdale, a tiny hamlet that hardly seemed significant enough to have a name, they found an inn. They were shown up a narrow, winding, creaky staircase to a small oddly shaped room that was a garden —flowered wallpaper, an old floral carpet, one chair covered with a chintz slipcover, a bed taking up most of the space of the room and covered with a spread printed with multicolored bouquets. A glass vase of silk roses stood on the chest of drawers.

A gracious, gray-haired, sharp-eyed woman who introduced herself as Mrs. Broome showed them the room. There could have been no doubt that she noticed Eva wore no wedding ring. Nevertheless, she referred to her as "Mrs. Scott," the name Bowen had given.

Eva and Bowen unpacked, and took a short walk partway up the hill behind the inn, from which they could begin to see the blue mirror of Derwent Water to the north. When they returned, Bowen said he wanted to take a nap before dinner.

"Of course, David. Last night . . . so much worry, so little sleep. You lie down at once." She turned down the bed while he took off his shirt and trousers.

"Oh, thank you!" He lay down.

She pulled the covers up around him and tucked him in.

"Thanks. Don't you think you ought to lie down too?"

She stood back and looked at him very seriously. "I think I ought *not* to lie down too. I think you need your sleep, David."

"I only meant . . ."

"I know very well what you meant—I am happy to say—even if you did not, yet. You go to sleep. While you are sleeping, I will call one of the women who works at my office, and the man in the flat next to mine, to tell them I shall be away for a while."

"Just over there, Mrs. Scott." Mrs. Broome indicated a glass door at the side of the lobby. It opened into a little closet—not really a room; but enough larger than a booth to contain a small table, next to the pay telephone, and a chair. Eva put her address book on the table, closed the door behind her. She found a number and placed a call.

Turning, looking through the door of the booth, Eva

could see out the wide windows that ran across the opposite side of the house. Then she turned abruptly, as though to face the person who had answered her call.

She spoke animatedly, gesturing, smiling, as if the person on the other end could see her. She nodded, "Yes, yes, yes," and said good-bye and hung up. She found another number, dialed again. Her second call was shorter, but she replaced the receiver more slowly. She stood for a moment with her hand still on it. She turned. She sat on the little chair, facing the door, staring toward the view, her hands together in her lap.

That view of intensely blue sky with primrose-tinted clouds was reflected in the booth's door. Mrs. Broome, who sat writing at a secretary, glanced toward the booth from time to time and saw Eva's figure as floating in it.

Time passed. The clouds shifted, an infinitesimal drift of one form into another, seeming not to move at all. After a while, Eva did focus on them; and then she tipped her head to one side and watched them. Deep sadness came into her face, as though she was now fully aware of separate moments, of the beauty of each, and that none would ever come again.

Finally, she rose, and turned to the phone, and —without looking up the number in her book—dialed again.

Bowen was asleep when she returned to their room. Very carefully, she lay on the bed next to him, on her side, looking at him.

They had a drink before dinner in the inn's bar —which was also its library; a comfortable room with books along one wall and wide windows presenting a view up the valley on the other. The only other guests were an English couple who didn't give their names, but did offer extensive advice about walking in the area. The four of them ate dinner at the same time, but at tables set in opposite corners of the dining room. Evidently to prove false the reputation of English country cooking as boiled and bland, Mrs. Broome's offerings were oily and over-spiced. Bowen and Eva told each other they enjoyed the meal, though, and drank a bottle of fairly decent wine with it. They skipped coffee in the lounge, went directly to bed, and made love giggling about the way the bedsprings squeaked.

On Monday first thing in the morning they drove the eight or ten miles up to Keswick and bought small backpacks and yellow foul-weather suits—although the weather continued glorious. "Best to be prepared," the other guests had warned them. They returned to the inn, changed clothes, and carried a picnic lunch up onto the fells.

"Oh, they are magnificent!" Eva exclaimed.

"Yes." Bowen gazed out over the worn, round mountains. Then, "No," he corrected himself. "The *Alps* are magnificent. They're so huge, rugged, thrusting. These . . . they're so *old*. Ancient. They must have been old mountains—must have known what it was to be mountains—ages before the Alps even thought about being anything but a swamp. And the spirits here"—he paused, his head turned as though listening—"there are spirits here, you know."

Eva nodded solemnly.

"They must have come here—collected here, like a vapor—when the earth first solidified."

Bowen and Eva were the only guests in the inn on Monday night.

"Slow, this time of year," Mrs. Broome told them. "Busy on the weekends, of course; but not many people during the week. Pity: I think it's one of the loveliest times of the year."

Eva and Bowen agreed. They were up early on Tuesday and planning a hike, even though the sky overhead was milky-hazy, and that to the northwest leaden.

"Rain likely before afternoon," Mrs. Broome warned.

"We won't go too far," Bowen assured her. "And we've got our rain suits."

They were on their way by eight-thirty. They walked out from the inn, swinging clasped hands. Crossing the velvet-green valley, they reached the road that ran southward from Keswick past Borrowdale and into the hills opposite where they'd visited on Monday.

A van and a sedan were already parked three-quarters of a mile north on the road. There were three men in the van, two in the sedan. They had driven up from London the night before. One man watched with binoculars.

Bowen and Eva went south along the road. Only a two-lane country road at best, after about a mile it narrowed and its surface was rougher as it headed up toward a pass between lines of hills. A little farther on they went by a small farm—cottage and barn—and in another two hundred yards Eva saw the sign pointing to the footpath they wanted to follow to one of the summits.

In the valley bottom, and partway up the sides of the hills, the trees and grass still held the lively greens of summer. As Eva and Bowen climbed, though, they seemed to go forward toward the dead time of the year. The grass became dun-colored, and bracken spreading in great patches across the slopes was pale yellow, bright yellow, gold, new copper, tarnished-penny copper.

"Like melted and all poured together, but not mixed," Eva said.

"Yes. I've never seen anything like it. I wish we had some real sun on it."

"Yes. But yet it is very beautiful. These plants . . ."

"Bracken."

"They are like golden feathers."

"Right. Wait!" Breaking off one of the huge fronds, Bowen held it at arm's length above her head. "Now you can ascend the mountainside in state, O Queen of the Fairies."

"Oooooh!" Spreading her arms with an undulating gesture, Eva pirouetted. She danced two steps up the hill, and Bowen followed, waving the frond.

"Wait, wait!" she cried out. "You must not be my plume-bearer. You must be the King of the Fairies. Here." Pulling a silk scarf from her neck she tied it quickly around Bowen's head.

"What are you doing?"

"Be still." She broke off three fronds, and began to stick their stems through the band so they stood straight up at the back of his crown. "There!"

Bowen turned his head slowly from side to side. He nodded gravely.

"Oh, David!" Eva clapped her hands together and bounced. "I would not have believed you could be even *more* dignified. But you are!"

"*Anopheles quadrumaculatus,*" Bowen intoned. He

raised his hands palms forward beside his head and proclaimed, *"Veni, vidi, vinci . . . VUM!"*

Half an hour later, all the whiteness had dulled to gray. What had been gray, blurry, off to their left, now coagulated into a lumpy blue-blackness obscuring the farther ranges. The air that had been still began to move, first in gusts, then steadily; and it was cold.

"It's coming up quicker than I thought it would," Bowen said. "We'd better get out of here."

As they went back down the trail, the colors that had seemed so distinct on the range of hills across the valley began to fade into a single, dull brownish-purple mass. The contours lost depth.

"We'd better put on our rain gear."

They paused and pulled on the yellow trousers and slickers.

The rain began before they reached the bottom; not a downpour, but a sullen drizzle. Behind them, the massy cloud had descended below the level of the summit they hadn't reached, and was groping its way down to the valley with fingers of mist. The opposite range flattened to a silhouette, then became only a denser grayness. Finally, it disappeared entirely.

Everything in the landscape faded and lost definition —a neutral, untinted gray of cloud and rain overhead and in the distance, the purple-gray of the nearer hillside, the greenish gray of the closer trees and pastures. Only Bowen and Eva were distinct, tiny in the misty vastness, but clear in those yellow suits as they wound their way down the last bends of the trail.

They came down onto the road, Bowen leading. He turned, waited an instant for Eva, took her hand. For a moment their figures were blurred by raindrops, as if they might be losing their solid forms, able to disperse into the aqueous air and disappear. Then the wiper swept the windshield, and they were fixed in space, targeted in the clear arc it left.

The van had driven up the road to a point beyond where the trail went off from it, turned, and parked. The three men waited and watched—the driver and the man beside him in the front, the third looking between them from behind.

Going back toward Borrowdale, the road rose slightly. Just beyond where the stone cottage and barn nestled into the hillside below it, it turned abruptly to the left before descending again. The side of the hill had been cut straight down there for its passage. In that section—perhaps sixty feet long—the top of the bank was ten feet above the roadway.

As Bowen and Eva approached the beginning of that cut, the driver eased the van out from the narrow shoulder. He rolled at only a walking pace at first, increasing speed gradually so no engine whine nor rush of tires would alert Bowen and Eva to his coming. They heard him only as he started up the incline behind them.

"Uh-oh. There's a car coming," Bowen warned.

Seeing Bowen turn, the driver pressed the accelerator.

"We should have been on the other side." Bowen had kept them to the side of the road where—in most other countries—they would have faced approaching traffic. He must have forgotten that in England cars drive on the left.

The van was coming up too fast for them to cross in front of it. Bowen pulled Eva's hand, and they stepped to the side and put their backs close to the nearly vertical bank. He kept her to his left so that he was the closer to the oncoming vehicle. They watched with cautious apprehension as the van swept up, with surprise when it slowed just as it reached them, then with shock at its stopping abruptly abreast of them.

Instantly, the passenger door opened, and a man started out just beyond Eva. Bowen stared at him, gaping; then, reflexively, snapped a look the other way. Another man had flung open the van's rear door and was coming around fast on Bowen's right. In an instant Bowen must have seen that the weapon in the man's hand wasn't a gun, but a hypodermic needle.

As if merely continuing the turn of head and shoulders he'd made in looking in that direction, Bowen pivoted on one foot bringing the other up and around in a slashing kick that caught the man across his ribs. Completing the *mawash geri* in unbroken motion, he put that foot down and his weight on it, cocking up the other leg and driving it like a piston straight back into the man's stomach. Still without pause Bowen shifted weight, spinning once more: a dancer, a discus thrower, a dervish. The man was doubling over. This time Bowen's roundhouse kick—the point of his boot—hit the man's head just in front of his ear, hurling him sideways against the earthen bank. He slid down it.

Constantly flowing, no movement ever ended but only fulfilling the one before—coiling smoke, swirling cloud—Bowen swung to complete his circle, rocked back, and then forward again to meet the charge of the front-door man. Taking a blow but swinging so it didn't hurt him, seizing the thrusting arm and pulling enough to throw the man off balance, Bowen drove a fist into the man's solar plexis. The man fell forward from the waist, his knees buckling, and staggered backward as though trying to sit on a chair that wasn't there.

Eva stood beyond him, both hands over her mouth.

Bowen shouted, "Eva! Run!" whirling to check behind him and then leaping, dashing that way past the rear of the van and back down the road.

After sprinting fifty feet, Bowen chanced breaking his stride and darted a look over his shoulder. The driver's door was open, the driver getting out. The van's body was closed—no windows in its sides back of the forward doors. The driver must not have been able to see Bowen fighting, must have assumed (for the few seconds the fight had lasted) that—two against one—he was being easily subdued. He must have seen it wasn't so only when that one partner staggered backward into his view. By the time he was out of the van and running, Bowen had doubled his lead.

Perhaps Bowen feared that despite the lead he might be run down. Perhaps instinct directed him to dart for cover. He could have had no plan; but he veered left across the road and leaped, hurdling the low stone wall into the pasture there and making for the barn and cottage. Whether he thought rationally that contacting any other people would bring the police, and he still feared that; or whether he simply bolted like any hunted animal into the nearest hole, he sprang into the barn as soon as he came to it instead of going on to the cottage.

The pursuer had slowed as Bowen approached the buildings. If Bowen had gone to the cottage, or there had been other people around the barn, he would have retreated quickly. He stopped, waited a moment. No sound of voices reached him. No one came out of the barn. No one seemed to be looking from the cottage.

The man climbed over the wall and trotted toward the barn. As he came to it, he halted again. He looked, listened, cautiously.

A long, low building—only seven or eight feet high at the eave running along the front—its ridge rose to barely twice that. The wide door was at the near end of the front side, and four oblong window holes —unglazed, unshuttered—at head level were set at regular intervals in the same thick wall beyond it.

The plank door was closed. The man walked past it carefully, and to the first window. Standing away from it, he looked in as far as he could see down the length of the building toward the far end. He walked on, looking through, until he could see back to the end wall beyond the door. Then he stepped up to it and scanned again.

The man didn't put his head into the window, but he came close enough to see the layout and structure inside the building. Along that front wall was an aisle ten feet wide. Between the aisle and the back wall were several large sheep pens. A loft, filled with hay, ran all along above the pens. The loft rested on thick square wooden beams running front to back.

Evidently sure he had time, the man prowled down the length of the building, peering carefully through each window from a little distance away. He moved quietly; only occasionally did his shoe scrape one of the pebbles on the bare ground where water dripping from the eaves had worn away the grass. He made his way back to the door.

From what the man had seen, Bowen could not be hiding anyplace on the lower level except tightly up against the front wall—crouching under the windows or standing next to the door. He would have to be either there or up in the hay.

Carefully, the man pulled back the peg that moved the inner bar that slipped into the wall to hold the door closed. He stepped back, paused, then kicked with the flat of his foot with a force to slam the door all the way around on its hinges, crashing back against the inner wall. The bang echoed, a flat, ringing crack, in the long stone chamber.

At once, after the kick, he stepped backward and crouched. A cool-headed, clever opponent might have expected the door to be kicked open that way, might yet leap out to take him by surprise.

Water from the drizzle, collecting along the edge of the slate roof, dripped in separate, quiet, little splashes.

If a clever opponent didn't seize the attack that way, the next most likely tactic would be to stand against the wall by the door—with something he'd found to use as a club, if possible—and slash at the intruder.

The man backed a step farther away, so when he sprang forward he took two steps for momentum to carry him well inside as he bounded through the doorway. His feet came down on the dirt floor wide apart, solidly. He landed crouching, arms up and out in front.

Bowen wasn't standing against that wall.

In the instant while the man was perceiving that, and beginning to assume Bowen must be up in the hay, Bowen struck.

From his tight crouch on the beam above the door, where he had been leaning, cramming himself into the angle of the roof, he shifted left and rose—still bent over, again with his back pushed up hard against the roof to keep him in place.

When he'd run into the barn, and slammed the door and shot home the bar and scanned for any weapon, all he'd seen had been a rope coiled on a peg nearby. He'd grabbed it, then looked to find a way, a place to use it. He'd been able easily to climb from the nearest sheep pen to the beam, and then to walk on it to the door. Crouching there, he'd doubled the rope to make a loop, measured out enough of it to reach nearly to the ground, coiled the rest of the doubled strands and hung them on his left arm. Then he'd pulled up the loop, holding some of the slack in each hand.

Now, spreading the loop open between his hands, he threw it out and down over the man's head—less than a yard below his perch—whipping one side, wrapping it around the man's neck. Then he jerked.

Gagging, choking, staggering, the man grabbed the rope with both hands, pulling to relieve the pressure on his throat, to yank Bowen down. He might have done it. His weight was less than Bowen's, but he was strong, and Bowen's position on the beam was precarious.

Seizing both lengths of the rope in his right hand, pulling up with all the strength of that arm, Bowen threw the coil of rope from his left over the opposite side of the beam. Without allowing the rope to slacken, he clasped it tightly between forearm and chest. Then he leaped backward off the beam. He dropped to the ground, partly sliding down the rope, partly being lowered as his weight outbalanced the other man's.

The jerk that snapped Bowen's opponent upward choked him and hurt his fingers gripping the rope; the steady pull that lifted him two feet off the ground left him strangling; but they didn't kill him.

As his toes touched the ground, Bowen gripped the rope tightly in both fists, bending his knees, letting himself fall backward, his torso half turned so that the man's kicking heels caught only his shoulder, and just once, before he was back far enough, low enough, to be out of their reach.

The man kicked as though he were deep underwater trying to propel himself to the surface. He pulled, elbows straight out in front. He lifted himself, slackening the rope between his hands and throat sufficiently so it no longer choked him. Then he hung there, gasping, swaying.

Bowen was on the floor, sitting, his legs drawn up, tensing against the weight that tried to pull him upright again.

The man gasped, wheezing. Each breath was deeper, held longer, evidently easier. He hung from his hands at one end of the rope; Bowen hung onto the other. The man began to force his elbows down, drawing himself up, bringing more slack to the rope between his hands and throat. He got his upper arms all the way down against his ribs. He turned his head from side to side within the loop.

Bowen let the rope go.

The man dropped. Unprepared, he hit on his heels, collapsed sitting, striking the ground, falling backward. Bowen kicked him in the head.

Bowen stood looking down at him, ready to kick again; but the man didn't move. Going around the sprawled legs, watching the prostrate figure, Bowen went to the doorway, peered out carefully past its edge.

He could see the van. Half of its rear end projected into sight beyond the earthen wall at the curve in the road, where it had been when he'd run from it. He couldn't see anyone there. Had either of the other men come after him? It would have been unlikely. Even the one he'd hit only once would have been out of action for five or ten minutes. The pursuit and fight in the barn had actually taken only five.

And where was Eva? He couldn't be sure she had run the other way, as he'd shouted at her to do. In any case, to get back to the inn—or away to anywhere—he'd have to pass the van.

He went to the man on the floor. Never turning his

back on the door, Bowen took the man's outstretched arm and tugged to roll him onto his face. The rope still trailed up over the beam. Bowen caught it, looped a clove hitch quickly around the wrist he held. There seemed no chance that the man was feigning unconsciousness, or that he would soon revive. All the same, Bowen moved carefully to lift the other arm, tying both wrists together, then tying the man's feet. Then he stepped away.

Eyes on the doorway, he slipped off the yellow rain suit and the nearly empty backpack he'd been wearing under it. He went to the doorway again, paused, listening, looked carefully, then dashed out and to the wall that bordered the road. He dropped to a crouch and ran like a four-footed beast, touching the ground ahead with fingertips to keep his balance, in the direction away from the van.

Scuttling that way, he reached the corner of the barnyard. Kneeling, he peered over the wall. He was out of sight of the van. He sprang up, vaulted the wall, ran across the road and climbed the hill. He went up fifty feet, then worked over at that level toward the place where the van was parked.

The trousers he wore for hiking were a dull earthy brown. His sweater was tweedy, brown with flecks of gold and olive. Even in sunlight he would have been difficult to see against the hillside. If anyone had picked out his figure through the obscuring mist, he would have seemed—at first—like a speck of the mountain moving. He moved rapidly, but in spurts —pausing for an instant, glancing over the ground a dozen feet ahead each time, choosing the places to put his feet, then running, bent over, his eyes on the road.

Then, had anyone been watching him, they might

have thought him an animal: not any gentle creature grazing, or one frightened, fleeing. His low loping was too swift, yet too controlled; like a wolf on a scent.

But even crouched, he was too upright to be taken for long for a beast. He would have been identified as a hunting man. Could his face have been seen, it might have been recognized—of course!—as that of one of his Scottish forebears pursuing a stag across a Highland slope. Or—grim and taut, but keen—as that of a spear- and ax-armed Gaelic warrior.

No one did see him. No one was at home at the cottage. No one else had gone out to walk near that place in the face of the oncoming storm.

He ran across an open place, went into the waist-high bracken. He couldn't run there, but pushing it aside—one hand and then the other—he worked his way swiftly over to a point above the curve in the road. Then he began to creep quietly downward. He bent lower. A little farther, he crouched, and finally, he duck-walked, his head just below the top of the bracken, his hands before his face, pushing the fronds away and slipping through them.

He heard a man's voice. It spoke only a word or two. Bowen froze, then went on more slowly, more quietly. He pushed a frond aside with his left hand, moved ahead, pushed one with his right—and there were no more! He had reached the open grass that stretched for a dozen feet above the edge of the bank. He could see the far half of the van's roof.

He crawled forward on his belly. The hillside sloped down at perhaps twenty degrees. Flat against it, he slithered forward until he was near enough to see over the edge. He found himself no more than ten feet above road level.

A man was leaning with his back against the rear of

the van. He held one hand over his stomach, rubbing it. He must only recently have recovered enough to put himself there—he hadn't been there when Bowen ran from the barn. The other man—the first Bowen had fought—had evidently been propped half up against the bank. Bowen could see only his legs, and they were sprawled in a way that suggested the man was still unconscious.

Eva stood between the end of the van and the bank, looking down the road toward the cottage. One fist was pressed against her chest at the base of her throat, the other against her mouth.

After a moment, he wriggled backward and then crept around to the edge of the bracken again.

The dying foliage, the deep humus underneath, gave off a rank smell of decay. Bowen crawled partway in, peering among the stems of the plants, groping. His hand found the top of a stone. He dug with his fingers, exposed enough to grip it, pulled it out. Then—still prone—he made his way back to the edge of the bank, reaching a point almost directly above the standing man. The man's head was barely six feet away.

He heard the man's voice again. He couldn't make out the words, but the tone was of annoyance and indecision—as though he wasn't sure whether he should stay where he was or go to see what was keeping his partner. Bowen heard Eva's voice.

All at once he must have realized why he couldn't understand what they were saying down there. Although their voices were muffled, they weren't too far away. They were speaking German.

CHAPTER

7

Bowen was lying flat. For just a moment he put his face straight down onto the thick wet grass as though to let his whole body sink into the ground. So completely did all energy seem to leave him that every molecule might quickly have been absorbed; he might simply have dissolved. Then he looked up, cautiously pulling backward and raising himself so that he rested on forearms and shins. The man and Eva were still looking toward the barn. Bowen brought himself up onto one knee. For one more long moment he stared down at them. Then, very slowly, so that there might be no abrupt movement to catch an eye, he cocked his arm back behind his head.

He hurled the stone.

Instantly, he sprang forward, leaping out into space to plummet to the roadside. Striking the ground, he dropped into a squat to take the shock of landing, and shot up to his feet again like a spring.

He came up ready to fight, but without need. His aim had been true. The man lay behind the van as though thrown there. Blood trickled from the side of his head.

Bowen wheeled to Eva. She stared at him, mouth gaping, eyes wide. Then she threw herself upon him, clutching him.

"David! Oh, David! *Mein Lieb! Mein Lieb!*"

He stood like a post. After a moment she pulled away from him, her hands still on his waist at either side. Then she backed one step away. She lowered her arms to her sides; lowered her shoulders. Although she held her head up and looked at him, she might have been a puppet hung over a peg.

"Let's go," he said. "Let's get out of here."

She looked vaguely from one prostrate man to the other, then back to him.

Bowen bent to check the man behind the van. "He's alive, but he'll stay down for a while. The other two'll come around sooner. Let's go."

Resignedly, docilely, the good little, obedient little girl, she turned and walked beside him, away from the van, back along the road that would take them to the inn.

No rain fell now, not even a drizzle; for the moment, the foul weather had simply settled itself lumpily as an unpleasant fog. Every so often Bowen wiped the moisture from his face with the back of his hand. Eva let it remain on her cheeks along with her tears. He strode purposefully. She stayed at his side as though only to be near him, like a well-trained dog.

"Well," Bowen said after they had walked for two minutes. "Well, just for the sake of clarity, so as not to leave anything still up for guesses . . . I mean, there isn't anything left to hide, is there?"

She must have taken the question as rhetorical.

"Is there, Eva?"

"No," she said very softly.

"No," he repeated. "So, we might as well clear up the odds and ends, fill in the details. All right?"

She walked on silently.

"All right?"

"Yes, David."

"So," he said. "Well, for a beginning . . . Let's see . . . Okay, what's the name of your home town, Eva? I don't think you ever told me, did you?"

"Wolgast," she said. Her voice, although soft, came out like that of some machine: a speaking weight-machine: A coin is put in, the machine speaks. No question of choice or feeling about it.

"Wolgast," he repeated. "Wolgast. Well, that doesn't do me much good. I don't know much about German geography, so I don't know where that is. I mean, not *exactly.*"

He wasn't rushing them, but she had to take three steps to his two. As on the night they'd met, the rhythms of their walking made a complex pattern. Although quick, the pace seemed easy for both of them. They had settled into it, seeming almost to be relaxed as they walked.

His voice sounded relaxed, even pleasant. It sounded like that of an ingratiating celebrity using his charm in a low-pressure television commercial.

"But I'll bet I will know where the city you worked in is, won't I?"

She walked beside him, keeping up with him. She didn't answer.

"Won't I? I mean, everybody knows where it is—if it's the one I think it is. What city did you work in?"

"Berlin."

"Got it! I had it right! I get the prize. Now, now for sixty-four dollars . . . There're two Berlins. Let me guess, Eva. Let me see if I've guessed right about which Berlin you worked in. Let me see now. Let me think it over and make sure I think I'm right." Without stopping, he twisted and jabbed a finger toward her. "East Berlin!" He looked at her through the next two steps, the expression in his eyes triumphant and hard.

"Am I right? Am I right, Eva?"

She didn't look at him. She stared on ahead, not looking at anything. "Yes, David. Of course." Perhaps the mist was dissolving her makeup. Her eye sockets seemed dark and sunken, but the rest of her face had a blank dullness.

"Yes. I thought so. I mean, of course I didn't think so. When we met, when you said you were from Germany—all this time—I just naturally assumed . . . God, I should have known better."

After several more steps he said, "And the 'company' you worked for . . . All that stuff, that heartbreaking story about 'Heinz' . . . That was a great story, Eva. You told that story . . . You were terrific. Believed it? God, I saw that bastard, I saw him raping . . . whatever . . . That was really clever, Eva; veering off there—when you told that part—not describing it exactly, leaving it to my imagination."

Bowen's hands had tightened to fists. He looked at them, opened them.

"Still gets me," he said. "You make that story up all by yourself, or did they write it for you?"

"It is true."

"Really?"

"It is true."

"There really is a Heinz?"

"Yes. Oh, yes, David, there is Heinz."

"And he . . . what? Chained you spread-eagled out on the bed and then he— What? What's the most horrible, bestial thing that I can imagine him doing? How perverted is my mind? The worse I am, the worse he gets, right? Terrific! I hope you didn't make it up, Eva. I hope they wrote it for you, because I'd hate to think you could think up a trick that is so—"

Her high moan came muffled from behind the fists pressed over her face. Bent at the waist, she twisted side to side, moaning on and on.

First he looked shocked, then stricken. His arms went forward as though to reach for her. Then, locking them across his chest, he glared at her. But his heart must not have been quite hard enough to let him stand so totally without compassion. He compromised by shoving his hands down into his pockets and looking away.

Eva's moaning diminished and stopped. For a moment she stood with her hands still over her face, taking quick breaths. Then she lowered them, raising her head, looking off to the side into the mist. "Why should you believe me?" she asked. "Let us go on." And she started away.

Bowen caught up with her in a stride. Without the bitter twist in his voice he asked, "Why should I, Eva?" as though it truly was a question. "If it's true, why would you keep working for them, whoever— It is German intelligence, isn't it? Some branch of East German intelligence?"

"Of course."

"Then what are you doing here? If that was a true story, what are you doing in England? Why are you still working for them?"

She answered without looking at him, as if she were giving a statement that was being taken down by a stenographer placed out of her sight. "It is a true story, David. The minister . . . the man who is Heinz's superior . . . arranged for me to come to England. I went first to the Federal Republic, under one set of false papers, then came to England with another. My job was arranged. It was done to get me away from Heinz, just as I have told you. But nothing is done only for such a reason—nothing so complicated, not for a person like me. I had to agree to be . . . What is it in English? To be asleep. To wait until such time as I might be of use."

"But why do it? Why continue . . . You're here, you're free."

"My family is not free."

"You mean they'd . . . put them in prison, or something?"

"I don't know. I am afraid . . . They—my mother is old, my sisters are loyal, my father was an official . . . They still have powerful friends. Perhaps they would not . . . I don't know.

"And I am *not* free. Gert Nagler—Heinz's men —they watch me. That is as I told you. Heinz still watches me—for himself. Even so far away . . . He doesn't care how far, as long as he knows— As long as I still am his! That boy—the one I told you I slept with, who helped me—they beat him. He didn't know why; they took his money, so he thought . . . But I knew. It was Heinz. You . . . I have been allowed to . . . because it is for Heinz. I still belong to Heinz!"

"You don't have to, Eva. You could find a way . . ."

123

"How?"

"I don't know how. But surely in two years . . . You could find a way if you really—"

"How!" she shouted at him. "Have you found a way?"

Bowen stared at the road just ahead of where he put each step. He took five of them before he answered.

"No." They walked another twenty yards before he spoke again. "When I spotted the guy following us, Saturday night: I really thought it was Gert Nagler's people, following *you*. When I'd first seen somebody watching us—Thursday night—I'd thought they were after me. But you explained it . . . Was it Gert's men, then?"

"Yes."

"So you called him, and told him I'd spotted them, and he should cool it, right? That was the call I overheard?"

"Yes."

"So when we were followed again . . . you knew who it was, while I still thought . . ."

Bowen's lips did crack into a kind of smile. "So, you must have thought my Mafia story was pretty funny." He shoved his hands into his pockets again as he walked. "Must have given you a laugh a minute. Better than the elephants. You played right along with it beautifully. I really thought you believed it. You really are a terrific actress."

"I did not have to act. I knew the truth of what you told me, David—what it meant to you. The details did not matter."

"Well, it was a good story, wasn't it? Really creative. When you mentioned that the guy looked Italian, I just took the real situation and . . . changed the names to protect the guilty."

"But I knew it *was* true, David. A lie that was true: I knew what was true for you, about you, in it."

"Well, then, I'm sorry I told it that way. It wouldn't have mattered if I'd told the truth, and I'd have felt better about it. I felt really rotten that I was deceiving you. I knew someday I'd have to tell you . . . but I hoped by then you'd . . ."

"Why did you lie?"

"I thought you'd feel better about thinking I'd worked for the Mafia than knowing I'd worked for the CIA. Isn't that funny, considering?"

"Yes, I suppose it is."

"I mean, there was a time in the States—you told people you worked for the agency; you might as well have said, 'I used to molest children, but I don't anymore.' Oh, not everybody, of course. Probably most people . . . the people who were Ellen's and my friends . . . Ellen, herself, thought it was terrific. Maybe I got sick of it, and them, just because I got sick about her. Anyway, I thought you—a European—and . . . The implications for us . . . You might have misgivings about being involved with a man the Mafia was after, but if you knew it was the CIA . . ."

After they'd walked for another half minute in silence, Bowen said, "Too bad about all the lies."

"Yes."

They'd walked halfway back to the inn by then. On either side the dull-green grass stretched away . . . a dozen feet? to infinity? Either seemed equally imaginable beyond the veil of mist. The road came out of the fog that dozen feet ahead, slid under them, and disappeared at the same distance behind: They might have been walking on a treadmill. There were no sounds save their own footsteps.

"You wanted what I know, didn't you?" Bowen

asked. "What material I was given to analyze. That would tell you what the agency knew, maybe how they got it. Reveal leaks, possibly expose agents . . . I never knew where stuff came from, but you'd know. Not even to mention what you could find out from me about what the agency knows—the actual product. Or what conclusions we'd reached. Yes.

"I never thought of myself as a spy. I just read reports and made projections like any other economic analyst. I never believed that anybody would . . . that you wanted what I know enough to . . . that you would actually try to kidnap me!"

"They wanted it."

"Just like the agency told me. They were right—the bastards. I thought it was only part of their trying to get me to stay working for them—if I wasn't going to be allowed to travel except where they could keep an eye on me, I might as well go on doing my stuff for them, right? Why not? I could make my own money on the side—they didn't care how rich I got. I really didn't believe they were right—that somebody might try to snatch me. Oh, I wasn't ever going to visit Berlin—or go to Germany at all. I didn't even go to Austria. But I never thought Switzerland, England . . . the other places I was planning . . . I got my fake passport just in case, but I used it as much to slip them as to protect myself from . . .

"How did it work?" he asked. "How did they pick me up? Your people. Where? When I came to London, or before—when I was in Switzerland?"

"I don't know," Eva replied. Her face was white and shiny, like a cold child's. Her voice had the quiet lack of feeling that comes between loss and grief.

He went on, "Well, anyway, obviously they picked me up. Found out I loved music. Got those tickets for

126

seats together for a concert I wouldn't pass up . . ." He looked at her, his eyes softening. "You really did enjoy that concert, didn't you?"

"Yes."

"Yes, you really do love music, too. I've never been close to anyone who seemed to respond so much . . ." Then the lines began to cut into his face again. "And the talking about books, and ideas, and . . . You really were the right woman for the job, Eva.

"I couldn't believe my luck—you seemed to fall for me as fast as I did for you. Inviting me to move in . . . 'Do you think this is happening too quickly, David?' That was really good—making *me* defend it. God, you are smart.

"I mean, if it had been only your looks . . . that would have made it more my own fault. Men are always making fools of themselves over pretty faces, over sex. We should know better. It's our own damn fault, but—

"Why couldn't that have been enough? The way you look would have been enough. But the music . . .

"I mean, what they really ought to do is send you over to Washington, and you could walk into the Pentagon and just stand there with your fingers against your cheek and look at them straight in the eye like you do, and give them that smile, and every general and admiral in the whole place would be falling over you trying to shove secrets down the front of your dress."

His stride lengthened, and his heels struck down hard on the macadam.

"And once they got their hands inside your dress . . . and once you got *your* hands on them . . . !"

She twisted to look at him, faltering in her step, but he stalked on.

"When I remember . . . 'I hope I won't offend you, Eva, if I say I'd like to sleep with you!' I could have saved myself the worry. If I hadn't said it, you sure would have."

"No, David . . ."

He hadn't heard her. "Offend you! Fat chance! God, it's a good thing I asked to go back to your apartment with you. It's a good thing I gave you some soppy poetry so you'd have an excuse. Otherwise you'd've had to trip me and get my pants off me right there on Waterloo Road!"

"David . . . !"

"Because you sure as hell weren't going to let me get away without getting me into you so I'd know what you could do—with all that training—and I'd be hooked and back for more! And then you could— You could just screw everything you wanted out of—"

"No! No! No!" Flinging her hands up, pressing fists over her ears, Eva screamed and suddenly broke forward, running, tottering down the road. She stumbled, caught herself, lurched on two more steps. Veering, she staggered to the shoulder of the road and suddenly half sat, half collapsed.

Bowen halted for a moment, then came to her. When he reached her, her hands were over her face, and she was rocking, sobbing. He stood looking down at her. After a while, he put his hands into his pockets. The high agony seemed to work its way deeper into her; her sobs subsided into moans, lower, softer with each breath. Finally, she was silent. She sat as though in shock, facing the fog.

He let himself down, half beside, half behind her, looking at a different sector of the gray blankness.

"I fell in love with you. I didn't expect to," she said. "And then I did, and then I . . . I didn't know what to do." She spoke as though reciting a tale she'd learned but didn't understand.

"How could you do it?" he asked. "What were you thinking?"

"I don't know. I could not have been thinking. I thought . . . because we loved one another . . . I thought, somehow . . . Eventually I would tell you . . . you would find out, and then . . . You would agree to tell them what they want to know, and they would say it was enough, I had done enough, and they would let us go away together . . . I believed, I thought because we loved . . ."

He turned his head to look over his shoulder toward her. "But you called Gert Nagler to come and grab me."

She twisted just a little, not enough actually to face him. "No. I didn't know he would— I meant only to report, so he would know I . . . So he would give me more time."

"But we were free. We were clear. We could have gotten away. Why report at all?" Suddenly he must have remembered. "Oh, your family."

"Yes. No. I don't know. I don't know why I cannot . . . Because I have always . . . Because they own me! Heinz owns me! My dead father owns me! Everyone owns me! I don't know what . . . I don't know *how* . . . !" She spun onto her knees to face him. "Oh, David, help me. Tell me what— Tell me how! I love you. I need you. Help me!"

For a long moment he looked at her. He reached and, very gently, touched her knee. "How can I help you, Eva? What should I do for you? Tell you what to do?"

She sat back. Tears started again. Not sobbing, she looked at him and simply wept.

"What could I do?" he asked again. "Maybe I could kick Heinz out; your father, if you think that's where this comes from. But I'd be just taking their place. I'm not going to tell you what to do, Eva." All of his customary concentration and focus had returned. "I love you, Eva; I do. But not this part of you. There's so much about you to love. But not this part. This part isn't worthy of the rest of you. And you've got to deal with it yourself, because that's what it's about."

He looked upward, turned his head, seemed to realize the drizzle had started again. "It's raining. My God, what are we doing sitting here— We've got to— *I've* got to move. When those guys . . . or more of Nagler's men, or the CIA guys trace me . . ." He stood up quickly.

Eva remained on the ground, looking up at him. Her face, so drawn, showed the skull beneath the flesh more clearly than ever. "What will you do? Where will you go? How?"

"Not sure. I'll have to try to get out of the country, somehow; that's obvious. And I guess"—he looked down at her—"it wouldn't be smart for me to tell you any more, even if I knew."

"Take me with you, David. I want to go with you."

He shook his head.

"Please. I ask. *I* want to. You see? I decide. I will leave them: my family . . . all of them. I will. I can." She reached up, put her hand against his hip. "You don't tell me. *I* ask."

"How can I? Now?" He touched her cheek with his fingertips.

"David! Take me with you!" She came up to her knees.

He stepped back away from her. "Eva, there's no way . . ."

130

"I will leave them. All. My family. Everything. I will. I can, with you. Please. Please!"

"Don't, Eva! Don't. I want to remember how much I loved you, not that I couldn't trust you."

"You must! You must trust!" She struggled to her feet.

"Maybe so. But I think I'll try to find somebody who hasn't already—"

"Already! Yes! Already it has been done—I have betrayed you. You know. But also you know"—her voice tottered as though to keep itself upright under a crushing weight—"I love you. Oh, David, you must —you must—know I do love you."

"I'd have to be crazy . . ."

"Be crazy. Oh, David, be crazy for love. We have such love that comes not to everyone. We must . . . For love, I will—I will try—*I will* be strong and free myself. For love of you. For love of me, trust me that I will."

He stood just out of her reach. Gradually, Eva appeared to accept the distance. She lowered her outstretched arms, and—except for her eyes, for her looking out at him—seemed to withdraw into herself.

"Oh, God," he said. "I'll never be able to trust you, Eva. I'll never be able to trust . . . and you'll never . . . It's hopeless. It's . . ." He stood for a moment, speechless; then straightened and set his shoulders back. Spreading his arms, he stepped toward her and she flung herself toward him.

CHAPTER

8

Eva saw Bowen's eyes flick to the rearview mirror again. She twisted to look through the back window. "You think someone is following?"

"I don't know. There's a gray car . . . been about the same distance behind us for a couple minutes, now."

"I see it. It is not the one that was on the road."

Driving away from the inn, toward Keswick and the route that would take them south, Bowen and Eva had passed a tan sedan by the side of the road, parked not far beyond the end of the trail they might have used on their hike had they reached the summit and continued, making a circuit instead of returning the way they'd come. Two men inside had stared at them with amazement. The men should have been able to watch the lane into Borrowdale, but the heavy mist had allowed Bowen and Eva to walk back to the inn as though invisible.

They had walked quickly, and—for the most part —in silence. Once, Eva had asked, "What do we do, David? Where do we go? There may be more of them. They will come again."

"Yes. I know. I'm thinking."

Later, Bowen had instructed her. "When we're there, you go straight up to the room and pack. I'll check out, and make a phone call. I've got an idea for getting out of England. I'll have to call a travel agent. Pack my things for me. I'll wear what I had on when we came."

Eva nodded. She didn't ask him to tell her his plan.

Driving away from the inn, as soon as Bowen had seen the parked car, he'd floored the accelerator. Eva had stayed turned in her seat all the way to Keswick, but the tan car never came into sight behind them although—as they went down the valley—the mist thinned, and she could see for half a mile.

"I guess—if it was them—they went to see what happened to their buddies," Bowen had said. "We ought to be able to get away clear."

Now he said, "Maybe they had even more people, lying farther back—in case we did get through."

"I don't think Gert would have so many men."

"Who knows? Maybe he brought them in—a planeload. Maybe he's got help from the Russians. I don't know."

"The car has turned off."

Bowen checked in the mirror. "Yes. Well, then maybe he wasn't one of them. Keep an eye out, though. Paranoia aside, it's probable they'd have another team or two lying back in case we slipped through. Or, if they did grab me, they'd very likely shell-game me around. I mean . . ." He hesitated, shooting a sideward glance at her. He had been speaking as though thinking aloud; as much to himself as to Eva. "That's what I would imagine. From spy movies I've seen. I guess you're the one who would know about these things."

"No. I sat in my cubicle and translated documents."

"Well, I don't know, either. I just think we ought to assume the worst."

"Yes. They will not give up easily. And now that they know that you . . ." Her look was half admiration, half appraisal. "You *are* a fighter, David. You told me, but I did not imagine . . . And you reacted so quickly, as though you were not surprised to be attacked."

"Well, as I told you, you can develop a way of being ready for things. But I won't surprise them next time."

She turned suddenly toward him. "It is too dangerous. Perhaps we can escape them, but we can never be sure . . . There is only one way: call the CIA. They will protect you."

"No. They . . . I've already thought about it. Sure, all I'd have to do is call London, and I'll bet they could get to me anywhere in England inside two hours—Hell, contact the local police, they could pick me up in fifteen minutes. Armed guard all the way to the plane; I'd be back in New York in half a day. Safe and sound.

"But they'd never let you come along, Eva. Even if they don't know already who you are—and I'll bet they do—they'd investigate. They would never let us be together, never let you into the States—unless it was as a prisoner, unless they thought they could get something from you."

Tight-eyed, Bowen looked ahead as though concentrating only on the road. Then he said, "I don't know if we can be together, Eva—after what's happened. I'm trying to trust you, and at the same time, I don't. Do you understand that?"

"Yes," she said very quietly.

"I don't know if it can work that way, if there's any hope. But we'll try it. It's *worth* trying. So, as long as we're trying, I'm not going to let *them* decide we can't be together.

"I've got to work a way to escape from the Germans entirely, and at the same time keep us together. A way to keep the CIA off our backs long enough for us to find out if we do want to stay together. And then . . . a way that they'll accept your being with me; know you're not a danger."

"How could that be?"

"Well . . . I'm not sure. I'm working on it. But the thing is, Eva, I'm not going to tell you the details. You understand? You'll just have to go along with me, not knowing. Knowing *why* I won't tell you. You understand? You still want to try?"

With fingertips she wiped one eye and then the other. "Yes."

Traveling southward, they passed from the rain and mist. A mottled pall of cloud still grayed the light, but even inside the car they could tell the atmosphere was drier.

"We should be coming up to a town soon," Bowen said. "How about some lunch? I'm starved."

"Oh, yes. I am also."

But just before they reached the sign advising them of the turnoff, Eva warned, "David, another car has been keeping the same distance behind us for several minutes. It could be the one that was parked by the road."

"Yes. I've seen him. He's too far back to be sure. I'm going to go off here, anyway; see if he follows us."

Bowen slowed gradually, and used his blinker; the car two hundred yards behind had ample notice. But it swept on past the exit.

"I guess we're okay," Bowen said.

No one seemed to follow them as they drove for several miles over a secondary road. They came around a hill and found themselves approaching a small town. Ahead, a sprawling, half-timbered building stood beside the road. "Look. There's a pub."

Bowen glanced around the oak-paneled room. A man and a woman perched stiffly at a small round table near the fireplace, showing they weren't the sort of people who frequent pubs. A single man wearing his tweed hat even indoors sat at another table in a corner, slumping in his chair, staring into his pint of beer as though it were a crystal ball. Bowen turned to the barman, whose red face suggested he knew well that nothing was half so precious as the stuff he sold.

"Can we get something to eat?" Bowen asked. "I guess we're a little late . . ."

The barman nodded. "Aye, you may. There's a portion of steak and kidney left, and"—he surveyed the counter behind him—"some of the shepherd's, and peas and carrots. And I can always do you a sandwich."

Bowen consulted Eva, and ordered. "And a lager and a half of bitter." As the man filled their plates, Bowen said, "I thought you'd be busy—there're so many cars outside."

"Aye. It's the sheep sales. Today's the second Tuesday. The herders all carry in their flocks, and there's great buying and selling. The pens are on the other side of the village, and only the lorries are let through, so everyone parks their autos here."

Eva and Bowen carried their lunches to the rear of the room, to a table that seemed secluded and more secure, from which they could watch the door. As usual, Bowen sat so that his back was to a wall. The other couple had finished their meal, and left a moment later.

"How is it?" Bowen asked.

"It is fine. It doesn't matter. I have hunger, but no appetite."

Bowen put his hand on hers. "Eva . . . It's going to be all right. We got away from them. I think . . . I'm *sure* we'll get away from all of them. We're together. It's going to be hard; we don't know what the future . . . But we are together. We're doing it." He looked into her eyes, then winked and smiled. "Cheer up, love."

Eva turned her hand and squeezed his fingers. "Yes," she said, sitting up straighter and smiling back at him. "What delicious shepherd's pie!"

Parchment-colored shades tinted the light from the chandelier and wall sconces. An electric fire glowed in the fireplace. It was one of the more successful fakes: The plastic coals were very realistic, and the flickering —if not looked at directly—seemed that of real flame. The warm room felt like a haven not only from the dismal weather, but from any distress.

When they had nearly finished eating, Bowen said, "Maybe we can find a room here—in this town—to stay for the night. What I'm planning . . . There may be a way to get out of England, to a place I want to go, without passing through one of the big embarkation points. The call I made this morning . . . It seems possible, but I have to call back . . . work out the details. Anyway, we wouldn't leave before tomorrow afternoon at the earliest. As soon as we're done with lunch, let's walk into the town and see what's around."

At the moment Bowen pushed his plate away, the lone man in the corner—as though suddenly awakened from his trance—drained the last of his mug, rose, and went from the room.

For a moment Bowen and Eva were alone with the publican, who had spread a newspaper on the bar before him. Then two men entered. They were young, muscular and tough-looking. For an instant Bowen studied them, and they looked back at him, with suspicious appraisal. Then they spoke to the barman in a language that—however unintelligible to a speaker of standard English—clearly wasn't German. Replying in the same dialect, the barman began filling mugs for them.

"I am really on edge," Bowen said, shaking his head.

"Good." Eva put her hand on his. "I am sorry there is need to be on edge, but we both must be."

. Scores of cars parked in neat ranks at either side and behind the pub separated it from the town. It stood like a sentinel out from the stone row houses lining the road, which narrowed as it passed between them.

The stone of the houses was grim gray-brown; they were roofed with dark slate. All of them seemed to be residences. So narrow was the sidewalk between their facades and the street that Bowen's and Eva's shoulders touched as they went along. The narrow doors were closed; none had glass in them. While they might sometimes open suddenly to let someone scurry in or out, they would never be left ajar. Curtains hung over each small window like gauze eye patches.

Some buildings had tiny shops on the ground floor —a chemist, a stationer, a butcher. Passing a woman with a shopping basket on her arm, Bowen had to step off the curb and let Eva go ahead. The woman didn't thank him, or even smile. They saw only her and two others in that section of the road.

The road curved slightly to the right, and Bowen and Eva could see that it led to the village center, to a stone cross. Going toward it, they discovered that their east-west road intersected a north-south one, and the meeting had been celebrated by the cross and by an unexpected generosity of village square around it. The cross stood three steps up, in the center of an octagonal island. Bowen and Eva went up the steps to look around.

On the east side of the square the road they'd been on continued between rows of houses again. A small wooden barrier had been set there to prevent vehicles from entering. A policeman rocked on his heels near it. About fifty yards beyond, the road reached the green and open countryside on the other side of the village. Knots of men stood in the street just past the last of the houses.

"That must be where the sheep market is," Bowen said. Looking over the men's heads, he could see trailers for transporting livestock drawn up along the way. "Maybe after we find a place to stay we could walk up and see it. Would you like to do that?"

"If you like."

"If *I* like?"

"I would like that."

"Good."

"Thank you, David." She touched her cheek to his shoulder, and he squeezed her hand.

"Actually," Bowen said, peering over his left shoulder at the houses lining the road to the north, "I don't see anything that looks like an inn." He pivoted suddenly, turning so that he might look south, "But there's bound to be—"

"What's wrong?"

"I just caught a glimpse of a guy behind us. He was leaning forward just enough to see us around the curve of the street. When I turned, he ducked back. Come on." Taking Eva's hand, Bowen walked quickly across the little square to the street leading toward the sheep market. He nodded casually to the policeman as they went into it.

"David, we should ask for help from that policeman."

"No. Maybe I'm wrong. And anyway, going to the police would be the end of us."

"But, David—"

"Only as a last resort." Bowen spoke in a tone of calm command. "Let's see if it really is anyone following us, and try to lose him, first."

Bowen and Eva reached the groups of men standing in the road. Covering himself behind one, Bowen looked back along the street.

"There're two of them. I'm not sure, but I think one of them was the driver of that car we passed by the road in Borrowdale."

Eva's hand tightened on his arm. Looking directly into his eyes she said, "I don't know how they found us."

"I know," he said. "There's no way you could know."

"What do we do?"

"Stay calm. Keep away from them. Watch for a chance to get away."

The groups of men in the road were the fringe of a crowd that began beyond the line of trailers parked along the roadside. Bowen steered a way between two trailers, and into the mass. He worked through to the sheep pens.

The pens were made of movable sections of rails and stanchions, set up in four large side-by-side blocks. Aisles four or five feet wide separated them. Men were crowded into the aisles and all around the outsides of the pens almost as thickly as the sheep in them, looking at the sheep, talking about them, prodding them with canes.

The men might have seemed a collection of country squires. All wore flat, billed caps, and jackets of good tweed. A few of the younger ones were dressed informally in colored, open-necked shirts, or heavy sweaters; but the majority had on white shirts and narrow, four-in-hand ties of subdued hue and pattern. Only the men's leathery, creased, and windburned faces, strong and sinewy hands, identified them as accustomed to hard manual labor in the out-of-doors.

At the far end of the pens, opposite the road, a platform had been set up. Two men stood on it. One seemed to be an auctioneer, the other held a clipboard. More livestock trailers were parked at angles beyond the sides of the block of pens, and along that far end, flanking the platform.

Holding Eva's hand tightly, Bowen began with polite but inexorable pressure to force his way up one of the aisles. He could feel her trembling. "Are you okay? Don't worry, we'll get away."

"I am afraid, David. I know what kind of men they are. And I am sick that they have found us."

"Yes. It's scary, but it'll be all right. I'm sure." He gave her a tight smile.

After a moment, she returned it. "Yes," she said, standing straighter.

All of the colors of the scene seemed chosen from a

single, restrained palette—green, gray, and shades of tan and brown—the grassy field beyond the market area, the hills rising in the distance into fog, the clouds lowering overhead, the woolens of the men's clothes, the creamy gray of the sheep themselves.

"Can you see them?" Eva asked, her voice steady. "Are they coming after us?"

"I can see them." The ground rose slightly toward the platform, so Bowen could look over the heads of the crowd down to the road. "They're back at the side of the road. Back at the edge of the crowd." The two men were swaying, craning to look, but not to find him and Eva. They had found them. "They're just keeping us in sight."

Dressed as they were, Bowen and Eva might have blended indistinguishably into the crowd. But Eva was the only woman in the place, and her hair—that color and gleam like white gold—was a beacon. And the dourly courteous sheep men—as soon as they saw her next to themselves—pulled back and nudged their neighbors to step aside to let her pass.

Eva's hand went to her head. "My scarf is in the car. If I could find something to cover my hair . . ."

Although the crowd grew denser, Bowen's pressure and the deference of the men toward Eva allowed them to move steadily. They worked their way slowly nearer to the front.

"If we can find something to cover my hair, perhaps we can hide ourselves in the crowd, go around behind the houses on one side or the other. What do you think?"

"I don't think there are enough people out on the road, and they'd spot us when we got close to the houses. And even if we got back into the town, and then they spotted us . . . There were only those couple of shops; hardly anybody on the street. And this town—all stone row houses, no place to hide—it'd be like being trapped in a canyon."

Accepting his estimate with a nod, she looked calculatingly toward the fields beyond the platform. "We could perhaps slip out that way. The trailers would screen us."

"They'd see us, eventually. And it wouldn't do us any good to be running around out there in the hills. What we need to do is get back to the car. I think we'd better just wait."

"But, David . . ." Her grip on his arm was tightening, as though both to express and control a rising fear. "They can wait, too. As long as they know we are here . . ."

He put a hand on hers. "Look, we've got a kind of a balance here. They can't take us out of the middle of a crowd—or anyplace where there are people around. On the other hand, obviously they realize I don't want to attract attention myself—go to the police, or anything. As long as we can keep some distance, we're okay. I think we should just be cool, and wait for an opportunity."

"They will know we are going to try to go back to the car. They could simply go back now and wait for us there."

"If they do, we'll deal with that then."

Bowen and Eva had not been the only people moving close to the platform. There seemed to be a sort of current to and away from it.

"I'm getting the picture—how this place operates," Bowen said. "The buyers are going around looking at the lots of sheep, and then they come up here and bid on them. Then they move off. Most of them hang around—maybe they're going to buy or sell some more, maybe they're just watching—but some of them leave.

"What we can do . . . we can work our way down toward the road again, and when several of them head back into the village, we can go along."

"But, David—"

"If those guys start closing in, then I'll have to throw it in and shout and get help. But it's worth a try. Come on, we'll go back toward the road, and watch for a chance."

Once again Bowen led Eva through the crowd, down another aisle toward the road. He paused by the next to last pen.

"Yes," he said. "They're just watching us. They're not going to come after us in here."

Eva leaned against the pen, gripping the top rail, staring toward the men who had followed them. "I'm very frightened, David," she said lightly, as though remarking on the weather.

Bowen stood close behind her. He put his hand over hers. "Well, if you are, you're handling it just fine. It'll be all right. If we have to, we'll wait until the market is over, and everybody'll be leaving at once, and we'll—"

"But if we could— David! There is another!" A third man had come up to the first two. "I know him!"

One of the original followers inclined his head to locate Eva and Bowen for the newcomer, who then began to make his way along the line of trailers at the roadside. Slightly taller than the average height of the local men, he could be seen easily as he passed the aisle where Bowen and Eva were standing and took up a position at the other end of the pens.

"Boxing us," Bowen said. "Do you see any more?"

Eva looked back and forth over the crowd. Bowen

did, too. He seemed to focus for a moment on a ruddy-faced man wearing a tweed hat. Then he scanned slowly, and fixed on the pair of Germans at the town end of the market. Swiveling his head, he tracked across the crowd to find and stare at the third, taller German.

"I don't see anyone else," Eva said. "Do you?"

"No. I guess not. I guess there're only the three of them. But I'm not going to wait for more to come. Okay, let's do it," he said. Gripping Eva's shoulders, he put her on his left side. He took her hand, folded her arm under his. "Just keep moving," he said.

For an instant she seemed about to pull away. Then she drew herself erect as he had done, setting her jaw like his. Because the crowd was thinning, they were able almost to march toward the road.

As they reached the line of trailers, the taller German on their right began to move toward them.

"Keep going," Bowen said.

They went between two trailers, out into the road. The taller German came between two others. The pair of Germans at the town end came around and stood at the side of the road ahead.

Bowen paused. One of the Germans ahead crossed to the other side. Two sheep farmers standing in the middle apparently reached agreement in their discussion. Shaking hands, they turned toward the village, and began walking as though to celebrate it with a pint at the pub.

"Okay. Here we go." Bowen and Eva fell in four paces behind them.

The taller German wasn't alone. He had a partner whom Bowen and Eva hadn't spotted before, standing across the road. The two of them began moving up behind Bowen and Eva. They might have closed in, but four young men, laughing and trading jibes in their incomprehensible dialect, came rollicking from between the trailers and commandeered the space there. One seemed to be telling a long, boastful, and preposterous story. Gesturing widely he skipped and wheeled to keep ahead of his fellows, sometimes walking backward, regaling them in spite of their slurs and hoots.

They all reached the houses. All four Germans stepped up onto the sidewalks at either side, the others stayed in the street. The Germans moved at the corners of a nearly perfect parallelogram, keeping their positions as though on parade. Within that box the two old shepherds strode side by side, hands in pockets, with the long, loose-kneed gait of men who hike over rough ground all day. Then came Eva and Bowen—she with head high, like a queen going to the block, he looking as relaxed as a matador; then the young men, almost over-running Bowen and Eva, falling back as two of them made the passes of a mock fistfight.

The formation proceeded toward the mouth of the street at the village square. Bowen checked from side to side, and behind, sizing up the Germans. All four were stocky, hair black—or it might be dark brown. Jackets and trousers, gray, or brown, or brownish gray. If their objective had been to kill him, they could have done it and melted away in a moment, and no one could have given a useful description of them. They all looked tough, though. Even the slightly taller one behind on the left who smiled maliciously when Bowen caught his eye.

The first pair of Germans reached the square. They paused, one on either side of the street.

"Hello, Ian!" one of the farmers called to the policeman who still stood guarding his barrier. "Soon be over now." He and his fellow paused to exchange a word with the officer.

"Keep going," Bowen said to Eva.

The leading Germans might have heard him. They proceeded across the square, one and then the other glancing back to assure that their quarry didn't attempt a break to the side.

Freed from the confinement of the rows of houses, the young men's exuberance carried them around Bowen and Eva. Brawny, burly, boisterous lads, as they passed each took the opportunity to glance at Eva. But they'd been brought up in the ways of country courtesy. They nodded politely, and their smiles were bashful. Two even touched their caps, one said, "Evening," and the fourth—the one given to walking backward —turned and asked, "Are you here for the sheep sale?"

"We're just tourists," Bowen answered.

"Ah," the young man exclaimed, "Americans, are you?" His eyes flicked once to Bowen, but he kept his focus on Eva.

"Yes," Bowen said. "We've been up in the Lake District. Walking."

"Ah, walking."

Bowen smiled and nodded.

"They're Americans," the man announced to his friends, speaking over his shoulder, as though they hadn't heard every word of the exchange. "They've been in the Lake District, walking." He wheeled around and fell into step beside Eva. He introduced himself at once as "Robert Dowd, but call me Bob. And what brings you here?" he asked her.

"We stopped to eat," she answered.

"You're not American. What are you, then, Swedish?" He looked at Eva appraisingly, as though he'd heard all the stories about Swedish girls.

Now that the ice had been broken, the other young men also fell into rank beside Bowen and Eva. All three of them seemed shyer than their companion; they let him handle the conversation.

He was the man for the job. As they walked along toward the pub—six abreast, taking up most of the roadway—he kept up a constant stream of questions and comments. When he asked, "And where do you come from?" Bowen answered, "New York," and Eva said, "London," and the young man bubbled into a long comparison of country versus city life.

Sometimes his friends shot barbs, leaning forward to sight on him—and, of course, on Eva beside him. But even without that excuse, they leaned forward and back as they walked, sneaking glimpses of her.

Bowen and Eva did glance at Bob, and sometimes at the others, for politeness. Mostly, they watched the Germans ahead, and—trying not to do it too often —the ones following. The Germans kept their distance. As they all approached the pub, the one on the left ahead, and then the one on that side behind, crossed to join their partners. Evidently they were prepared simply to keep Bowen and Eva boxed until their newfound friends departed.

The two leading Germans went past the pub and into the area beyond it where Bowen had parked. The two following turned into the area between the pub and the village, no doubt to approach the car from that side.

"Perhaps these gentlemen would like to have a drink with us," Eva suggested brightly.

Bowen looked hesitant for an instant, but Bob responded at once.

"Oh, now, that's very generous of you; and we'd be

pleased, I'm sure. But, you see, the bad luck is, it's afternoon closing hours. They won't open again for"—he looked at his wristwatch—"nearly a quarter hour. But we do thank you for the offer. Very kind of you. And—if you're not going to stop in the village —you'd best be on your way quickly. The sales should be nearly over, and in a few minutes now—although this is only a country town—we'll have a traffic tie-up that would do a sizable city proud."

They all went past the pub. Bowen scanned the parking area. He'd taken a place between two cars halfway into the lot, in the hope—was anyone following—that his car might not be seen from the road. He couldn't see the Germans. They could have ducked in anywhere to wait in ambush.

"Can we offer you a ride?" he asked.

"Ah, thank you. That's very kind of you. But we've our own transport."

"Well . . ." Bowen gave Bob and his companions a regretful smile, looking at each of them. They were solidly built, strong-looking young men; they might well have been the kind who brawled in barrooms for amusement. The Germans would be trained fighters. Still, the odds would be five to four; Bowen also was trained, and he was on guard against surprise.

They all paused at the corner of the pub before going into the car park.

Late afternoon: The light seemed to have given up all attempt to penetrate the overcast, and was withdrawing rapidly. What remained had the bleakness of the background in a painting of Napoleon retreating from Russia.

"Maybe another time," Bob said. Bowen smiled and shrugged, and they all started into an aisle between two rows of cars. "You really should stop awhile," Bob was saying, "we haven't the mountains here, but there's fine walking . . ." when Eva clutched Bowen's arm.

"David—!"

Bowen followed her line of sight. Back toward the road, beyond the row of cars on his left, two men were getting out of a van. Despite the distance, despite the gloom, Bowen recognized them as the ones he'd fought that morning.

CHAPTER

9

Bowen could see his own car over the roofs of others parked in one of the lines perpendicular to the road. Two of the Germans were standing beyond it, in the aisle on the other side. The ones from the van stood in the same aisle, close to the road. The third pair came around from behind the pub.

Six to five, now.

The German who had smiled at Bowen did so again. The two whom Bowen had beaten that morning looked viciously angry. The other three kept their faces blank as cast iron.

Bowen halted. Bob and his friends went on a step, Bob still talking. Then he, and they after him, stopped, turning to look questioningly at Bowen.

"Bob, I think maybe we're in for some trouble." Bowen nodded slightly down the aisle at the Germans there, then swung to glance back toward those by the road.

Bob looked, then grinned. "Ah, no. They're really good fellows, and we're all sober law-abiding citizens —at the moment."

Bowen did a take of incredulity, then snapped to look toward the road again. A black car with a blue bubble-light had just pulled into the parking lot. It stopped before passing the Germans standing in front of their van. Two policemen got out of the rear. There was a third, plus the driver, in the front. The ones who had come out carried the wide-gauntleted white gloves British policemen use when directing traffic.

"Hoy, Tim," Bob called. "Come to put the world on the right course, have you?" He nodded at the other policeman, "Teddy, hoy."

"Hoy, Bob. If we hoped to do that, we'd start by putting you lot away." He acknowledged the other men, "John, Tom, Trevor."

For a moment, Bowen and Eva stared in amazement at the men bantering back and forth. Then Bowen gripped Eva's hand. "Come on. Let's get out of here." He started them toward their car. That seemed sufficient impetus to set everyone in motion. The four young men drifted with Bowen and Eva, still calling back over the line of parked cars to the policemen. Tim and Teddy started to stroll to the road. The Germans all drew back, and then hurried toward their own vehicles.

"Ah, here we are, then?" Bob said. He and his companions halted in front of the car with Bowen and Eva.

Bowen unlocked the door for Eva, then went across

the front to the other side. Bob stood away so that he could pass, then came to Eva's door when she was inside. She rolled down her window.

"You'll be on your way," he said. "Pity you can't stop longer, we could show you the sights. There's a ruined chapel beyond the hill there, if you care for that sort of thing. If you fancy something a little more lively, there's Sukey's disco on the South Road. Do you dance?" he asked.

"Yes."

"Oh, I can imagine you do. I can just imagine."

"Well," Bowen said, "thank you. For your company." He offered his hand to the nearest man, then to the other two.

Reluctantly, it seemed, Bob came to the front of the car and shook Bowen's hand in his turn. "Do look us up, if you pass this way again."

"We certainly will."

Halted where it was, the police car blocked the aisle that the van would have to use. After Bowen left his parking place, the four young men, walking abreast again, filled the other aisle. If the Germans had pulled into one of those aisles, or honked, or otherwise shown an urgent wish to leave, perhaps the men or the police car would have moved to let them. The Germans must have considered it indiscreet to call attention to themselves by revealing such a desire.

"We must have at least two minute's lead," Bowen exclaimed gleefully. "At least that. They won't know whether—when we got to the center of the village—we turned north or south; or—if they turn south, too —whether we took the left or right fork back there. We'll soon be untraceable!"

He seemed to feel secure enough to keep the speed of

the car to forty—not any too slow for the narrow, winding road, but not too fast. Still, to be sure, he checked frequently in his rearview mirror.

The road followed the course of a small stream that meandered around the nearly treeless hills. Sheep country: meadows of rich-looking grass cropped short by grazing; stone walls, built without mortar, bordering the road and running off for miles to the sides; a cottage here and there. A lovely countryside, but broad, empty, and lonely.

They had driven three miles when Bowen suddenly exclaimed, "No!"

"What!" Eva whirled to look back.

"There's a car coming up on us. Wait till the road straightens again. He's at least a mile back, but he's coming up fast." Bowen pressed his own accelerator. "Coming at that speed . . . it's probably them."

"How could they . . .?"

"I see only one of them. They must have been in the other parking lot—on the other side of the pub—they must have gotten out before anyone could . . . they must not have been blocked in that one. Hold on!"

The road bent sharply left. Bowen took the corner fast, skidding into the other lane. "Bad news," he said calmly. "This is not the kind of road for a high-speed chase."

Another turn swept toward them. Bowen braked, and took it more slowly than the one before. "We're more likely to end up wrapped around one of those stone walls than escape them."

"How could they know which road we took?"

"They couldn't. Couldn't *know*. Must've guessed right."

"What can we do?"

"Not outrun them. And there's no place to hide. If

we come to another fork, and they can't see which way . . ." Bowen spoke quietly, as if to himself, most of his concentration apparently on the road. "I don't think we'd better count on staying ahead of them long enough . . . I think I'd better . . ."

Ahead, a side road led off to their right. Looking in that direction Bowen could see a high structure on a rise of ground a mile or so away. As they sped up to the junction, he read aloud from the signpost there. "Chapel and Crypt." He hit the brake, then powered around the turn.

"What are you going to do?"

"Stand and fight."

"David! No!"

"I've got to. You just do what I tell you."

The side road curved and climbed, rising in a long sweep to the top of the low hill, ending in a flat area where a sign directed visitors to "Park in Designated Spaces Only." Neat white paint lines demarcated six, a pathetic attempt at restoring order to the ruined place. Bowen pulled into one of them. "Come on!"

He and Eva were out of the car at once.

"Where? What can we—"

"I don't know"—Bowen threw open the trunk of the car—"hide someplace. Ambush them. It'll only be two of them. Give me half a second surprise—" The Germans' car was turning onto the road to the chapel. Bowen rummaged in the trunk. He found and jerked out the handle for the jack. "Come on!"

"What if they have pistols?"

"They didn't this morning. I'm no use to them dead."

"David—!"

"Come!" He grabbed her hand.

They ran up four broad and worn stone steps to

reach the chapel's floor. For a moment they halted, looking one way and another.

All that was left of the chapel was a tall section of the far end wall and a bit of one side making a corner to it. Part of the frame of a window stood high in the end wall—carved stone molding down one side, the half of the rise of a high-pointed arch. The building's stone must once have been silvery gray. Now it was pewter and soot, pitted, and encrusted with lichen. Only those two pieces of wall remained—and the stone floor. Grass grew between the stones, but their understructure seemed intact—few were heaved or fallen.

The Germans' car was halfway up the side road to the chapel. Bowen and Eva had less than a minute's lead.

Bowen took a step forward, pulling Eva. "Maybe hide behind the wall— What's that?"

He was looking down. Just ahead was a milky-colored rectangle in the floor. "It's Plexiglas. There's another. What . . .?" He scanned back and forth more carefully, his eyes going to the back of the floor area.

"What do those signs say?"

At the corner where the two wall fragments met and at what would have been its opposite at the other side of the end wall were white signs with black arrows pointing at an angle downward.

"To the crypt," Eva read.

"Come on!"

The Germans pulled into a space away from Bowen and Eva's car. While coming up the side road, they had seen Bowen and Eva run toward the back of the chapel and disappear. There were two of them—the taller one who had smiled sardonically at Bowen, and a younger man with the build of an iron-pumper. They went up onto the chapel floor and prowled toward the end wall. They saw the two stairways leading down to the crypt. They exchanged a few words. Moving at the same speed, they started down—one on each side, to keep their quarry between them.

The steps were worn and rounded, descending to the crypt that stretched below the whole chapel floor. Everything was stone. The clicks of the men's footfalls rang down the stairs and ricocheted back at them. The crypt held the dampness and cold of the day. It stank of mildewy dankness, of old urine and ancient rot. Gray light filtered down through scratched and weathered Plexiglas skylights; no more light than at late dusk, but enough to reveal a stone forest. Running front to back, four rows of thick, cylindrical pillars—like the petrified trunks of thousand-year-old trees—supported the heavy sweeps of the double-vaulted ceiling.

The men paused at the stairways, their eyes adjusting to the dimness, scanning the space. In only a few moments, they could see its volume. They could see some of the low rectangular pedestals on which sarcophagi had rested. From the corners of the room, though, the columns blocked large areas from sight.

The smiler spoke, his gutteral words rolling down the room. While his partner kept in place, he walked all the way across the end of the room to peer into each aisle, then returned to the center one. Looking down it he could see one lidless stone sarcophagus in the center of the room.

The younger man made a suggestion, his voice reverberating softly like distant thunder. His colleague in the center began to walk forward, on guard, looking left and right, ready to see Bowen and Eva pressed against the far side of a pillar. The chamber magnified the soft scrunch of his footsteps.

Suddenly, a soft, high moan lifted, undulating, echoing through the gloom. Both men started as though speared with shafts of ice. Again the sound rose, keening, agonized, angry. The older man, in the aisle, shuddered visibly; but—hands lifted, prepared to meet a human enemy—he crept forward toward the sarcophagus from which the groans were coming.

His partner set himself to sprint across the room if Bowen was using the sound as a distraction to cover a dash for the stairway there.

Up on its pedestal, the stone coffin's sides were nearly three feet high. The German had to reach its foot before he could see over and into the darkness well enough to make out Eva's figure clearly. Then he recognized her, lying half on one side, her wrists evidently secured behind her, a scarf tied across her mouth.

He flashed glances either way to check for Bowen, then rushed to the side of the coffin to lift Eva. He leaned. Bowen sprang from his crouch behind the coffin's head. The German caught the movement, jerked himself upright.

Bowen had been hunkered with his right hand behind his back so that when he came up he could swing it around wide at full strength. The jack handle smacked the German's skull with a loud, flat crack that hung for a moment, ringing.

Looking upward, seeing the blow hurl the man away, Eva screamed. Unclasping her hands, which she'd held behind her, tearing the scarf away from her mouth, she screamed again, and the vaults screamed back. She scrambled, clutching the side of the sarcophagus to pull herself up.

"Down!" Bowen shouted. She twisted, and saw the muscular German running toward them. "Get down!" Bowen shouted again, but Eva froze.

Seeing Bowen, seeing the iron brandished in his hand, the young German skidded to a halt a yard from the side of the coffin. Bowen sidestepped cautiously around it. He was half-crouched, his left arm bent at chest-level. His right arm was extended out and back, holding the jack handle upright. Still as a stone pillar, himself, he stared at the German as though daring him to move first. Then, never off balance, he stepped again, one foot crossing the other. Slowly, he brought his right arm across his body, first in front of his left shoulder, his weapon straight up. He stepped forward once more.

The young man looked at Bowen, clearly stunned to recognize him as the aggressor. He inched backward. Then—eyes narrowing, jaw setting—resolve firmed his face. He attacked.

Bowen's stance seemed to dictate that he'd make a rightward slashing blow. The German feinted to invite it, then lunged obliquely to come in under and behind it. But Bowen had been inviting *that*. Spinning backward he whirled full circle. Once again he brought the jack handle full around to strike his opponent's head at maximum force, and that crack rang back from the walls, and Eva screamed.

After the bellman left, Bowen went to the window. He lifted a slat of the shade, looked out.

"Airshaft."

He went to the dresser, glanced into and then closed

the drawers—all three of them. He looked into the bathroom. "A little grundgy in the corners and around the fixtures, but not bad."

Eva stood near the bed, as she had since they'd been brought to the room; stood like the suitcases the porter had deposited in the entryway.

It was a small room, the walls painted a dismal, muted mustard color, bare except for two cheap prints of noble-looking horses, and an unframed mirror over the chest of drawers.

"Not exactly the Dorchester," Bowen said. "But it'll do for a night or two. How's the bed?"

Eva glanced down as though only then realizing there was a bed in the room. She touched it, sank down to sit on it. "It is fine."

"Musical, like the one in Borrowdale?"

After a moment she pressed the mattress with her palm. "I think it is new."

"Well," Bowen said as though that settled something. He looked from side to side surveying the little room. Then he sat in the single armchair that was squeezed into the corner between the window and the foot of the bed. "Well. I think we can relax, now. There's no way they can find us here."

Eva nodded. She slipped off her shoes, swung her legs up, and lay on the bed.

"You look exhausted," Bowen said.

"Yes."

"Why don't you sleep for a while. I think I'll take a shower." But he didn't move. "You were terrific today, Eva. This afternoon. I know you were scared, but you really handled it. You were right there."

"Thank you. You were very strong, and calm, yourself, David. But we were lucky. Those boys walking with us; and then the police. What would we have done if we hadn't been so lucky?"

"I don't know. Run, yelled for help. I don't know."

"We cannot expect always to be so lucky. When they find us again."

"Maybe they won't find us again."

She closed her eyes for a moment and sighed. "They have ways . . . they have people, everywhere. And if they do find us . . . you will believe . . . You will believe I told them."

"No." He paused. "I guess it would depend on the circumstances. I know you didn't tell them today. Somehow they followed us down the motorway —those cars we saw: They probably were shifting off, taking turns. But you couldn't have told them. I know that. You see?"

She looked at him, and then at the wall again. "Another time, you may not know. You will never trust me. This is hopeless, David. For a time, today—this afternoon—I allowed myself to deceive myself, to hope perhaps . . . But you will never trust me; you cannot love me."

For nearly a minute, Bowen sat looking at her, silent. Then he said, quietly, "Of course I don't trust you, Eva. And I *don't* know if I'll ever be able to. But I do have hope, and I am in here trying. I am not a quitter, Eva. I don't think you are, either. You're tough. You're a fighter. A survivor. So—goddammit—don't you crump out on me now!"

When Bowen came out of the bathroom, toweling his hair, Eva still lay on the bed. After a moment she opened her eyes, saw him. He was tanned to the waist. Light from the lamp at the corner of the room by the chair emphasized his muscles as he moved. He looked strong, his body hard. But her gaze at him, her smile, was wan.

"Did you sleep?" he asked.

"I rested."

"Feeling better."

"Yes. A little. I think so."

"Good. Why don't you take a shower, too? It's a good shower. Does wonders for you."

"Yes. I will."

As Bowen crossed to the chest of drawers, Eva got herself up and—with her back to him—took off her sweater and skirt. She put on her purple-splotched wrapper over her underclothes and went into the bathroom. Bowen continued dressing until he heard the shower start. He waited another moment, listening, then went quickly to the head of the bed, lifted the receiver of the telephone on the night table there, and—looking at the bathroom door—placed a call.

"You are awake?" Eva asked in a whisper.

"Yes."

"What time is it?"

"I don't know," he said softly. "Three or four o'clock, probably."

No light came through the shade over the window on the airshaft, nor from under the hallway door. The man in some room nearby who had a chronic cough must finally have fallen asleep. Every guest in the hotel must have been asleep: All were quiet, and the distant hum of the elevator hadn't been heard for an hour. Eva and Bowen lay side by side in total darkness. They might have been in a diving bell deep under the sea.

"Have you been awake long?" she asked.

"No. I was asleep until just a little while ago."

"Are you all right?"

"Yes. I just . . . Things going around in my head. You know."

"Yes. Can you tell me?" No one could have heard them talking, but that sense of lying close together in the secret hour of the night kept Eva's voice just above a whisper.

Bowen also continued speaking softly, his pitch low. "Oh, how I feel about you—both sides of it. How I feel about myself. Both sides of that, too."

"Yes?"

"I think I'm seeing a way to make all of it work for us: love, anger and vengefulness, trust and suspicion, getting away, being able to stay together . . ."

"How?" Eva sat up.

"Well . . . First, tell me some more about Heinz. The way he acted with you. If he's the head of a division, or whatever it is, of an intelligence service, he's got to be a smart man, shrewd, in control of things. He can't be flakey. How could he have been so jealous —shown his jealousy by using his men to watch you, ruined morale in your section?"

"It was a madness, David. As I have told you."

"You mean an aberration: He's not usually like that? He's never done anything like that before?"

"No. Exactly. Except . . . There was a story . . . Not really a story, only hints. That when Heinz was young, many years ago, he hunted down a woman . . . All that anyone would say—it was something whispered to new girls; it was like a legend, like a superstition that is passed along, and no one knows the origin—that a girl must never finish with Heinz before he was finished with her or he would . . . No one would say what he would do, only that he would hunt her down.

"And once—before the end, a long time before,

while we were still happy together—Heinz said that if ever I left him for another man, he would find us even if we ran away and hid in a cave at the tip of South America. He said he—I thought it was a joke. I had been teasing him about a new typist on the third floor, warning him that if he 'interviewed' her I would . . . I was thinking up fantastic, horrible things—I said I would put ground glass in his underpants, I would pour instant glue on her typing chair . . . He said that if ever I ran away with another man, he would find us and, with his own hands, he would make us into bratwurst. Then he held his hands up, big, and ran at me, and . . . It was a joke. It was love play. We were laughing all the time. We made love. Why are you asking this, David?"

"I've thought of a way to use his jealousy. It's a way to help us get away, first of all. And then, it's a way to prove to the CIA—when we tell them about it, eventually we'll have to . . . And to show me, Eva, and —maybe most importantly—to prove to yourself that you're finished with him. That you've cut yourself off."

"How! What?"

"By calling Gert Nagler."

"What!"

Now Eva was up on her knees, straining toward Bowen, trying to see him in the darkness. His voice came to her from the head of the bed, deep, soft, calm, disembodied.

"You call Nagler. You tell him you've tricked me. After all, none of those guys knows what happened between us after I got back to the van. You can tell him I haven't tumbled to the true story—that I think what's going on is that he's still after both of us because of Heinz's jealousy. You tell him what we're doing —when and how we're getting out of England."

"David— I don't understand!"

"Well, of course, it won't be the truth."

"I don't understand."

"Think about it and you will. First, it'll throw them off us. Instead of looking for us—maybe looking where we are, maybe finding us—they'll go for where we aren't. But the real point is that after we're gone, Heinz'll know. He'll know you tricked him. From what you say about his jealousy . . . After you do this—trick him, actively help me to get away, run away with me—there's no going back for you.

"Your doing that, Eva, will prove you've changed sides."

The telephone ringing woke them. Enough pale, colorless light was seeping into the room through the window-shade slats so that Bowen could see the receiver and grab it before the third ring.

"Hello?

"Yes."

Eva propped herself on an elbow, staring across the bed.

"That's right," Bowen said.

"That's right."

Eva sat up, as though looking at the telephone on the table might let her see who was speaking.

"Yes," Bowen said, without expression.

"Yes.

"No, later.

"Yes. Good. Okay." He hung up.

"Who was that?"

"The travel agent. I called him last evening—while you were in the shower. He thinks he can get us on a flight. He'll know for sure in a couple hours."

"When?"

Bowen found his wristwatch by the telephone. "God, it's almost nine-thirty. Well, we should know before noon, then."

"I mean, when will the flight be?"

"That's what he's going to tell me."

"I meant . . ." She sighed and turned and lay against the pillows.

Bowen sat back beside her. "Soon," he said after a moment, without looking at her.

"Thank you. I shouldn't have asked you."

"I don't know when, exactly. You'll see why—why working this out is tricky—later. And I . . . I don't want to tell you about it now."

"I shouldn't have asked you," she said again. "I am sorry."

"It's okay." He didn't touch her, but he did look at her. "We should be leaving either tomorrow or the day after. We're— I'm hoping for tomorrow."

"Thank you, David."

After they'd eaten breakfast, after returning to their room, Bowen said, "I've got to go out for a little while, Eva. I've got to call the travel agent back, and I . . . want to do it from outside. And I want to do some shopping, pick up a few things. Will you be all right here?"

"Yes, David. Of course." She spoke lightly, and even managed a small smile for him.

"I hope you don't mind . . . I . . ."

"It is all right, David. I understand."

"This'll all be over soon."

"Yes."

He embraced her, and she lifted her face and kissed him. Then, as he pulled back, she said, "Have you thought . . . While you are gone, I might use the telephone."

Looking at her, with his arms still around her, Bowen said, "If you want to make a call, you should go down and use the pay phone in the lobby. Otherwise it'll have to go through the switchboard, and I could find out."

After a moment, he kissed her lightly again, then turned away. "I'll be back as soon as I can. It won't be long."

When Bowen returned, Eva was sitting on the bed with her legs up reading a newspaper. "Hi," he said. "It took a little longer than I thought it would." He went past the foot of the bed to put a plastic bag on the chest of drawers. "Have you been okay?" he asked cheerily, positively, like a doctor visiting a patient in traction.

"Yes. I became a little bored, so I went down to the lobby and bought *The Guardian.*"

"Good."

Then they held each other's eyes for a moment.

"I hoped you wouldn't mind," she said, trying to keep the light tone.

"Of course not."

After just an instant, he smiled, and then Eva tipped her head to give him her seeing-in-through-the-cracks look.

"I might have used the telephone while I was there," she said.

"Did you?"

She shrugged. "Why did you give me that opportunity?"

Sitting on the bed, Bowen said, "Well, maybe because we're leaving the country in an hour from now, and I knew we'd be out of here before anybody you called could reach us. Or maybe I hired a private detective to sit behind a newspaper down there and watch the booth. Maybe it was a test. Or maybe"—he smiled at her again—"maybe I did just decide I had to trust you. Which would you rather believe?"

Not returning his smile, she said, "And if I did not call, David, maybe it was because I have changed sides, or maybe it was because I suspected a trap. Which will you believe?"

Bowen nodded. "We are leaving tomorrow, like I hoped. What we're doing, we're going out from Leeds with a charter tour—to the Caribbean. We'll end up on a British island. The tour's supposed to be for people from the midlands here. A plane's being brought in for them instead of making them go down to London or wherever. Leeds isn't a regular transatlantic embarkation point—there shouldn't be anybody on duty especially to watch for us. And, even if we're on a list, putting ourselves in the middle of a group like that . . . So, now you know."

He reached, putting his hand on hers. "What *I'd* rather believe is that you didn't call because we're together."

"Oh, David," she said, gazing at him.

"Yes." He smiled.

"Perhaps. Perhaps."

"Yes."

She looked about the room for some distraction. "What is in your package? What did you buy?"

Getting up from the bed, Bowen took a box out of the plastic bag on the chest of drawers, opened it. "It's a radio. Portable—plug-in or battery. I thought it would be nice to have some music, maybe the news. Here, and when we get to the island . . ." He hesitated.

"But the main thing . . ." Then he rushed on, "It's also a tape player. And recorder—built-in mike. I've been developing my idea—my plan. I thought—if you're willing—we'd make a tape for Heinz."

He paused, looking over the radio he was holding up before him, looking directly into her eyes. She returned his stare, just as steadily. They were as silent as though listening to the thing he held in his hands ticking.

Then Bowen continued. "We wouldn't want old Heinz to think—when you call Gert Nagler, misdirect him—we wouldn't want Heinz to be able to think that maybe you were forced to do it. I thought you might like to . . . express some of your feelings toward him. You might like to tell him, directly, what you think of him."

"David . . ."

"It would go further—it would go all the way beyond just calling Nagler—to prove you've broken with him. And I think it would be good for you to do something that might really hurt that son of a bitch and make you feel you have some power."

Eva stared at Bowen for a moment, looking shocked, incredulous, afraid. Then a brightness and intensity flared into her eyes, and—although her lips were thin and tight—she smiled.

"Yes. Yes! I would like to do that. What a good idea, David."

His smile matched hers. Then he said, "You think for a minute what you're going to say." He pulled the wire from its compartment in the back of the radio, plugged it into the socket by the telephone table.

"Yes," she said. "There is much I would like to say."

"Tell him what you think of him, and that you're going away with me—that you're helping me get away.

Tell him we're in love." He took a tape cassette from the plastic bag, removed its wrapper, put it into the player.

"Yes, David, I will tell him. But I think I will try to hold in my anger. Better, I think, I should try to be calm. Better he should not think I have lost my head, that I do not know what I say."

"Probably right. Well, tell him anything you want. Speak in English, Eva. I want to know what you're saying. But say whatever you want. However you want. Say it in a way—put in things that only he would know—so he'll know you're not reading a script."

Eva nodded.

He put the player onto the night table. The black plastic and brushed metal gleamed. Eva had swung around and come up onto her knees on the bed, facing it. Bowen touched it, then turned to her. "I've set the volume up. I think it'll pick up everything you say from where you are. Just speak naturally. Okay?"

"Yes."

Bowen pressed the play and record buttons.

Eva had clenched her fists in her lap. She began speaking. "Hello, Heinz, you pig. It is Eva. I am speaking to you from a hotel room where I am staying with my lover, David Bowen." Her voice was strong, but calm. "You meant to use me to trap him, but he has freed me from you. I love him. He loves me. He knows everything, yet still he loves me. We are going away together. I am helping him. By the time you hear this, we will be far away, where you never will find us. We will live together. Perhaps we will marry. We will be happy together."

She lifted her eyes from the machine to Bowen. She extended her hand, and he walked around the foot of the bed to take it.

She turned to face the recorder again. Her voice trembled, but she kept it under control. "I love him, Heinz. Truly, completely, with all my heart, and my soul . . . and my body.

"In time, Heinz, we will not think of you any longer. Now, when I think of you, it is with hatred. You are a cruel, vicious animal. You think you are refined. You think you are sensitive. You listen to Mozart—like that Sunday we went to the Gewandhaus—and you close your eyes and say, 'How exquisite, how tender!' But you have no soul, you are a snake swaying when the snake charmer plays."

Her grip tightened on Bowen's hand. She leaned farther toward the tape. "But it is wrong to compare you to an animal. No animal is so depraved. No animal is so consciously vicious. As I think of you, more, my feelings go from hatred to disgust. You are depraved, and disgusting. You are sick. You are pathetic. You think you are strong and powerful, but you are weak."

She turned to look up at Bowen. He nodded, and smiled.

Still looking at him, she said, "I know this now because I have met a man who is strong—so strong he does not have to prove it to himself by being cruel to people. Now that I have met him, I know what I felt for you wasn't love, it was only the infatuation of a young girl who knows nothing." She looked toward the radio. "Because I knew nothing, I thought you were interesting and exciting; but you are only old. You are old, so you have gathered many clever things to say; you have learned many little gestures and poses. They are all tricks—like an old dog knows tricks. Like an old dog howls when he's told, 'Sing,' but he has no music."

Bowen put his other hand on her shoulder.

Eva went on, "Like our learning to do sex from

books—not from love, but tricks from books. Bathing together—the oil of roses you had sent from Bulgaria. Oh, yes, you learned the tricks, Heinz. You learned to perform skillfully. But now I know even that was nothing more than tricks. I know because David is skillful, but his skill comes from love, and so it is far, far better than yours. From David I have such love, and in bed such pleasure because of his love, that I know now what I did not know then—that you are only a sick, old man with nothing inside you.

"I tell you this, Heinz, to say good-bye. In English, 'good-bye,' not *auf wiedersehn.'* I will never see you again. After a while, I think, I will not think of you. Now I hate you, but already that is passing to disgust. In time, I think, when David and I think of you, it will be to laugh at you. And then we will not think of you at all."

For another moment she stared at the machine. Bowen could feel her nearly shaking. He was gripping her hand already. He tightened his other hand on her shoulder. She clutched it with her own free hand, twisting to look up at him. He bent, and kissed her.. Her fury, fear, the thrill of revenge, all seemed suddenly to be transmuted and discharged as lust. She pressed her mouth hard against his, her lips moving, her tongue.

He broke away for breath. He looked at her, at the machine, then back at her, and smiled crookedly. "Why don't we really give Heinz something to remember us by?"

For an instant, Eva looked shocked. She began to shake her head.

"Remember, Eva, 'Living well is the best revenge.'" He slid a hand down to her throat.

She smiled and half closed her eyelids.

"Tell Heinz what I'm doing now," Bowen said, sitting on the bed beside her.

"David is putting his hands on my back, Heinz. At my waist. Under my sweater."

"Tell him how that feels."

"It feels wonderful. David has fine hands—very strong. But he touches me so gently. He knows how to use his hands—how I want him to use them. Sometimes gently, sometimes hard—but never too hard. Now he is moving them around me, to the front. He is holding them there. He moves only his thumbs, very slowly, very lightly."

"Tell him how it feels."

"It is exciting and thrilling when he does that, because I know that he will move his hands up onto my breasts. But he doesn't do it right away. He lets me anticipate it, and it is exciting for me to anticipate.

"Now his hands are moving up, pushing my sweater up. Now—" She gasped.

After a moment, Bowen spoke. "That interruption, Heinz, we were kissing, then. There will be interruptions like that, but don't go 'way. We'll keep you informed."

Eva giggled.

"I've still got my hands on her breasts, and she's—Wait, Eva! Not yet. She was starting to unfasten my belt. Not yet, Eva. There must be at least forty minutes left on that tape, so we want to make this last."

CHAPTER

10

L ooks to me like steak and chops are the only things
to have, again. I'll have the steak this time; you
want the chops?"

"Yes. That will be fine."

"Same wine as last night—that Rioja?"

"Whatever you like, David. Yes. I really don't care."

Bowen signaled the waitress, ordered. When she had
gone he said, "What's the matter, Eva? You've been
mopey ever since we woke up."

"I'm sorry, David. I am unhappy about what we did:
the tape."

"Why?"

"Not the first part, when I spoke to Heinz, telling
him . . . I mean, after . . . What we did. At first, when

174

we were doing it, it seemed exciting. It was thrilling to . . . show off, to know how hearing us would hurt him. I would like to hurt him. But not that way, David."

Bowen studied the table just in front of him. He moved his fork so that its distance from his plate equaled that of his knife. "It sure does prove you've broken with him. That's an important thing for you. For us. Don't you feel good about that?"

"It makes me feel ashamed."

Bowen slid his water glass to his right, centering it above the point of the knife.

"It makes me feel dirty," Eva said.

Bowen moved the glass a half inch away from himself, then a quarter inch back. "Then we'll erase it."

Bowen went to the other side of the bed. He moved the radio from the bedside table to the dresser. He stood in front of the dresser, solidly. He took the cassette from a drawer, put it into the machine, pressed the control buttons until he found the end of Eva's speech to Heinz.

"Okay," he said to Eva, his back to her. She had halted, standing on the other side of the bed, watching him. She heard a click.

"I've got it on fast forward and erase. It'll only take a minute."

They both stood, as they were, listening to the quiet whirr of the tape, Bowen staring down at it, Eva looking at his reflection in the mirror over the dresser. His body blocked the player from her view.

There was another click.

"Done," Bowen said. "I'll rewind it." He pressed that button. Then he opened a drawer, took out a small manila envelope. He carried it and a sheet of notepaper around to her. "Here. Put in a note. Just say, 'For Heinz,' and sign it. Address the envelope. Send it to Nagler in London." He gave her a pen from his jacket pocket.

Eva sat on the bed and wrote.

Bowen took the note, wrapped it around the rewound cassette, and put them together into the envelope.

"Okay, that's done," he said.

Bowen slipped the envelope into his jacket pocket. "Well, all set?"

"Yes." Eva sat on the edge of the bed. Their bags stood near the door, ready.

"Then I guess it's time for you to call Nagler. Then we'll go."

"Yes." She rose and came around the bed. "What do you want me to tell him?"

He put his hands on her hips. "Tell him we're in Canterbury; and we're going to take the Hovercraft ferry from Folkstone to Calais early this afternoon. Tell him I'm still madly in love with you." He kissed her cheek. "Tell him that I still accept your story about Heinz—the jealous industrialist—and that his guys've been after us because of you. And that I haven't gone to the police because I'm afraid then the CIA will find me. Say that because I'm so in love with you and afraid for you I haven't let you out of my sight, so you haven't been able to call before now. Tell him you've only got a minute; and if he starts asking anything you can't handle, say I'm coming and hang up."

"All right." She gave Bowen a quick, nervous smile. Then she said, "But . . . I will have to speak German, David."

"I know."

"With two words I could signal that what I tell him is false."

"I know. Why are you telling me that?"

"I suppose because I want to be sure you know what you are doing: that you truly trust me."

"Okay." Bowen drew away from her, but didn't look away. "I know you could tip him off that you're lying. But you can't tell him where we are or where we're going without my understanding those words, so I'm not taking any immediate risk. I guess, love, if we're working on honesty I ought to make that clear to *you.*"

After a moment they managed small smiles for each other.

Eva went past him to the telephone, lifted the receiver, placed her call through the hotel operator. Bowen went around to her side of the bed, and sat. Perhaps he hadn't wanted to stand where he'd been or to sit in the armchair so close as to seem to be monitoring and ready to snatch the phone from her hand. He sat with his back to her; and when she said, "Gert? Eva," and began speaking rapidly, breathily, in a hushed voice, he stared at the floor apparently trying to discern a picture in the carpet stains.

Bowen pulled to the curb in a ten-minute parking zone just beyond the post office. "You'll be all right here?" he asked without giving it any particular inflection.

"Yes."

"I'll only be a couple minutes."

"Good," Eva said, smiling as though not taking any special meaning from his reassurance or from his leaving her alone in a public place for the first time in three days.

Neither of them could have been more casual without taking off their shoes.

While Bowen was inside the post office, she sat quietly, watching traffic and the pedestrians on the sidewalk next to her. Sometimes she looked into the rearview mirror. Bright, pale straw-colored sunlight shone onto her side of the street, but the air was chilly, and people walked briskly. Men passing the car glanced at her, but only seemed to notice her in the way she was used to. None loitered, or appeared to be watching her. So when Bowen returned and asked, "Everything okay?" she was able to say, almost as if bored, "Yes, I am sure everything is all right," even though her fingers were twisted tightly together in her lap.

"Good." Bowen started the car. Then he reached over and squeezed her hands. "Well, love, here we go."

They grinned at one another, then Bowen pulled into traffic.

For several minutes, finding their way out of the city occupied them. Finally, when they were on the highway for Leeds, Bowen said, "Okay, let me tell you what we're going to do.

"We'll go into Leeds, find the railway station, and leave the car there. We could leave it at the airport, I'm sure; but—assuming the CIA is trying to find me and tracks me through the rental agency—they'll think we took a train."

"David, if they could track you through the car rental . . ."

"Sure, they've probably been trying to trace me ever since we slipped them in London. They may have gotten the British police to help them, and put out an inquiry to all the rental agencies, and had a report back—say Sunday night or Monday. But we only used the car for a couple hours on Sunday, and for a quick run into Keswick on Monday. The only time we were really on the road was Tuesday, most of which we spent out in the boondocks. The car's been sitting in an underground garage since then. We've got less than an hour's drive now. If we can make that . . ."

Eva shifted in her seat so that she could watch through the rear window.

"What I'll do," Bowen continued, "I'll leave the car in one of the Godfrey Davis parking places at the railway station, with the keys and papers in it; not go to the desk to turn it in. By the time anybody realizes it's there, and reacts, and the agency or the police get on it, we'll be a continent away."

He pulled out to pass a slow-moving trailer truck. Traffic on the highway was heavy, but flowing quickly.

"Where we're going, Eva . . . The plane, the tour we're traveling with, is going to Antigua. When we get there . . . Ellen and I went down to the Caribbean many times: Antigua, three or four other places. I know of a guy on Antigua who has a small charter boat. We'll take a short cruise—without going through any embarkation formalities—to Montserrat. It's one of the smaller islands, not touristy. We'll take a cottage there. This is the off-season; I'm sure we won't have any trouble finding one.

"So, first of all, the CIA may never be able to trace us out of England. Even if they do, they'll lose us again in Antigua. They might be able to find us eventually, but I doubt they'll try that hard. I mean, it's not like I'm a high-level defector carrying the secret of how to build a rail gun. They aren't going to put the entire agency on me, or try to mobilize every police force in the Western Hemisphere. After all, the Caribbean is a place they would have let me travel, anyway."

Eva broke in, "But now that I am with you . . ."

"Of course. They won't like that, which has been my point all along. Still, I think they won't be able to find us quickly—or that they'll even put up the kind of effort that might find us sometime soon. And by the time they do . . . And whether they find us or not, eventually I'll contact *them*. We don't want to spend the rest of our lives hiding. We'll just wait long enough to prove that my being with you is okay."

"David, there is a car . . . It has been back there for several minutes now."

"Which one?"

"The brown one. Do you see it?"

"Yes. It may not mean anything. We're all traveling at about the same speed. We'll watch it."

After another minute, Eva said, "Still he is there. I think you should do something, David."

"I don't think it's . . . Okay, you're right. We should find out." At the first opportunity Bowen slipped into the slow lane behind a creeping tank truck.

"What are you doing?" Eva asked incredulously.

"I was already over the speed limit. We'll do it the other way."

Bowen snapped the switch to put his flashers on. At twenty miles per hour, he and the tanker made almost as much of an obstacle to traffic behind them as though they'd been standing still. Cars flashed past at nearly three times their speed. A huge hauler roared up behind, racing with the momentum of a runaway locomotive, and then—at the last possible instant, it seemed—swung to the side and passed them.

"Here he comes!" Eva called out.

The brown car swept by as if pulled along like a leaf in the truck's slipstream.

"Was he watching us?"

"He did not look at us when he passed. I don't know."

"Probably wasn't anything, Eva. If he slows down and waits . . . If he doesn't, then either he wasn't following us, or he's lost us. But I don't think he was following us. I'm sure we're okay."

"David, there is a man— I am sure I have seen him before."

"Where?"

"Over there, beyond the ticket counters."

"Which one?"

"Wearing the hat. The one with the tweed hat."

Eva and Bowen sat in the airport's entry lounge. Bowen had allowed more time for them to reach the airport than they'd needed. When they'd arrived at ten-twenty the position at the ticket counter with a big poster-board sign above it, *Samuel's Sunshine Holidays,* was empty.

"Well, they did tell me 'check-in from ten-thirty,'" he'd acknowledged.

After ten minutes a middle-aged couple had come in and gone to that counter, looked at their watches and the lobby clock, and—after some discussion—taken seats in the lounge as close to the counter as possible. Then came a young man wearing a brand-new polyester jacket and trousers; and then a young woman in a tight yellow dress and spike heels. The single man and woman took seats a little distance apart, and alternated appraising glances.

"I don't know," Bowen said, studying the man in the tweed hat carefully. "I don't think . . . Where do you think you saw him?"

"I don't know, but I'm sure . . ."

"The pub! He looks like the guy who was sitting in the corner when we had lunch in that pub, on Tuesday."

"Yes! It is him! What can he be doing here? David . . ."

"I don't know. I don't like it. But I don't know how . . . It'd be a pretty unlikely coincidence; but I don't see how anybody could have known we'd be here. And I can't believe we could have been followed."

"We must have been, somehow."

"I just don't see how— It doesn't matter. If somebody knows we're here . . ."

"What will we do?"

"I don't . . . I'll have to think. We'll have to . . ." Bowen paused, staring at the man who stood looking up at a monitor displaying flight times.

Evidently having acquired the information he wanted, the man dropped his eyes and surveyed the lounge.

"I'm not sure," Bowen said. "It looks like that guy in the pub—a lot like him—but I'm not sure. Are you? Are you positive?"

"I think . . . I saw the man in the pub only when we came in; my back was toward him . . . But I think —But we cannot risk . . ."

"You're right, of course. There's no point to this trip if somebody . . . We'll have to break for it, and try to find another way. But . . . It's going to be hard to get anything this good again. Let's hang in for just a minute and see. Maybe it's not him. I mean, you're not—we're not—positive."

"But, David . . ."

"Just for a couple minutes." Bowen continued to

stare at the man with his measuring-it-down-to-the-eighth-inch look.

The man glanced back and forth over the room again. Then, apparently finding the sign he was looking for, crossed and went into the men's room.

"Okay," Bowen said, rising. "I'm going to find out."

"David, no!"

"Yes. What can he do?" Bowen scanned from side to side. "I don't see anybody else here who looks suspicious. You should be okay for a couple of minutes. I'll be right back." He looked down at Eva with a tight-lipped smile that was not reassuring, squared his shoulders, and strode across the lobby.

A young woman wearing a bright-orange blazer and beret came through a door behind the counter and put a case up on her work shelf there. Even as she was opening it, the middle-aged couple who had arrived next after Bowen and Eva was at the desk. Smiling, the clerk shook her head, and the man looked at his watch. After a moment the clerk glanced up, evidently realizing the couple was still there. She said something. They didn't move. Apparently, they weren't going to give up their places.

The man in the tweed hat came out of the men's room. He went back across the lobby to the newsstand, bought a paper.

Three minutes passed. Then Bowen came out. He caught Eva's eye and smiled.

"It's okay," he said as soon as he reached her. "It wasn't him." He sat. "It did look a little like him —which is to say, he and the guy in the pub both look like one of those English character actors who's in every British film you've ever seen. But close up . . . I could tell it wasn't him at all."

"You're sure?"

"Absolutely."

Other people were arriving for the tour. The persistent presence of the first couple at the ticket counter had drawn a second. By the time the woman there had arranged her papers and was ready to begin giving out tickets and boarding passes, many of the holiday makers were in line. Bowen and Eva remained sitting. He held her hand tightly.

"Lots of people are coming in now," he said. "We'll wait until there are a few more ahead of us, and then get in line, and then by the time we go through passport control there will be as many behind us, too; and we'll be in the middle of the crowd."

"Yes. David . . ."

"What?"

"The gate there, the booths . . . it is a regular passport control station; it is not something temporary, arranged only for this flight."

"No. I'm sure there are regular flights to and from the continent. It's just not normally a transcontinental embarkation point."

"Why would the CIA have only transcontinental points watched? Why would they think we would go only to America? Surely they would alert the passport officials everywhere."

"Sure." Bowen used his "Don't you worry, little lady" voice, his "I've thought of everything" tone. "What I'm gambling on is that they'll expect us either to try to get out of one of the big places to anywhere, or out of a smaller one—even by boat—to the continent. They'll be watching both of those. I'm gambling that they won't figure—won't know about, won't think I'd know about—something like this: a transatlantic flight out of a regional airport. They won't expect it, they won't be watching for us in a group like this, and we'll just go through in the middle of the crowd."

"But, David, precisely because it is so unexpected for us—an American and a German—to be traveling with such a group . . . If the passport officers have been alerted at all, we will stand out."

"It's a gamble. Anything we try would be. It seemed to me to be the best one. I just don't know what else we could do."

Doubtful, Eva stared back at him wide-eyed with tension. Then she gave that quick shrug and smile she always used to show it didn't matter.

"We're together," Bowen said to the woman behind the airline counter as he laid their passports in front of her. "The tickets are in my name—Stuart."

"Thank you very much." The woman flashed a smile without really looking at him, glanced at the passports —checking names, expiration dates—without really looking at them either. It was her job merely to make certain the tourists had passports, not to authenticate them. She checked down her list, put a line through his name. "Have you luggage to check through?"

"No. Just carry-on."

She peered over the counter. "Very well. Please put these tags on them, if you would." She found and handed him two packets. "Here you are, Mr. Stuart: your plane tickets, boarding passes. You are arranging your own accommodation on Antigua, I believe."

"That's correct."

"Please proceed through passport control, over there"—she gestured—"and the security check, to the departure lounge. And"—suddenly, she gave a smile as bright and broad as the tropic sun painted on the poster above her—"we wish you a very pleasant holiday."

Bowen stepped to one side, slipped the tags around the handles of his and Eva's bags, then led her to join the next queue.

"A couple more minutes," he said. "Once we get past the passport control, we're clear."

"Yes."

"How are you doing?"

"Fine." Eva gave him a quick smile. "I am, of course, terrified."

"You surely don't look it. You look great. You look like a woman I'd like to fly away to a tropical paradise and live happily ever after with." Eva's fingers lay on his forearm. He put his hand over hers. They stood close together, smiling, and gazing into one another's eyes like a couple come straight from the church; they might still have had rice on their shoulders.

All along the line travelers were chatting, introducing themselves, telling one another what a jolly holiday they'd be having. The single man in the polyester outfit and the woman in yellow had somehow arrived on line simultaneously. More people came from the ticket counter and took places behind Bowen and Eva, but they—like the ones ahead—seemed to recognize the magic circle around the happy couple, and didn't attempt to break it.

The tourists inched forward—move ahead, pause, move, pause—each traveler coming to the stainless steel railing, waiting there, going on to one of the two passport officers, presenting an identity for inspection. All of their papers, surely, were in order. None of the people ahead of Bowen and Eva was stopped for more than fifteen seconds. Yet all of them—as their moments of truth approached—looked apprehensive. Their holiday grins faded or seemed forced, like the jokes some made to the officers, who smiled politely although they must have heard them all before.

Each officer sat in a booth solidly walled up to the height of the chests of those presenting themselves, glass walled above. But, clearly, it wasn't the officers who were confined. They sat on high chairs, looking down on those who came before them to have themselves approved. The line moved along, each person approaching, waiting, being nodded on, disappearing around the booth. The line moved steadily, regularly, yet each person's release seemed a special event that set no precedent.

Eva spoke softly, "What should I say if he asks why I am traveling with this tour?"

"That you want to take a holiday in the Caribbean."

"But why would I be with *this* tour, not one from London?"

"The truth, Eva: You were traveling up here in the north with a friend when we got the idea of going to the Caribbean. I inquired and found out about this flight. It's convenient and inexpensive. That's all there is to it. It's the truth. If you don't act like you think something's wrong with it, he won't think so either."

"Yes. I'm sure . . . but . . ."

"Be sure. If they've been alerted to watch for us, then we're done for. They'll recognize us at once. If they haven't, then there's no reason for them to be suspicious."

They moved another two steps closer to the railing. Eva looked slowly, casually around the entire lobby.

Gleaming ground stone and concrete floor. High-impact plastic. Steel—brushed, plated, anodized. No lint-attracting textures. Every surface was slick and smooth. Durable. Hard. There were no niches, alcoves, hide-behinds of any kind; no cracks or crevices or crannies where even dust might lodge and escape the mop or cloth. Clean and simple lines—mostly straight, the few curves flowing to carry the eye on, none curling back upon itself or spiraling inward to rest. People might rest in the seating area, briefly; but the machine-molded chairs weren't meant for settling-in. *To the Gates, To Ground Transport.* To and from; everyone was on the way to or from somewhere.

Bowen and Eva reached the railing. He put her ahead. "There isn't going to be any problem," he assured her, quietly, speaking into her ear. "I'll meet you on the other side of the booths."

The people who had been just ahead of them presented their passports through the openings in the glass walls. Bowen squeezed Eva's shoulder. "You okay?"

"Yes, David. I am fine."

One of the officers wore a beard, neatly trimmed. Both looked like good-natured chaps, of happy disposition. They smiled their polite smiles and wished every traveler a pleasant holiday. They also looked as though they had seen every face before and heard every story that might be told to them; as though however many people they let pass, none slipped by them.

One of the booths cleared. Eva went to the window and presented her passport. Bowen watched the officer stare at her for a moment with a look of special interest. Perhaps the interest was more personal than professional. Eva seemed to know how to handle it. She looked back steadily, pleasantly. The man looked down at her passport. He asked a question.

The other booth cleared. Bowen had to go to it.

Eva said, yes she was a resident of Britain; yes she would be returning. The officer stamped her passport.

He slid it to her. "Have a pleasant holiday," he said. She stepped away from the booth, turning to wait for Bowen.

At the other booth, the officer put Bowen's open passport down on the counter. He stared at it, then sharply up at Bowen. Then he stamped the passport and pushed it through the window.

"You see?" Bowen said as he took Eva's arm. "Nothing to it."

CHAPTER

11

They were rocked gently, and if they went outside the powerboat's cockpit and looked over the railings they could see the prow parting its white furrow, the foam streaming alongside. Only that gave them the sensation of moving. The cobalt sea seemed sculpted and set into little ridges and shallow gouges; blue, blue with only now and again—and gone—the crest of a whitecap. The mountains of Montserrat, a faint but clear silhouette blue-gray in haze, had been in view ahead of them all the way from Antigua: the shape higher, broader, the color darker, greener each time they looked; changed, but never seen changing.

"It is like a dream!" Eva exclaimed, gazing through the window in the front of the cockpit.

"Yes," Bowen said. "It is. It will be. It'll be wonderful."

Then the island had contours, and then textures —the thick, jungle forests on the steep cones of the hills, the smooth yellow-green of cleared fields, the ragged palm trees. They could see the cut of a road, houses, individual trees. Finally, rounding the southern tip, they came to the jetty at Plymouth town.

The immigration and customs official there might have been the one from Leeds—the bearded one —flown over ahead of them, his skin stained walnut as a disguise. He wore a neat, white tropical shirt-jacket, open-collared, and his nose was different, but the look he gave Bowen was the same: cordial but suspicious. He seemed, finally, to accept Bowen's story about coming to the island on impulse, purely on holiday, having been there before and loving it, for a visit of only perhaps a month, coming by boat (instead of flying) for the pleasure of it— He seemed to accept the story, and gave Bowen and Eva entry permits, without necessarily believing a single word.

Bowen hired a cab at the stand by the dock, told the driver he'd pay him just to wait and keep their bags in his car. Then—as he'd told Eva he'd do—he set off for a real-estate office to see about a cottage. "I know there won't be any problem; there are vacancies even in midwinter." She would wait there, sitting on a bench under a palm tree. "When I get back," he said, "we can walk up to the main street and buy some clothes and some groceries."

"Oh, David! It is paradise!" Eva stood on the terrace that opened directly from the living room. As soon as they had entered the house and seen the view through the window wall opposite the front door, she had rushed across the room to open the sliding glass panels. For a moment—hands clasped before her, shoulders raised in rapture—she gazed over the flowering shrubs along the wall at the edge of the lawn below the house, out at the shining, peacock sea.

The house had been built into a hillside that sloped steeply down for half a mile farther toward the sea and then fell in a cliff to the water. Two other houses neighbored it, but they were set higher—one to the right, one to the left—so nothing blocked the view. All around and above the houses the hillside was thickly forested. The road from Plymouth ran along near the cliff; the track from it that passed the three houses, going between theirs and the other two, wound upward at the right. Eva and Bowen could see the road and track when standing on the terrace or at the living-room window, but when they sat the bushes bordering the lawn were high enough to screen them, and they could feel themselves totally alone.

Eva spun to face Bowen, her head back, radiant. "Paradise! Oh, David, David!" She flung her arms wide, and threw herself into his embrace.

They had left England in the morning, flown all day, cruised in the powerboat for an hour and a half, and it was still only late afternoon when they were settled in Montserrat. Not caring about the island's time of day, they adjusted the louvered shutters to make the bedroom as dark as possible, and slept.

They ate their supper at midnight, at the glass-topped table on the terrace, by the light of two oil lamps.

Bowen, of course, set out a plan. "Tomorrow, we'll go back into Plymouth and stock up on groceries. And there's a newsstand where we can get paperbacks.

We'll call a cab—I don't think we need to rent a car, not right away. I thought we might just like to stay around here, by ourselves, for a while. It's only about a ten-minute walk down to a beach."

"Yes. Whatever you think is best."

"I don't mean I think we have to hide out, Eva. I think we're safe right now, and will be for a while." Bowen took Eva's hand. "We'll just have to live in the moment, and worry about the future when it comes."

She squeezed and smiled. "Yes."

The next morning they let the brightening sky bring them awake, then dozed in one another's arms for another hour.

Then Bowen made breakfast while Eva was showering.

When she saw what he'd done, she protested. "I will cook."

"I think we should do it together, or take turns."

"No. I will cook, and take care of the house. You will sit in the sun and turn brown so you can disguise yourself as a native of the island."

"Eva, you don't have to—"

"Yes, David, I do. You are paying for everything. I cannot imagine how much . . . I must do something. Perhaps someday we will have a modern marriage and both have to work outside and inside the house as well. For now, I will cook. I am a good cook. You will be pleased."

"I'm sure I will, but I *like* to cook."

Finally, Eva had been persuaded to let Bowen set out breakfast and—occasionally—help with supper. But she would not tolerate his doing any other housework.

After breakfast, Bowen called his broker in New

York—he could dial directly from the cottage—and talked for nearly half an hour.

"Everything's okay for now," he told Eva afterward. "One of my longshots has paid off well enough to offset the expense of coming here; so I'm about where I expected to be at this time. He's going to send me some stuff to look over, but—the way I set up my accounts —there isn't anything I have to watch closely."

They walked, delighting in each new prospect of mountain and sea as it unwound before them. Every person they passed on the back roads or the tracks leading through fields, no matter how grave-faced, dignified, reserved, wished them a cordial "Good morning."

By mid morning the heat of the sun was too great, and they returned to their cottage to read. They lunched on their terrace, napped, and then walked down to the beach.

"You are a terrific swimmer!" Bowen exclaimed when they came out of the water.

"When one learns to swim in the Baltic, one develops the habit of swimming vigorously. You are a very strong swimmer, yourself, David."

"Well, I told you: Ellen and I used to come down here—somewhere in the Caribbean—nearly every year. I like to swim."

Then they lay for an hour or more sunning, and enjoying the breeze in the shade of the palms.

That day set a pattern. Bowen bought them masks and snorkels, and each afternoon they would go out beyond the gentle surf and swim slowly back and forth for hundreds of yards through a sea so clear and glowing it seemed to be liquid sunlight.

Sometimes they called a taxi and went to one of the

restaurants in Plymouth for dinner. They liked best the Oasis, where the proprietor came out on the veranda during the evening and entertained his guests by tying knots in a rope, cutting them off, and then pulling the rope out whole again.

They would go back to the cottage and sit on the terrace looking at the stars, the waves' phosphorescence; holding hands, talking. They would go to bed, sometimes to make love, sometimes merely to lie close together until they drifted into sleep.

They met their neighbors. A young married couple without children were in the house above and to their left. Two athletic-looking young men were in the other house. Like Bowen and Eva, they seemed to be enjoying quiet holidays, staying close to their cottages rather than traveling about the island. Regularly one pair or the other would use the beach when Bowen and Eva were there. They all chatted pleasantly whenever they saw one another, but none seemed interested in socializing.

"Ahhh!" A gasp of horror from Eva, in the bathroom, one morning.

"What's wrong!" Bowen dashed to see.

"My nose! My face!" Eva stood goggling into the mirror. Seeing him appear behind her, she threw a hand over her face.

"What's wrong?"

"I am peeling. My skin is peeling. I have tried so hard not to take too much sun . . . I always burn . . . Oh. Oh. Go away."

"Why? What's the matter?"

The other hand over her face, too. "I look horrible. I am ugly."

"Eva . . ." He came to her, hands on her shoulders,

turning her around, pulling her hands down. "You are silly, that's what you are. It's only a little peeling, not much at . . . You are not ugly. You are just rosy. You look full of life. You look . . ." He put his arms around her and held her very tightly.

"What are you looking at?" he asked, suddenly aware of her gaze on him.

"You."

They were lying on the two chaises, set foot to foot on the terrace.

"Well. Any particular reason?"

"No. I was only looking at you reading. I like the way you read."

"You like the way I *read?*"

"Yes. You read a book the way you listen to music. So much intensity."

Eva put the casserole into the oven and came out to join Bowen on the terrace. He was sitting in one of the oversize wicker armchairs staring at a sunset sky turning yellow-green, a sea changing to violet.

"May I sit with you?"

"Of course." Bowen moved a little to one side.

Eva curled into the chair beside him, tucking her shoulder under his arm, drawing her knees up tight across his lap, laying her head on his shoulder, twisting her hands one around the other under her chin and against his chest. "Is this all right?"

"Yes. Very cozy."

"Yes." She snuggled closer.

Silhouetted clouds hid the sun, but cadmium-colored rays shot up in streaks.

Bowen turned his head and touched his lips to Eva's forehead. She sighed and wriggled slightly, snuggling again. But, after a moment, Bowen shifted in the seat, pulling away enough to look at her, at the way she was cuddled to him. "Eva, tell me . . ." he said softly. "What was your father like?"

"My father?"

"Yes. Tell me about him."

"What?"

"Anything. What did he look like?"

"Why?"

"I just want to know about him. I know he was important to you. I want to know more about him."

"He was tall, and very thin. His hair was completely white. He was . . . We went often to the sea. There were stones there. Put there, out into the water, for protecting the beach. Very big, sharp stones—rocks. Angular, but—from the sea—also softened. That was my father.

"He was fifty-six years old when I was born. Seventy-nine when he died. I know him only as an old man. He did not meet my mother until after the Second World War. She was much younger than he. When Hitler came to power my father was only eighteen; but already he was a member of the Party—the Communist Party. So he escaped east and worked with the Russians during the war."

"What was he like?" Bowen prompted. "You say he was like a rock. I think, before, too, you said he was stern."

"Yes. But not harsh. I do not mean he was unkind to us. I think . . . Of course, German men are trained from when they are little children not to show emotion —not to feel very much. And I think . . . during the war . . . the work he was in, the things he saw and had to do . . .

"I think he loved us; I believe he did. I would see

him looking at my mother sometimes, when she was busy, when she did not see him looking. And he was proud of us, my sisters and me. I know he was disappointed not to have a son. And so he expected us to do well in school, and to have careers, as I have told you. And we did do well, and he showed us he was proud of us."

"How?"

"He would say, when we had perfect marks on our examinations, he would say, 'Eva, Lotte, Anna, you have done well. I am proud of you.' When we were small, he would give us a candy. When we were older, there would be some present. A little book of poems for me, once."

"What if your marks weren't perfect?"

"Then he would say we had done well, but we must do better. Always he expected us to do our best, of course; but he did praise us for whatever we did."

"Yes. But it doesn't sound as though he was exactly . . . demonstrative."

"No. No, that was not in his nature."

"He probably didn't hug you or kiss you."

"Oh, yes. Each evening, before we went to bed, we would go to him and he would kiss each of us."

"On the mouth?"

"No, David! He was our father. He kissed us on the forehead, of course."

"Well, I wasn't meaning to suggest anything . . . sexy. But what I mean . . . Did he hug you? Did he ever pick you up and swing you around?"

"No. That was not his nature."

"Did you ever sit in his lap? Like this?"

"I don't . . . Perhaps, when I was quite small . . . I don't remember."

"Yes."

Eva pulled upright on the edge of the chair, staring at him. "What do you mean? What is the point of this, David?"

"The point is . . . Eva, I like it that you're so affectionate, physical. That we touch each other so often —aside from sex—just to show affection. I like it that you wanted to squeeze in here and sit with me in this chair. But when I looked at you—the way you were sitting—you were like a little girl curled up in her daddy's lap.

"I'm not your daddy, Eva. I don't want to be, I'm not going to be. And that's what's worrying me. What happens when— I mean, are you really through with Heinz? After what he did to you—sure, you say you hate him. I'm sure you do. But even after he started treating you badly—back in Berlin—you stayed with him. Okay, maybe you couldn't get away. Maybe you really couldn't. But—until the very end, you didn't break with him completely. You didn't fight, scream —throw things, break dishes over his head: If you couldn't get away from him, then you could have been so bitchy you'd make *him* want to leave *you.* And then once you were in London—for two years . . . You couldn't slip out of the country? You couldn't go to British intelligence, or the CIA, offer to defect—give them information, work for them—in exchange for protection? Did you *try*? Did you?"

"No, David, I didn't think—"

"You didn't think you could do it, that it would work. Maybe it wouldn't have. But you didn't *try.* And I can't help but wonder, Eva, if you didn't try because —somewhere, down inside you—you didn't want to; you couldn't."

"I have broken! How can you say that, David? I am here. With you. The tape . . ."

"Yes. But what happens when you— If you ever hear from Heinz, if you ever meet him again?"

"That can't happen."

"No. Of course not. I just mean . . ."

"I don't know, David. I did not think I was being a little girl sitting on her father's lap just now. But perhaps you are right, that I was. So I suppose, David, that we must wait until the occasion arises. Unless you do not wish to take the risk; unless you wish not to wait."

"I told you, Eva, the first time we met: I told you I like risks."

"Calculated."

"Yes. When there's a good chance of winning. When the prize is worth it."

"You think I am worth some risk. How nice."

"Yes, I do. Quite a lot of risk. And I think the chance of winning is better if I tell you that I think there is a risk."

Enough light came into the bedroom from the sky so that Eva could tell Bowen wasn't asleep. He lay on his back. She raised herself on an elbow to look at him. "Is something wrong, David? You look sad."

"No. Not at all. I was just thinking. Happy thoughts, actually. It's only my face: If you have a face that naturally looks a little sad, then you can think anything you want—check over your grocery list, tell yourself jokes—and people think you're pondering the destiny of the universe."

"I do not think you were telling yourself jokes."

"Well, no. You're getting to know me too well. But I wasn't sad. I was thinking of a lot of things. Memories. That concert—the Schubert quartet. Dinner in the

Greek restaurant. The hills in the Lake District that first day, in the sunshine."

"Yes." Eva blessed them with her smile. "Beautiful memories."

Bowen put his hand over hers. "And I was thinking . . . Eva, I want to know . . . About when we met. About before I learned the truth."

From the way she stiffened, he might have stabbed her. Putting his arm around her, drawing her close, Bowen kissed her gently, then again, and once again.

"I want to know what you were feeling then. It's important for me to know. We're close together, so you know it's all right. But tell me."

Returning the pressure of his fingers, but looking away, shaking her head, Eva said, "I have told you, David, I don't know."

"You said you didn't know what you were *thinking*, that you weren't thinking. But I know you were feeling things. When we first met— You had to start something with me. Those were your orders. You must have been apprehensive. What would I be like? Would I be interested in you? Right?"

"Yes. Of course. And I felt sick. Angry that I was being made to do this thing. Angry and ashamed that I was being used. Ordered by people I despise to meet you, entice you, go to bed with you if that should be necessary—and they and I assumed it would be. To be a whore for them. With a man who would disgust me—I was disgusted with myself, so I expected you would disgust me. And then to betray you.

"And then I saw you, and we talked, and you did not disgust me. I liked you very much. If I had not been sent to meet you . . . I would have *wanted* to meet you."

Bowen kissed her again. "And then?" he prompted.

"And then . . . I don't know, David! I became so confused."

"Yes. I know. I mean, I understand. You had conflicting feelings. After we made love, were you . . . disgusted?"

"No. David, I truly wanted to make love with you. I was still disgusted, ashamed, with myself because I was deceiving you; but I was *not* deceiving you. I was not like a whore, with no love for you. So . . . I was, already, thinking—not thinking—that there would be a way."

"Yes. I understand. And then, the second morning, when you invited me to move in with you: more than one thing then, too, right?"

"Yes. Of course, it was part of the plan. Not that it would happen that way—not necessarily that you would move in with me. The plan required only that you would want to be with me. But when I came into the kitchen and saw what you had done . . . You had given me the bright, warm, yellow springtime sunlight after a dark winter night—all my life a winter night. You nourished me—oh, yes—perhaps only a slice of whole wheat toast and a coffee; but nourishment, from your hands.

"Yes, I felt more than one thing. Pleased, I suppose, that the plan was working, that what I had been ordered to do I could do. But . . . oh, David . . . such joy!"

"So, Eva, what it amounts to—our story—is that you were an agent sent to seduce and entrap a man, but you fell in love with him."

"Yes."

"Well, he fell in love with you."

CHAPTER

12

Bowen's and Eva's life in paradise ended after exactly three weeks.

Ten days after they came to the island, a large parcel covered with U.S. Postal Service stamps had arrived for Bowen. He set brochures and other papers from it in piles on the dining table that stood at one end of the living room.

"Ah," she said, "bringing home bacon."

"Yeah. I thought I'd take a chance they wouldn't see me and deport me if I drudged a little. Since we never eat in here, I thought I'd use this table and"—he gestured toward the credenza set against the wall behind him—"this top drawer. Okay?"

"Of course."

"I like to keep my things all in my own order, so don't move anything. And don't go into the drawer, okay?"

"Certainly, David."

On the twenty-first morning, Eva confronted Bowen after breakfast. "David, you must this morning walk by yourself. It is now three weeks that we have been here, and I must thoroughly clean the house."

"You've been dusting and sweeping every other day. It's not dirty."

"It is three weeks. It is time to clean thoroughly."

"Eva . . ."

"David. About this, I am the boss."

"Why today? Why not tomorrow?"

"Why not today?"

Bowen couldn't seem to think of a good reason.

"Out!" Eva ordered.

"Okay. But don't disturb any of my things, okay?"

"I will keep all in perfect order."

So Bowen put on his hiking boots and went out—he said—to explore a footpath that his map showed winding around the side of the hill above the cottage.

Eva began scrubbing, scouring, and polishing. She started in the kitchen, then tackled the bath and the bedroom that they were using. After an hour she returned to the main room. When she reached Bowen's table she lifted each small stack of papers with care while she dusted, returning each to exactly the same location. Then she paused for a moment, looking down at the papers. Then she turned to the credenza and pulled open and looked into the top drawer. With one finger she pushed at the corner of the irregular sheaf of sheets and booklets there, moving it slightly to one side. She froze. Then she lifted out the papers and stood for a long time staring down into the drawer.

"Hi," Bowen called across the living room from the entry. Eva was sitting on the terrace, her back to him, looking out at the sea. "All finished? Can I come in now—I promise not to track in a single grain."

Evidently not considering her failure to reply significant, he sat on the little wrought-iron bench and began removing his shoes. "That was an interesting walk. There's a side trail—doesn't show on the map—that leads right out to the top of the cliff." Still reporting on his excursion, he finished with his shoes and padded across to the terrace in his socks.

"Hi," he said again, brushing the top of her head with his hand, leaning to kiss her forehead. Then he straightened. "What's the matter?"

Eva turned her head to look up at him—only that, no other movement. She looked at him steadily for a long, long moment, from somewhere very far back. "I found the pistol in the drawer," she said.

"What? What were you doing, looking in that drawer?"

"Why is there a pistol?"

"What were you doing, looking in that drawer!"

"I knew you had bought rubber bands. I took one from that drawer three days ago. I thought today to put them around your papers on the table, to keep them as you had arranged— It does not matter why I looked in the drawer!"

"It sure as hell does matter! I told you not to go into—"

"You told me not to disturb anything! You did not say it was forbidden; that you had a secret, that you are—what? Bluebeard with your secret, forbidden room! But this is not the point! It is not the point, why did I look into that drawer. The point is, why is there a pistol there today? Why is there ever a pistol?"

"There's a pistol there because we are escaping from people who tried to kidnap me, remember?"

"You said we were safe. You said there was no longer danger. How could there be danger from them, David? How could there be danger from Heinz or Gert—any of those people—Unless . . . unless you believe that I . . ."

"I don't. I don't believe that, Eva. But with people like that—spies, the East German intelligence service —how do I know what they can do? Where they might have agents, be able to trace us? I mean, I don't see how, but still . . . I just wanted to have some insurance."

"Where did you find a pistol? How could you buy one, here?"

"You can get anything, anywhere, if you've got the money."

"Here? On this island? Even the police do not carry guns. Who would sell you a pistol? And if there was such a person, how would you know him?"

"There are ways. There always are people. You can find out—"

"How did *you* find such a person? And how did you find a man who would take us away from Antigua illegally? We did not give up the entry permits that we had filled out on the airplane when we came there. I did not think about it then; I was thinking only how clever you were to find a way that we could not be traced. Now I think, I wonder, how did you know a man who would do such a thing?"

Bowen was standing erect, in his customary posture; yet for once he seemed unrooted. "I do that, Eva," he said after a moment. "I plan escapes. When I travel, wherever I am—some people, when they travel, they always figure how they'd get out in case of fire. I always figure how I'd get out if someone were after me."

Eva stared up at him. "Why?"

"It's a game for me, a hobby—I don't know, maybe it's a compulsion. Like back in London—that alley at the end of the dead-end street—the first time I saw it, I thought, 'What a place for an escape.'"

"And do you always buy a pistol?"

"No. But this time the escape, the danger, is real. I mean, it has been. I'm sure we're safe now. I'm sure, but I guess I also wanted that insurance."

Eva continued to stare at Bowen in silence. Then she turned to look out at the sea again.

"You don't believe me," he said.

"No. I know you are very skillful in making escapes. But now I do not believe this is from your cleverness at the spur of the moment, only, or that it is a 'compulsion,' or a game."

"What do you believe?"

"I believe . . . I have been sitting here thinking, trying to understand . . . When I think about this pistol, about many things about you . . . David, you are not who—what—you have told me you are. I believe something goes on here that I do not understand."

"What?"

"I do not know. I cannot imagine. But something."

He stood looking down at her, and then, finally, off to where the sky and water met in a barely discernible line. "Do you still believe I love you?"

A moment passed before she gave the slightest of shrugs. After another, she looked at him. "I believe; I do not believe. I don't know."

Bowen squatted beside her. With one hand he pried open one of her fists. "I told you I was working on a plan, Eva, for us. I told you I wouldn't tell you all about it. Pretty soon, I think, all this will be over. Until then you'll just have to trust me."

"Trust you?" She worked her fingers free again. "Who are you?"

Eva looked across the table at Bowen; looked truly at him for the first time in nearly an hour.

"Have some lunch," he'd said when he'd finished putting bread and cheese, sliced tomato, on the table. That was the first thing he'd said—the first words between them—since she'd pulled her fingers free of his grip, and he'd risen and gone back into the house. He'd gone to the credenza, pulled out the drawer, and looked at the pistol. Then he'd walked into the bedroom and made a telephone call. Then he'd come back into the living room and sat on the couch there, staring at the back of Eva's head. Finally, he'd gotten up and prepared lunch.

"I am not hungry."

"You should eat something."

She'd taken her place without further argument, as though merely dully obedient. She'd eaten a little, slowly and mechanically. Then, suddenly, she looked at Bowen.

"You did not erase the tape!" she said. "The lovemaking—you did not erase that!"

Bowen didn't look away. After a moment he went on chewing, evidently on a piece of clay, and then managed to swallow it.

"It is for Heinz!" she said. "This—coming here, bringing me here—the tape: It is for Heinz. It is to make Heinz jealous; to make him—from his madness about me—to come here, himself, and to trap him!

"Of course! Escaping from England . . . How it was possible, so easily, to 'escape.' The boat from Antigua . . . the pistol . . . At the sheep market—those young men, the police! Oh! Oh, I thought you were clever, so clever. I did not begin to know how clever you are!"

Bowen sat back in his chair, still without looking away from her, still without replying.

"Yes?" she demanded. "Yes?"

"Yes," he said. "That was my plan. I told you I had a plan—*have* a plan. After those Germans tried to take me at Borrowdale . . . I called the CIA: my 'travel agent.' I told them that if they would let us get away—help us to get away—and let us stay together, I thought we might be able, we'd try, to trap Heinz. That would be the price, and it would prove you were okay, so they'd let you into the States with me, afterward."

"I do not believe you."

"Well, it's the truth. That's why I've been trying to tell you, to prepare you, so when you found out you'd believe—"

"Believe? I believe that you have this plan, but not the rest. You are too good at this. You are too clever, too skillful at escaping, at knowing when you are followed, at fighting. These are not the skills of an accountant. You are an agent, aren't you? This has been your plot from the beginning, hasn't it? You arranged to meet me—"

"No—"

"All the time they thought—Heinz, Gert—they thought they were trapping *you,* and all the time, you—"

"No, Eva. How could that be? You—it was arranged for *you* to meet *me*. I was the one who spotted the CIA, who let you know they were following me."

"So that we would have to run away from London. So that we would begin the escape that eventually would bring us here!"

"It was *you* who brought those guys after me in the mountains!"

"Yes; and that played directly into your plan! Better than you could have hoped. I felt such guilt; and such love when you forgave me and accepted me again . . . Oh, that was *so good* of you! So generous! You had to struggle so long about it! I was filled with such gratitude and love, I never questioned . . . I was so eager to help . . ."

"It's not like that!"

"Isn't it, David? David? *Is* that your name? Is there a David Bowen?"

"Yes there is, goddamm it! I am. Everything I've told you is true!"

"True! The Mafia? Escaping? Finding someone to sell you a pistol because it is your *hobby?*"

"I'm sorry, but I had to . . . But everything about who I am—"

"Lies!" Suddenly seizing the edge of her plate, Eva swept it up, flinging bread and cheese back over her head, then smashing the plate down on the edge of the table, shooting shards in all directions. "Lies!" Screaming again, "Lies!" and "You bastard, lying bastard!" she lunged, grabbing for the platter at the center of the table between them.

Bowen dashed his glassful of wine into her face. "Stop it," he said as firmly as a bank vault closing. Either the shock of the wine, or that calmness in his voice, broke the rush of her anger, if not its intensity.

For a moment she glared at him before wiping her face with her napkin; and even then she never looked away from his eyes.

Bowen stared back just as hard. "What is it, Eva? What is it—really? I've told you all along there was a plan—a plot, if you want to call it that. What's new, now? Only that you know what it is: that the plot is to capture Heinz. But that's what's hitting you, isn't it? That we're going to get Heinz."

"No! It is *not*— It is that you have lied to me. Lied to me, and used me. Lied to me, pretending that you love—"

"I do love you."

Crossing her arms tightly to herself, Eva twisted to face the sea.

"Okay, Eva: I told you some lies, and I have used you. I didn't see any other—"

Eva sprang from the chair, stalked away to the terrace balustrade.

Bowen rose, came partway toward her, then halted. "You'll see. I guess there's no point in trying to convince you now. After we take Heinz, then either I'll ask you to go back to the States with me, or I won't. Then you'll know."

"You will not take Heinz," she retorted without turning. "He will never come here."

"That's the gamble. We're gambling that what you told me is true: That he is crazy—out of his mind, doing crazy things—because of you. Maybe he *isn't* that far gone, but what did we have to lose by trying?"

"He will not come."

"Maybe not. But two of his men arrived here yesterday on the afternoon plane. Two guys, West German passports, of course; but there's no doubt."

Eva had turned, at last, to face Bowen with a look of incredulity.

"That's why I didn't want to go out this morning. I didn't go for a walk, I just went . . . someplace out of sight, and waited.

"Steve McCluskey, the guy who's running this, told me—when I called him before lunch to say you'd found the gun and were on to me—that they've just rented a car. They'll probably get to us—drive by to check us out—sometime this afternoon."

"Heinz will not come."

"You may be right. But a group of three 'Austrians' already have reservations on the four P.M. plane the day after tomorrow."

For nearly two hours Bowen and Eva sat on the terrace, on chaises set on diverging angles. Each held a book, neither read. Bowen looked at Eva often, sometimes for minutes at a time. She never turned to him.

At about two-thirty, the phone rang. Bowen took the call in the living room, watching her as he did. Without turning, she lifted her head, listening.

"Right," Bowen said.

"About ten minutes?

"Right. Okay."

He put down the telephone and crossed to the doorway. "They're on their way," he said. "Should be here in about ten minutes."

"How did they find us, David?"

"You sent them a card. There's one they sell at the Vue Point hotel showing the view from there across the cove, looking toward us. It actually shows this house, on the hill here. You circled the house."

"I see."

"You must have done it sometime when we were in

Plymouth, and you were by yourself for a few minutes. Just a 'wish you were here' card. To someone in London who got it to Nagler. Not signed with your real name, of course."

"But in my handwriting."

"Of course. No problem—all the samples you left in your flat."

"Why did I send it? I have broken with them; come here with you; made that tape. Why did I let them know where we are?"

"Maybe you're still working for them—you didn't break: Pretending you did was the only way you could continue working on me. Or maybe you did, and this is a trick. But even so, the card says you're here. Heinz is checking that out."

"He will discover the trick."

"I don't think so. That is, McCluskey doesn't think so. These guys, Heinz's men, they're being watched from very far back. Local people, mostly. We're out here by ourselves—just two other houses, ordinary-looking tourists, around us."

Without breaking her steady stare at Bowen, Eva shook her head slightly. "You underestimate Heinz," she said.

"Well, we're trying not to do that. I'm going to have to ask you to do something, now. I want you to sit on the balustrade—over there. You can sit on it with your back against the wall of the house. Take a cushion from one of the chairs, if you want. Take a book."

After a moment of looking at him levelly, Eva asked, "Why would I sit on that railing when there are comfortable chairs on the terrace?"

"You can get the breeze better that way. You can see the view better. Nobody's going to ask. Just do it, Eva, please."

"And when they arrive, am I to wave at them?"

"Just keep reading."

Walking with the dignity of a captive empress, Eva took up her book, went to the balustrade where Bowen had indicated, and sat as he'd directed.

Bowen looked at her for a moment, then moving brusquely, went to the credenza. He opened the drawer, took the pistol from under the papers, returned to the terrace door.

Eva regarded him. "I thought you believed there would be no trouble," she said.

"We do. These guys aren't being subtle at all about asking about you, looking for us. They have to be just scouts—check out the situation, bird-dog us, then pull out before Heinz goes into action. But in case we're wrong . . ." He pumped a bullet into the chamber, checked the safety.

"Accountant," Eva said, and opened her book.

At the expected time, the car with the two Germans turned from the main road onto the track. It climbed around slowly up to the houses, the men inside staring out like any sightseeing visitors. Bowen stood back in the living room, where he could watch them—and Eva—without being seen through the glare on the glass wall. As they passed the house, he crossed to look through the louver-covered window on the road side.

When the men reached the end of the road they paused for several minutes, as though simply enjoying the view. Then the driver backed and turned and headed the car downhill again, and the men drove slowly down to the main road and away, evidently to continue exploring the island.

Bowen put the pistol into the drawer. He called, "Okay, Eva. You can get down from there now."

She did get down, after a moment—as though she'd chosen to, not because he'd released her.

For the next three hours, Bowen and Eva again held their books without looking at them, or (occasionally) did read a little—the same page several times. At a little before six, Bowen got up and said, "Well, I think I'll take a shower and change clothes." Eva took no more notice of the announcement than did the palm trees at the edge of the lawn. When he returned to the terrace, she rose and passed him and went into the bathroom herself.

After they'd sat at the table in silence for ten minutes, Bowen dutifully eating and Eva picking at the supper he'd made, he slapped down his fork and said, "Goddammit, Eva: I don't think *you* have got any right to act this way toward *me* because I didn't tell you the complete truth. Or even because I've used you. After what you did to me; after I accepted it and forgave you."

"Accepted? Forgave? Or *made use* of what I did?"

"I've told you—"

"You have told me many things that are not true."

"That doesn't mean that none of it—the most important things— The day after tomorrow you'll know the whole truth. You might at least give me the benefit of the doubt until then instead of jumping to the worst conclusion you can imagine."

She looked directly at him then and said, finally, "Very well. I shall try to suspend my judgment. But you may, perhaps, understand that I am angry and afraid; and you may give me the right to be mistrustful."

Bowen nodded, and Eva nodded back to him, and

after a moment she said—with an almost disembodied politeness—"This chicken is very good, David. Thank you for preparing it."

Throughout the remainder of the evening they sat at a distance from one another, silent for the most part, now and then speaking a sentence or two in the tone with which civilized divorces are concluded. At ten-thirty the phone rang. Bowen answered.

"Heinz's men seem to have bedded down for the night," he reported on returning to the terrace. "They sent a long telex to Frankfurt this afternoon. In code —they've told people they're businessmen looking over possibilities for resort development. Undoubtedly it confirmed that we're here, gave our location."

Eva accepted the news without comment.

"I think we can go to bed too, if you're ready," Bowen suggested. Then in response to the look she gave him over her shoulder he said, "I'm tired, and I imagine you are too. Despite that, we probably won't really sleep much. And tomorrow's going to be tense. So I think we'd better try to rest a little."

She rose. "Yes. If you don't mind, I think I shall use the other bedroom."

Bowen stared at her levelly for a moment, then looked away. "I'd rather you didn't. I'd rather we were together."

"Why? Do you think I am going to run away? Where could I go?"

He didn't look up, and then she went on. "Do you believe I will try to call those men? To warn them? Why would I do that?"

He shook his head, but still wouldn't meet her eyes. "I don't believe anything like that, Eva. But . . ." with his head tipped to the side he did look up at her,

". . . you're not sure about me; well, I guess I'm not really sure about how you feel about our trapping Heinz. And no matter what *I* feel, I think it's important that—in the unlikely event that anything does go wrong—I want to be able to say we were together all the time."

For an instant Eva swelled, as though about to explode again. Then she sighed.

"So," Bowen said quietly, "I'd like us to use the same bed. I'm not going to 'force myself upon you,' Eva! For God's sake. I think we should sleep in our clothes, anyway."

"Why?"

"Those guys may have gone to bed now, but they might wake up later. They'd never get near us; they couldn't move from that hotel without being seen. But if they tried, we'd be called and taken away from here."

"How do you know they are the only danger?"

"Because McCluskey—the CIA—knows the identity of every person who's come to this island since we arrived."

So Bowen and Eva lay on the one bed, side by side, not touching. "Good night, Eva," Bowen said after a while, and turned toward his edge. "Good night," she replied, turning to hers.

In the neighboring houses, the young couple and the athletic young men also napped in their clothes, lying on top of the bedcovers. One member of each team slept while the other sat back from a window, scanning from time to time with the night-vision equipment. On all the previous nights, since the watch began—as soon as "Eva's" card had reached London—the partner off duty had actually gone to bed. This night, however, they, and the CIA people back in Plymouth, and their hosts from British intelligence and the local police, all kept themselves ready to move quickly. Of all the people on the island involved in the operation, only the two Germans put on pajamas and crawled into their beds and slept the night through.

At a little before three A.M. Heinz's attack team came out of the water at Isles Bay.

CHAPTER

13

Within minutes the four men had opened the waterproof bags they'd floated-in with them, stripped off their swimming gear, and dressed in the commando's uniform of black trousers and high-necked pullovers, soft-soled shoes. They didn't pull on their hoods just then. They checked their weapons, put the things they were abandoning out of sight behind the trees at the edge of the beach, and started up to the hotel.

The people of Montserrat say they have no crime because the island is so small: No one steals, since all the thief's neighbors would know if he had something new. So the parking lot outside the hotel was only dimly lighted. The young man at the desk in the lobby wasn't in any sense a guard. No one ever arrived at the hotel in the early morning hours; all the guests were asleep by then. Other than a little record keeping, he seldom had anything to do but to stay awake for the unlikely possibility that some emergency might occur.

While two of the Germans broke into cars, the other pair walked directly through the wide-open glass doors into the lobby. They strode in briskly, the first focusing on the night clerk behind the desk, the other scanning everywhere else. In step, quick-step, they crossed the lobby. The young man saw them, was starting to rise, his face still modulating between surprise and greeting, when the nearer German, swiftly extending the natural swing of his arm, brought the silenced pistol level and fired three fast shots as he continued walking. He went on, right up to the desk, looked over to assure that the clerk was dead and had fallen out of sight, then turned on his heel and started out again. The other man had halted, but spun to fall in beside his partner and exit with him.

The Germans could have knocked out the young clerk. That would have been sufficient to keep him from reporting the theft of the cars—if he'd even heard it. But Heinz wanted to make a point to the CIA about trying to trap him.

Bowen came awake. He looked at the illuminated clock on the dresser. Three-forty-seven. Eva seemed to be sleeping; but then carefully, as though not to disturb him, she scratched her cheek. Bowen got up.

"Where are you going?"

"Just to get a drink of water. Do you want one?"

"Yes, please. Thank you," she replied, polite as a telephone operator.

In the kitchen, Bowen poured water from the refrigerator jug. Drinking down his own glassful, he poured another for Eva. As he returned across the living room, he paused. He had closed and locked the front door on the uphill side where the track passed, but had left the sliding glass doors in the terrace window wall open. For a moment he stared at them. Going to the doorway, he checked that the screened panels were latched, then went back to the bedroom.

By four-thirty, the four men were in the edge of the forest behind the houses uphill of Bowen's and Eva's cottage. They had come through the trees from the valley road around the hill, out of sight of the houses. Before driving there, they had gone north to isolated Little Bay, and left one of the cars. The small power yacht from which the men had swum to the island was already approaching Little Bay, keeping well offshore, cruising throttle-down for silence, showing no lights.

The men now wore their hoods and black gloves. As they crept down from the forest they were virtually invisible. One pair headed toward each of the houses. Elsewhere in the night other creatures moved too. On the black sand beaches, little land crabs peered from their holes and then scuttled swiftly sideways and pounced. In the jungle, snakes that tourists never see glided silently beneath fallen, rotting palm fronds. Lizards among dark rocks scurried and snapped up insects and crouched still as the stones again. The four men moved like fleeting shadows, over the low fences and across the lawns.

Each house had its balcony-terrace on the downhill, sea-facing, road-facing side. Each had a ground-level entrance on the uphill side with both wood-paneled and screen doors. The night was balmy; by opening the glass panels to the terraces and the solid rear doors a gentle breeze from the sea could be allowed to waft through, cooling the houses from the heat of one day and against that of the next.

The four Germans were quieter than the night itself. That breeze from the sea rustled the palms. Frogs and toads peeped and trilled in damp ditches. Somewhere, far back around the hill from where the houses stood, a dog barked, another replied, a donkey brayed, sheep bleated. The four Germans set their soft-soled shoes soundlessly on the deep grass.

Keeping very low, showing no silhouettes against the deep black of the forest behind them, they peered in through the ground-level doorways, and then at the corners of the windows of each hill-facing room. Then they took positions hunkered down to the sides of the doors, checking their watches.

Four-forty-five: the shadows sprang. In one living room the watcher fell forward, head smacking the table in front of him. In the other, hit first in the shoulder, the watcher started rising, spinning, then crashed backward as four more shots struck him square in the chest. His partner, shot from the bedroom window, died without ever waking. In the other house the sleeper—in a sea-facing bedroom—woke at the sound of his partner falling, knocking the table over. Throwing his feet over the side of the bed, he was reaching for the pistol on the table there when one of the Germans, coming through the doorway, hit him with a burst from a silenced submachine gun.

Bowen had been asleep, had come up to consciousness, had lain awake for half an hour. He lifted his head to look at the clock again at three minutes past five.

To the distant west, sea still merged into sky without any horizon line; nearer shore and directly overhead, though, blackness was becoming blue-gray. Inland, behind the houses, the shapes of the Center Hills began to stand forth.

Putting his head down again, crossing his arms on his chest, Bowen stared at the ceiling, evidently resigned to not sleeping anymore. Eva breathed regularly. Bowen listened to her. In three minutes he was asleep, dreaming.

If Bowen or Eva heard the sound of a nine-inch knife blade slicing the wire away from the frame of a terrace door screen, they must have incorporated it into their dreams. Their first consciousness of danger was when a firm-voiced command woke them, and they started upright and saw the four black figures in a half circle at the foot of the bed, pointing guns at them.

Eva sat at one end of the couch, Bowen at the other. Two of the Germans, holding their submachine guns casually but carefully, faced them from chairs drawn up to the sea-facing window wall, one to the right, one to the left. They had removed their hoods and gloves. The other two Germans had left the house.

Eva sat erect, but without showing any tenseness. Bowen—either very calm, or trying ostentatiously to appear so—had slid down in the seat to put his head on the couch back, his legs straight out in front. For all his air of relaxation, though, his stare at one of the Germans had its customary concentration.

The German looked him up and down. "Do not have too great a confidence," he said. "Do not make a mistake. Your friends in the other houses, they have been neutralized."

Bowen didn't stiffen or sag, but his face must have tightened, for the man smiled. Eva didn't react at all.

After a moment, Bowen turned to her. "Well, I guess you were right, Eva. I guess we did underestimate Heinz."

She didn't respond.

"How do you suppose he got on to the setup?"

She gave the slightest of shrugs.

Bowen asked the man who had spoken to him, "How did you know about the people in the other houses? Those guys who drove past yesterday . . . they couldn't have spotted them in that one pass. Did you send in other people we didn't pick out? One-day visitors from a cruise ship, British nationals, took a little drive around the island, a little walk in the woods behind here, and sailed away again? Swam somebody in one night and out the next? That's how you guys must have come in, obviously. But what would have made Heinz that suspicious? What would have made him think this might be a trap?"

The man only smiled again.

"Why do you suppose he suspected a trap, Eva?" Bowen asked, turning just his head toward her.

"Because I told him, David, of course," she said without looking at him.

Then she turned her head and met his eyes. "I sent other postcards." Her tone was matter-of-fact.

With the serenity of a marble angel, she looked out at the sea again and said, "I flashed signals with a mirror from the terrace to a submarine. I used the radio transmitter that has been cleverly concealed in my teeth. I betrayed you, as you have always known I would."

Bowen continued to stare at her. Then he turned to the man again. "Or did you just take out everybody in the neighborhood, on principle?"

Again, the man only smiled.

Eva glanced at Bowen almost pityingly. "Did you really think Heinz would arrive at the airport one afternoon and walk into your hands?"

"We really didn't think he'd come at all. I told you: It was just a gamble, and we thought we had nothing to lose. We never figured he'd come if he suspected a trap; but if he did come, that would mean he didn't suspect, so he actually might just walk in under a cover."

"You are fools. You don't know Heinz. He is an expert. He is a master. He comes here, into your trap, because for him it is no trap at all. For him, you are children painting false mustaches on your faces, believing you are disguised."

"I didn't realize you still admired him so much."

"I know him. I respect him."

"Well. Great. Tell him that. I'll tell him. I'll tell him I gave it a good try, but I couldn't beat out the old silverback. God, maybe you did send your own postcards. You're still so much in awe of him, you might have. Tell him you did. The way you feel about him comes through so strongly, he'll probably believe you."

Abruptly, Eva rose and went toward the window. Both guards raised their weapons, but she spoke in German, and they lowered them. They had closed and locked the sliding glass doors. They let her stand looking through the window. After a moment, Bowen —moving slowly—got up and went to stand near her.

Although the sun had not yet cleared the mountains, its light filled the sky. Moment by moment the colors and details of the landscape sharpened. Standing at the window wall that made a postcard picture of the view, Bowen and Eva could see the entrance to the drive up to their cottage. The other pair of Germans had retrieved a car, and were on guard there. One of the men leaned with his elbows on the roof scanning one way and another with binoculars. The other lounged against the car, waiting. They could see the second car coming along the main road, from the north.

"There he comes, Eva," Bowen said.

"Yes. This time we will not escape."

"I'm afraid you're right. But would you really want us to get away, Eva? Isn't this what the whole thing has been leading to."

"I don't know."

"You don't?"

They stood at the glass wall, not close together, not far apart. Her left arm lay across her body, her right fingers touched her cheek. He stood squarely, hands down in his trouser pockets. They watched Heinz's car drawing closer.

"You were very amusing at the beginning, when we first met," she said.

Quietly, like old people reminiscing, they spoke of the night they'd met, while the car wound its way up toward the cottage.

When it arrived, the guards made Bowen and Eva move into the room, away from the window. One man covered them while the other went to the front door. A car door closed. A voice, almost inaudible, asked a question; another answered briefly. Bowen and Eva stared at one another long enough for a leaf to fall. Footsteps sounded on the flagstones, drawing closer, drawing them to look toward the door. The man who had gone out returned. And then Heinz came in.

Like the other men, he wore black; but his pullover was a hand-knit, textured wool sweater, and he had a short leather jacket over it, open. The other men were shadows. He was a dark star of infinite density.

By the time he strode the four steps through the entryway and halted inside the living room, he had scanned all around and was ready to focus exclusively on Eva and Bowen. He said three quick words, snapping his fingers and pointing, and the guard covering Bowen dropped the muzzle of his submachine gun to aim at Bowen's thighs instead of his chest. Then Heinz stared for a full ten seconds at Eva.

For the first two of them she met his eyes. Then she dropped her own. But without seeing him she must still have known he hadn't released her. Her head tipped forward. Then her hands, which had been clasped at her waist, fell away to hang slack at her sides. Finally her shoulders sagged. Heinz didn't force her to her knees with his stare, as it seemed he might have done. He turned it to Bowen.

He didn't ask Bowen anything. He didn't say anything. He didn't seem to expect Bowen to say anything. He just looked.

Bowen wasn't battered down, though, as Eva had been. He bore Heinz's eyes on him, staring straight back, for nearly half a minute. But then he spoke.

"I don't know if standing here looking at each other without saying anything is supposed to be a test, Heinz, but I'm not interested in taking it. The game's up, the joke's over, and we might as well finish it as quickly as possible. You've won, Heinz; but you've also lost. I'm not David Bowen."

After a moment Heinz tipped his head slightly to one side, then straightened it again. His eyes were gray, his hair silver; he might have had mercury for blood.

"Ask Eva," Bowen said. "She figured it out yesterday that I couldn't be the kind of guy I've been pretending to be. My name is Peter MacDonald. I'm CIA, and this whole thing has been a setup from the beginning."

Heinz did shift his eyes to Eva, who now seemed shocked to life again and was staring at Bowen.

"Ask her. I fooled her for a while, but she started being suspicious even back in England when I put away your guys who tried to snatch me. By yesterday she had it all: that I was sent to England as bait—the entire Bowen legend created as bait—for you. MIM5, the CIA, we knew who she was—who she was to you. The Bowen character was tailored so you'd use her to get him. You thought you were baiting me, but I was the fish who would grab your line and pull you overboard. Ask her if she hasn't figured that out."

Heinz did ask Eva, "Is this so?" But the answer seemed to be of minor interest to him.

Still looking at Bowen she answered, "Yes. That is what I think." Her voice was soft.

Bowen spoke to her. "I should apologize, I guess, for deceiving you, Eva; except that I think we're square." Then to Heinz again, "She really is terrific, Heinz. There were times when I thought my act was so good that she'd truly fallen in love with me and come over. But when we had it out yesterday it became clear to me that she . . . she's like the girl in the song 'Her Heart Belongs to Daddy.' She's just been staying with the game, staying on me, waiting her chance, like you must have told her to do."

For another long moment Heinz continued to regard Bowen in silence. Then he said quietly, "You actually suppose I will believe this?" one side of his mouth thinning into the hint of a smile.

Bowen shrugged. "I almost hope you don't. It'd really serve you—and especially her—right: poetic justice if you chop off her head because she's been so good at deceiving me. But I realize that if you go on believing the Bowen story you'll try to beat information out of me that I don't have. I'd really prefer for you to know the truth and just terminate me, if that's what you want to do, and get it over."

After a second Heinz took a quick breath and said, "I might consider this insulting to my intelligence, and be angry, if it was not so amusing."

Bowen shrugged. "Ask Eva what made her suspicious. Get details. She'll tell you. She'll do anything you say, Heinz." Bowen turned to look at Eva, directly into her eyes. "Or," he said to Heinz again, "I can show you something that might convince you." Raising his hands slowly to shoulder level, tipping his head in a way that seemed to ask permission and take it as granted, Bowen cautiously stepped to one side, stepped again, toward the dining-table end of the room.

"He has a pistol in the drawer," Eva said, her voice thin.

Bowen froze, then lowered his hands. "You see?"

Heinz nodded. The guard beyond Eva went to the credenza.

"The center drawer on the top," she said.

The man pulled out the drawer. *"Ja,"* he reported.

"This game is childish," Heinz said, his tone suggesting boredom more than annoyance.

"What I've told you is the truth."

"We shall see. We shall certainly do so without beating you; there are more effective methods that do not risk making damage to a valuable asset. The beating, or whatever, will come afterward. That is a personal matter, independent of what is your name. Eva . . ." Heinz spoke her name, and tipped his head toward the door.

Eva walked past him, head down. Heinz pivoted as she went by. One guard gestured with the muzzle of his submachine gun, indicating Bowen should follow, and started crabwise—keeping him covered—ahead of him. The other guard came after.

A third one of Heinz's men had stayed at the door. He held it open while all of them came out of the house. Two more men—the fourth of the attack team, and the one who had driven Heinz from the beach —had turned the cars to face down the dirt road, and were waiting in them with the motors idling.

As they approached the road, Heinz—in one step —came up with Eva. Taking her upper arm, he steered her to the second car. He said something in German to the men bringing Bowen; curtly, but softly, smoothly. Gripping Eva's arm, he waited beside one rear door until Bowen had been put into the back on the other side. A man got into the front, beside the driver, and pointed a pistol over the seat at Bowen. Then Heinz opened his door.

He spoke to the man covering Bowen, then to Bowen himself. "I have told him to aim his pistol between your legs. It would please me very much if you would give him a reason to shoot you." He guided Eva into the car next to Bowen, then sat beside her.

Then Heinz said one word. The driver snapped *"Jawhol,"* in reply, just like in the movies, and flashed his lights. The car ahead, carrying three men, pulled away; and Heinz's driver followed it closely.

Swiftly but smoothly they drove into the pale-blue morning, a morning tender and fresh as the newly opened bindweed that twined along the roadsides. Although the sun would not rise out of the sea for another fifteen minutes, night had passed. Few islanders, though, seemed to consider that a reason for getting out of bed. As the cars went north on the main road, they did pass one van loaded with people going to work at the hotel: breakfast cooks, two gardeners who started early in order to finish before the worst heat of the day, the morning deskman. By the time the van reached the hotel, the Germans would be starting down the last hill to the sea at Little Bay.

Bowen sat very still. The man who was twisted around in the front seat never took his eyes from him, nor varied the aim of the cocked pistol he held braced on the back of his seat and against the headrest. Sometimes Bowen stared at that man, sometimes at the back of the driver's head. Sometimes he turned his head—slowly, carefully—to look at Eva or Heinz. Sometimes he looked out the windows. Always he seemed neither to be looking for anything in particular nor missing anything. His usual intensity of focus seemed raised to a higher power.

Heinz spoke to Eva in German. His tone was solicitous; he might have been asking if she was comfortable. She replied, almost inaudibly. Heinz laid one hand casually on her thigh. After a few moments he rubbed his hand back and forth, slipping his fingers down and around. She sat slack, unresisting.

The cars climbed up through the hamlet of Cudjoehead, and down a long ridge toward the sea. "So, Eva," Heinz spoke again, in English this time, clearly for Bowen's benefit. "Have you truly been deceiving this man all this time? Have you been doing all your lovely, unspeakable tricks only so that you could betray him? Did you truly betray him just now by telling about his pistol, or did you only accept his so gallant offer of a way to deceive me?" Eva didn't reply. She was looking down, as though at her knees. Heinz went on, "Have you truly been Heinz's good golden baby rabbit?" His voice was as low and smooth as ever, only mildly chiding. "Oh, I think not. I think you have been a bad little rabbit, *ja?*"

Her head sank lower.

"But do not fear," he went on. "Heinz will give you the chance to prove you love him. And then, perhaps, all will be forgiven, and again you will be Heinz's golden rabbit, and his fluffy squirrel, and his good little mouse. You will like that, won't you?"

Eyes down, Eva didn't speak.

"What did you say?" Heinz asked softly, even gently. And when she still didn't respond, more firmly but even more quietly, "What, Eva? What did you say?"

Finally, in the tiniest voice, she answered, "Yes, Heinz."

At the bottom of the long descent the road turned right to parallel Carr's Bay beach. Fishermen had a weathered-board shack there, but it was closed. None of them were about the dinghies drawn up on the beach nor the three fishing boats riding at anchor fifty yards out. At the north end of the beach the cars turned from the main road, which headed inland again, onto the lesser one that wound around the cliffed hill separating Carr's Bay from Little Bay.

There were no houses along that road; none closer than half a mile away, high on another hill that was blocked from sight when the cars turned toward the sea again and began descending. They went down into a wide vale. The slopes on either side were open —grassy, scrubby, not densely forested like the other parts of the island. One surveying glance could assure that no person saw the cars going toward the beach. One such glance could assure Bowen that even if he broke away somehow, he would find no cover, no place to hide.

The green vale broadened to perhaps a quarter mile, ending at a row of palm trees and the cocoa-colored beach beyond them. The cars stopped at the line of trees. The driver got out, opened Heinz's door for him. Heinz stepped out, turned, and said, "Come, Eva," in the tone of a master to a well-loved and unfailingly obedient dog. Without raising her eyes, Eva slid across the seat and out of the car, and stood at heel beside him. Then the man covering Bowen waited for the driver to come around and aim his submachine gun at Bowen again, then nodded for him to get out.

From the other car, one man came to join those guarding Bowen, while the other two headed toward a dinghy pulled up on the beach. Heinz gave one of his quick, quiet commands. His three men fell in around Bowen—one on either side, one behind, all eight feet away, all with their guns pointed at him. One signaled him to start for the boat. Heinz took Eva by the arm again and followed behind.

Out toward the horizon the flat rays of the rising sun reached the sea and burnished it silvery blue and sparkling. Closer, within the island's shadow, the color was still a slumbering indigo. The line of brightness was advancing toward the island steadily; in a few more minutes the sun would clear the mountains, its rays touch the beach. In the still morning there was no surf to speak of. White lacey lines of foam flowed up the gentle slope of the beach, but there were no breakers. Perhaps fifty yards out, the dark-hulled powerboat floated without perceptible rocking. It was a small sport-fishing boat, with a cabin and an open afterdeck.

The men who'd reached the dinghy had pushed it stern first into the water, and were holding it just beyond where it began to float clear. Heinz's man had rowed him to shore, for silence; now the oars were stowed, and an outboard motor had been tipped into place.

Obviously, all eight people could not be carried in the dinghy at one time. "Cannibals and missionaries," Bowen said. Heinz gave an order, and Bowen was directed to climb into the dinghy and sit on the seat facing the rearmost one. One of the guards walked into the water with him, keeping his gun trained all the time.

Heinz spoke to Eva in German, gesturing at the water, as though apologizing that they had to walk into it; but he guided her firmly to the dinghy, to the seat behind Bowen, where he joined her. The two men holding the boat shoved it farther to keep it just afloat, and then two of the others waded out and took the seat at the stern. One of them, holding his submachine gun in both hands and bracing his forearms on his knees, took aim at Bowen's crotch again. The other pulled the lanyard to start the outboard. At the third try it caught. The men in the water gave the dinghy a final shove.

Low in the water—the weight of the passengers badly distributed—and with the motor grumbling out of character with the tranquil and languid morning, the dinghy made its way slowly to the yacht. So clear was the sea, so little disturbed by the boat's passage, that it seemed less a liquid than a transparent solid they glided over. They could see the lumpy, velvety bottom, green and yellow-green. A score of purple-black shapes like vertical pancakes shot away from them, and a quick, silver arrow.

The steersman brought the dinghy alongside the yacht, shifted to neutral, and held them in place with one hand. Heinz took Eva's wrist and climbed into the yacht, seeming to compel her to come up with him more by will than by pulling her. The steersman took his pistol from its shoulder holster with his free hand, pointed it at Bowen. Then the other man climbed aboard the boat. Finally, Bowen was signaled to go aboard, never for a moment without at least one weapon aimed at him. The steersman shifted, advanced the throttle, and headed back to shore.

As Bowen came over the railing, the other three stepped away—Heinz pulling Eva, who seemed without any volition of her own. For a moment all four stood still, there on the open afterdeck: Bowen and the man guarding him near the rail—Bowen toward the stern, the man six feet forward from him—Heinz and Eva half way across the deck. In that moment, Bowen looked first at the man with the gun, then at Heinz —whose pale eyes seemed almost to glitter, whose stern mouth seemed almost to smile—and then at Eva. Although still slack, still bowed in apparent abjection she had raised her head enough to stare back at him. Their eyes met for only an instant.

Suddenly, jerking the arm that Heinz held, unbalancing him, screaming, "Now!" she arced her free arm around, her fingers spread and rigid, driving them at Heinz's eyes.

In the fraction of a second while the guard snapped his attention toward Heinz and Eva, Bowen threw himself upon the man, carrying him sideways and backward, hurling them both over the railing. The man's hand contracted, sending one shot into the deck, and even as he fell he tried to twist the gun toward Bowen; but as they struck the water he released it.

Bowen, knowing what he was doing, what he intended, filled his lungs even as he fell. The other man, so surprised, could catch only half a breath before they plunged heads down below the surface. Together they sank, kicking, twisting, turning a slow somersault—the two of them like a single many-limbed body—righting themselves, neither trying to break free, each struggling to gain a superior hold.

With one hand the guard clutched Bowen's shirt to hold him from escaping; the other hand he brought up under Bowen's chin, forcing Bowen's head back, trying to break Bowen's bear hug. At the same time, he scissored his legs to add thrust to the buoyancy that was lifting both men toward the surface again.

Bowen let himself be pushed away. Grabbing the man's shoulders, the sleeves of his pullover, Bowen rolled backward, bringing up his knees, driving his feet into his opponent's stomach. A great bubble came from the man's mouth and rose wobbling irregularly. That kick counteracted the other man's. The two men hung in place below the surface in the clear but dappled water. Shadows from ripples above played over them, intensifying the sense of squidlike, seamonster swirling in their kicking legs, the writhing of the guard's arms as he tried to break Bowen's hold on his shoulders.

Now the guard's only purpose—instinctive, beyond plan or reason—was getting air: willing that his empty lungs would not expand and drag in the killing water, fighting to shoot himself upward out of it.

Bowen couldn't stay down much longer, either. Bubbles—one, and then another, and then a steady tiny stream of them—were rising from his nose. Still, he contracted backward, downward; his efforts opposing the other man's.

The guard's writhings became more frantic. A driving knee caught Bowen's side, knocking out half his remaining air.

Although their counter-movements kept them at a nearly constant depth, some current was drifting them laterally. The flutter of shadows on them solidified into a single blue shaft. Bowen must have comprehended what that meant. Suddenly he joined his own force to the wild flailings of the other man's legs. As he did he pulled his head down into his shoulders, swiftly shifted one hand to his opponent's chin, and shoved the man's head up as they shot upward and crashed into the powerboat's hull.

The man went suddenly limp. Bowen struck once more, knocking the German's head up against the hull again. Then he kicked away, shooting under the boat to break the water, gasping, on its far side. Taking full breath again, he ducked under, ready to fight or flee.

The guard lay flat, up against the boat's bottom, face down, arms spread wide as though flying. So clear was the water that even in the boat's shadow his black-clad figure was perfectly distinct in contrast to the red-orange hull. Even the wrinkles in his trouser legs showed sharply; even his eyes, which were open, staring as though watching for something on the sea's floor.

Bowen kicked to propel himself toward the boat's bow, came up beside it again. He could hear Heinz shouting. He could hear the dinghy's outboard motor coming toward the yacht. He went down once more, began swimming hard underwater past the stern and away. At the end of a breath, he surfaced, looked around. He was about a dozen yards from the yacht. The dinghy was closing on the yacht, still with only the one man in it. Heinz was standing near the powerboat's stern peering, scanning all around. Bowen couldn't see Eva.

Bowen treaded water, even kicking hard enough to thrust himself chest-high above the surface. Heinz spotted him, shouted, pointing. Bowen had come up south of the boat. If he continued swimming in that direction he could pass the cliff that separated Little Bay from Carr's Bay, and come ashore there. The striaght-line distance was less than half a mile; he could reach it long before Heinz's men could get there over the miles of winding roads. Bowen started swimming on the surface, away from the yacht. Then he went under again.

The man in the dinghy was racing full throttle to intercept him, swinging wide to put himself well ahead of where Bowen had been seen. Once in such a blocking position, he could speed across any line Bowen might take, and—through that pure, transparent water—see him from nearly a hundred feet away.

Bowen swam underwater with the utmost speed he could; smoothly—not losing his head and tiring himself without result—but putting deliberate power into every rhythmical kick of his legs, every sweep of his arms.

Swift and unexpected as Eva's thrust at Heinz had been, she hadn't blinded him. The tip of one finger touched his eye, the other jabbed the side of his nose; but with a lightning reflex he had parried, grabbing her wrist, using the stiffness of her own arm to throw her back a step from him. Swinging his other arm wide, he struck her full force—a slap snapping her head to the side, reeling her. Jerking her toward him again, he struck a second blow, backhand, unleashing all the power coiled into his arm from the first one. It hurled her sideward, staggering, falling to the deck. Tottering back a step himself, Heinz found his footing, shifted weight, and kicked with all his strength at Eva's stomach. She twisted just enough, just quickly enough, to take the blow on her ribs.

Then Heinz spun to look behind him. Bowen and the guard had vanished. He ran to the rail. He could see the two men suspended in the water, directly below the side of the boat, intertwined, grappling. Then they passed out of sight beneath him. He began shouting at the man speeding away from him in the dinghy.

Twisting, the steersman saw Heinz waving and put the boat around.

As soon as he saw the dinghy returning, Heinz spun. Eva lay prone on the deck, one hand to her ribs, making little gasping moans. He stalked past her to scan over the other side. Seeing nothing, he crossed once more, then went to the stern to look that way. It took no thought to realize that if Bowen broke free of his opponent under the water, swimming for Carr's Bay would be how he must try to escape. After a moment he saw Bowen come up for air. He signaled the man in the dinghy, then turned back to Eva. She wasn't there.

Two steps revealed her dragging herself, crawling forward along the narrow space between the cabin and railing, trying to reach the foredeck. She was still pressing one hand to her side. Each time she pulled herself forward she gasped. Obviously, her ribs were broken. Crawling seemed to be excruciatingly painful; so was simply breathing. Certainly she couldn't throw herself over the side and attempt to swim.

Heinz glanced over his shoulder. The man in the dinghy was reaching position. He'd be closer to where Bowen would next have to breathe, better able to spot him, than would Heinz from the boat. Heinz turned back to finish with Eva.

He didn't hurry. Moving away from him was agonizing for her; he let her do it. He stepped to the rear end of the cabin, halted. He let her drag herself another half length, took one short step along the passageway. He let her move again, took another step.

Pain twisted Eva's face. Tears streamed across it. She pulled herself forward once more, and Heinz took another step after her, and she sobbed, and winced at the ragged stab that gave her. If the railing had not prevented her, she could have rolled overboard, preferring to drown herself rather than let Heinz torment her. Since she couldn't escape, she could have lain there and let him do what he would and get it over. But as long as there was even an inch of space for her to move away from him she was compelled to take it. She put her forearm on the deck beyond her head again and—with another gasping groan—hauled herself up and over and down upon it.

Heinz had learned the mature pleasures of patience. He took another step, only enough to keep his distance from Eva constant. And then another, when she pulled herself in line with the forward end of the cabin, and one each time she moved farther out beyond it onto the short foredeck.

Panting, gasping, trying not to sob because that hurt so much more even than moving herself, Eva came at last against the convergence of railings at the bow. Heinz took his step, too. He paused, looking down at her. Perhaps he was deciding whether to kick her to death there or to drag her below for some more extended pleasure as they sailed. In any case, he stood feet apart, chest expanded, arms at his sides, looming over her, obviously enjoying a triumph.

Bowen hit him.

He had surfaced at the side near the stern, the boat blocking him from the sight of the man in the dinghy. That man's attention was fixed ahead to where he thought Bowen would appear, so he didn't see Bowen come up over the railing. Bowen had begun creeping up behind, just as Heinz passed the front of the cabin.

With all his strength, Bowen slashed his bladed palm, striking Heinz under his ear, then drove with his shoulder to hurl the man overboard. Heinz staggered, reeling, twisting away, shaking his head. His eyes, unfocused for an instant, fixed again on Bowen. Bowen leaped back, swung a kick at him. Heinz pivoted and stepped into it, taking the blow against his arm and side. He punched at Bowen, might have knocked him over; but Bowen grabbed him, held on to keep from falling.

Heinz didn't try to break away. Throwing his arms around Bowen, he kneed him. He caught the inside of Bowen's thigh; then Bowen regained his balance and twisted so Heinz couldn't do it again.

For a moment the two men struggled, locked together. Bowen was taller; Heinz heavier, his center of gravity lower. Both were strong.

And on the shore one of Heinz's men shifted his glance from watching the dinghy, saw the two figures grappling on the foredeck of the yacht, shouted, pointing. And then the others looked. And then the first was running, leaping, diving into the sea. And then the other two were following him.

Heinz was bear-hugging, twisting, trying to throw Bowen. Bowen freed an arm, struck with flattened palm to the base of Heinz's skull. The blow must have hurt, but it didn't break the German's grip. He had his hands locked behind Bowen's back, squeezing, forcing Bowen's breath out, not letting his chest expand for another. Heinz pulled his head tight down to his shoulders, wheeled right and then left to deny Bowen the solid footing from which to strike effectively another time.

Arms flashing, feet kicking up froths of foam, the three swimmers raced toward the boat. The man in the dinghy was sweeping in an arc, now nearly a hundred yards away from the boat, his eyes on the water.

Bowen struck at Heinz again, but the blow didn't carry full strength. Using his compactness, bulling at Bowen to keep him from setting his feet back behind him, cheek into chest, Heinz was on the point of bending Bowen backward enough to topple him.

Bowen twisted to save himself. Unrelenting, Heinz wheeled again. The movement brought him a step away from Eva, who was lying half up against the railing. Pain pulling her lips away from gritted teeth, she drew up her knee and smashed her foot to Heinz's ankle. The force of her kick knocked him off balance, weakened his grip enough for Bowen to twist and free himself, then whirl back and strike another blow. Heinz fell. His head struck the deck. He lay still.

Bowen turned to Eva, who started to smile in wonder and relief at him. Movement at the side of the boat caught her eye, and she screamed.

Bowen wheeled to see the first of the swimmers, water streaming from him, poised upright on stiffened arms, fists gripping the rail, about to swing up onto the boat. Two leaping steps, and he was in place to kick at the man's head. But the man, knowing he was in no position to fight, threw himself back into the water again. Surfacing, he called to his companions, directing them to the stern and the other side.

Flashing glances toward them and then toward the bow again, Bowen shouted, "Eva! Can you cast off that line? There!" He pointed.

Twisting, Eva saw that the anchor line was secured to a cleat at the point of the bow just beyond the railing.

"I try!" she forced herself to call back. Inching

painfully, she was able to reach through the railing and touch the rope.

Bowen darted to the afterdeck. The three men were swimming, treading water, positioning themselves. The one who had tried to come aboard before kicked toward the boat, reached for the railing, then took a stroke away again as Bowen lunged toward him. Instantly, Bowen checked and leaped toward the stern; and the man coming at it kicked around and held his place. Bowen turned one way and the other, ready to dash in any direction, and for a moment held the men at bay. They seemed for an instant like blood-crazed sharks, but they were far more terrifying. They were not confined to the water. They had only to move farther apart—one staying at the stern, the others going along the sides toward the bow, so one or two could keep Bowen occupied. The third, and then the others, could climb aboard.

Eva worked to slip a half inch of rope under the length of loop that lay across and held it; and then—a little easier, but still so slowly, so painfully—another three-quarters of an inch; and then a full inch.

Bowen spun and ran into the cockpit. There was a key; he turned it. The starter whined, didn't catch. He twisted it back to "Off," tried again. It ground and then did, and the engine caught and rumbled. If he put it in gear, the boat would pull against the rope and Eva wouldn't be able to cast off. But fear that he might start the propellor whirling would keep the swimmers away from the stern.

Bowen sprang back to the afterdeck again. Indeed, the stern swimmer was coming around to the port side. Bowen checked first to starboard. The man there had a hand on the deck and was reaching for the railing. When Bowen took a step toward him he released his hold, but remained floating, touching the side of the hull.

"How are you coming?" Bowen shouted.

Eva hadn't the breath or strength to answer. Without looking back at him she nodded and went on working at the rope. She had unlocked the first turn and was loosening the second.

Bowen strode up alongside the cabin, making the man on the starboard side kick out of reach, and dashed across to the port side. The man nearer the bow had vaulted out of the water and was about to roll over the railing. Bowen ran at him, and he threw himself back into the sea again. The third, who had been at the stern, was approaching the port side near it.

For an instant Bowen stood just aft of the cabin, legs spread, twisting one way and the other, seeing the man near the bow reaching for the rail again, knowing the one on the other side, blocked from sight by the cabin, might be climbing over it.

"Free!" Eva shouted, "Free!" shouting despite the pain.

Jumping into the cockpit, Bowen pulled the throttle back, shoved the other handle to the position marked "Reverse," and threw the throttle forward again. The engine thundered, the boat jerked, quickened, shot backward. One man in the water kicked away, one was grazed and spun off, the third clung to the railing against the drag of the water. Bowen saw him through the cockpit window, left the boat to steer itself, and came running out. But the man knew his disadvantage and dropped away again.

Back in the cockpit, Bowen shifted to "Forward," spun the wheel hard over, and turned the boat around heading at an angle away from the island so that they passed the man in the dinghy beyond effective pistol range. Bowen saw two looped cords attached to the dashboard, understood their purpose. He set a course parallel to the shore and slipped the loops over a spoke of the wheel to hold it. Then he throttled down and ran forward to Eva and Heinz.

Heinz seemed still unconscious. Bowen knelt beside Eva. Her face was ashen-white, the skin drawn tight. He tried to take her in his arms, but she exclaimed, "No! My ribs—I think my ribs are cracked. But nothing inside is injured, I think."

"Can I do something?"

"No. If I do not move . . . it hurts not too much. Better I stay as I am." She managed to smile wanly, and he grasped her hand, and she squeezed it back.

Bowen pivoted on his heels to look at Heinz. Eva could feel his hand quivering with the rage inside him. "I'm going to kill him," he said quietly, firmly. "I can kill him, Eva, without a moment's hesitation. It will never trouble my conscience. A man like him—I'll be doing the world a service."

"But then everything you have done to capture him will be for nothing."

"They'll know I tried—we tried. That's all I care about. It's all I've cared about since I thought this scheme up back in England when we were trying to escape. Killing him will prove that to you."

With her head back against the railing, Eva stared into Bowen's eyes. "I believe you," she said. For a moment she shifted her own to look at Heinz, then returned to Bowen. "If I tell you, 'Do not kill him,' will you believe it is because I wish to save *him?*"

"No. Not anymore. Never again."

"Good. Then do not kill him. Do not—you —become a cold-blooded killer, not even of Heinz. And let the CIA have him. They have paid. Those people who were in the houses near us . . . they have paid for him. Let them have him, and let him be gone from our lives forever."

After a long moment looking back at her Bowen said, "All right, Eva. You're right. I'll find some rope, and tie him."

"Thank you, David."

He released her hand and was about to rise.

"David?" she halted him.

"What?"

"You are truly David?"

"Yes." He turned to her once more, touched her cheek with his fingertips. "And you're Eva, my Eva. And from now on we'll never tell each other anything but the truth."

In spite of the pain, Eva laughed. "Oh, David, I don't think any lovers can ever do that."

THE BEST IN MYSTERY

- [ ] 51388-6   THE ANONYMOUS CLIENT $4.99
  J.P. Hailey   Canada $5.99

- [ ] 51195-6   BREAKFAST AT WIMBLEDON $3.99
  Jack M. Bickham   Canada $4.99

- [ ] 51682-6   CATNAP $4.99
  Carole Nelson Douglas   Canada $5.99

- [ ] 51702-4   IRENE AT LARGE $4.99
  Carole Nelson Douglas   Canada $5.99

- [ ] 51563-3   MARIMBA $4.99
  Richard Hoyt   Canada $5.99

- [ ] 52031-9   THE MUMMY CASE $3.99
  Elizabeth Peters   Canada $4.99

- [ ] 50642-1   RIDE THE LIGHTNING $3.95
  John Lutz   Canada $4.95

- [ ] 50728-2   ROUGH JUSTICE $4.99
  Ken Gross   Canada $5.99

- [ ] 51149-2   SILENT WITNESS $3.99
  Collin Wilcox   Canada $4.99

Buy them at your local bookstore or use this handy coupon:
Clip and mail this page with your order.

Publishers Book and Audio Mailing Service
P.O. Box 120159, Staten Island, NY 10312-0004

Please send me the book(s) I have checked above. I am enclosing $ _____
(Please add $1.25 for the first book, and $.25 for each additional book to cover postage and handling.
Send check or money order only—no CODs.)

Name _____

Address _____

City _____ State/Zip _____

Please allow six weeks for delivery. Prices subject to change without notice.

BESTSELLERS FROM TOR

☐ 51195-6　**BREAKFAST AT WIMBLEDON**　　　　　　　$3.99
　　　　　　Jack Bickham　　　　　　Canada $4.99

☐ 52497-7　**CRITICAL MASS**　　　　　　　　　　$5.99
　　　　　　David Hagberg　　　　　　Canada $6.99

☐ 85202-9　**ELVISSEY**　　　　　　　　　　　　$12.95
　　　　　　Jack Womack　　　　　　Canada $16.95

☐ 51612-5　**FALLEN IDOLS**　　　　　　　　　　$4.99
　　　　　　Ralph Arnote　　　　　　Canada $5.99

☐ 51716-4　**THE FOREVER KING**　　　　　　　　$5.99
　　　　　　Molly Cochran & Warren Murphy　Canada $6.99

☐ 50743-6　**PEOPLE OF THE RIVER**　　　　　　$5.99
　　　　　　Michael Gear & Kathleen O'Neal Gear　Canada $6.99

☐ 51198-0　**PREY**　　　　　　　　　　　　　$5.99
　　　　　　Ken Goddard　　　　　　Canada $6.99

☐ 50735-5　**THE TRIKON DECEPTION**　　　　　$5.99
　　　　　　Ben Bova & Bill Pogue　　Canada $6.99

Buy them at your local bookstore or use this handy coupon:
Clip and mail this page with your order.

Publishers Book and Audio Mailing Service
P.O. Box 120159, Staten Island, NY 10312-0004

Please send me the book(s) I have checked above. I am enclosing $ _____
(Please add $1.25 for the first book, and $.25 for each additional book to cover postage and handling.
Send check or money order only—no CODs.)

Name _____
Address _____
City _____ State/Zip _____
Please allow six weeks for delivery. Prices subject to change without notice.